FLAME OF THE DRAGON HEIR

FLAME OF THE DRAGON HEIR

S. R. BREAKER

Dear reader,

This book picks up mere days after 'The Curse of the Arcadian Stone: The Bridge' ends. Scan this code to listen to the audiobook for free!

 If you haven't read the earlier books in The Dragons of Arcadia and Nameless Fay series yet, you'll still find a complete story here — but you'll enjoy it more if you've followed our heroes' journey from the start.

Thank you for returning to The Land of Arcadia with me. I can't wait to share the next twist in their story.

Contents

Prologue

—

The figure with long, bright fuchsia hair stilled in her seat, swallowed by the cavernous hush of the darkened library.

Midnight shadows stretched long between the shelves, where candlelight guttered and waned, bleeding its last across the ancient stone. The air hung heavy with the scent of wax and time, of scrolls decaying in slow surrender, dust thick enough to taste.

Even the silence felt alive, pressing close, as if the ghosts of forgotten scholars lingered still, waiting for her to turn another page.

She had all but memorized the prophecy—a copy carefully penned, scrawled on old parchment, edges singed with soot, stained and worn through the centuries. A more precious artifact than its humble appearance denoted.

And despite its state, partly torn and ink-smudged, the words contained therein were testament enough. That the dying magic of the Land of Arcadia might still be recovered. An assurance that there was indeed a way to save all the realms.

Words that had given her strength and courage to take on her mission—even if she'd had to journey to a faraway, dangerous world no Fae before her had ever gone.

To bring back the one true hope for her people—for all the people.

And she had succeeded, returned home safely.

She'd felt nothing but relief, vindication.

That was, until she received today's letters, late with the dusk of the evening. More ancient scrolls entreated from faraway archives, and the last thing she had expected it to contain—a long-lost portion of the torn prophecy.

More ominous words. Not many, still incomplete, but it was enough.

Test. Chosen. Cost.

Her hands balled into fists, attempting for the words to mean something else. An effort all in vain, as she knew what they meant, as all prophecies came with a cost.

And the cost is the chosen...

A lump constricting her throat, she stared at the last of the flickering candles.

Gods and fates... What have I done?

***

PART ONE

- JOSH -

1

Again

Josh

I really think I've been thrown in this dungeon before.

The dim square space gave off mildew and rust. Flickering torchlight cast long, twitching shadows across the moss-slicked walls. Muffled clangs of metal and the rare distant thud of boots echoed through the corridors of the castle above, all woven into that low groan of centuries-old stone amidst the quiet of the night.

I tilted my head to one side to consider, my thoughts circling back to this notion once again, with the lack of anything else to do.

Well, maybe not in this dungeon cell specifically, but I at least knew I'd definitely been in this other world before.

Or maybe, actually, yeah...

Was this the exact same dungeon cell as before?

Frowning, I drew my knees up. Shifting on the cold floor, I rubbed my face with my hands in defeat.

It was hard to be sure.

It all seemed so foggy in my brain.

A few years back, my estranged/supposedly deceased/somehow magic-possessing father had wiped my memories. Super not helpful, that. But he'd revealed that I'd already previously journeyed to this world—this magical medieval land its people called Arcadia.

Whatever had happened to me at the time was apparently so traumatic that I had to forget all about it in order to go back to living my normal life on Earth.

Of course, that all eventually got shot to hell. As 'normal' was something I could no longer return to.

Those years I was back on Earth, I'd only kept having this nagging thought in the back of my mind that I was living a half-life. That I was missing something. That I didn't truly know my purpose or where I belonged.

Everything was blurred.

Except for her...

I glanced out the barred windows up at the dark sky.

I didn't even know her name.

Or I must have at some point, I supposed.

Long before she'd popped into my life on Earth last Thursday, dropping some major proverbial bombs, almost getting us both killed by those rogue Fae warriors who'd pursued her from this mystical realm, and before she'd summoned that brilliant bluish-white portal to bring us here.

Was it Monday now? I wasn't entirely sure if time worked the same here, but the sun had risen and set twice out that window. Two days since some big goons had thrown me into this dungeon. Two days since I'd last seen her.

Though I only needed to close my eyes to see her face. As if it had already been ingrained in my mind. Possibly even in the memories I'd lost all those years ago.

Those vibrant violet eyes, always full of wonder or marveling—or often annoyance at me. The way her nose would wrinkle when I inevitably said something she considered ridiculous or overly optimistic. Her long, bright fuchsia hair that always floated about her, blending into the dusky sky... How silky her hair felt between my fingers when I'd pulled her close and—

I gave my head a brisk shake to clear those thoughts.

My heartbeat raced at the mere memory. I was sure I would never forget that amazing kiss for as long as I lived.

I loved her.

I mean, it made no sense. I just met her.

But for some reason, I knew it—deep in my soul.

And for some reason, I had this notion, or perhaps it was a mere hope, that she also felt some kind of similar way about me.

I'm already betrothed, she'd said before we left Earth.

Complications.

I blew out a breath. Regardless, I had already resolved to stay by her side no matter what. I was certain I would be content as long as she was safe and happy.

Really, I should be pissed off at her.

Why had she gone on and on about my 'destiny' of saving this world to convince me to even come here, and then left me in a dungeon?

Sure, the food was okay. Servants delivered fresh towels and wash basins on a regular basis. I'd have said, for a dungeon, it was actually decent—possibly even too posh for a verified prisoner. Even the 'toilet in a pit', for this medieval world's day and age, was surprisingly humane.

Except given what she'd told me so far, I'd imagined I should have been an honored guest here instead or something.

I'd glimpsed how huge this castle was from the outside when that portal spewed the two of us up directly at the edge of the forest along its borders.

I thought maybe they had to hold me here while they made preparations. They surely could spare one room among the dozens, maybe even hundreds, they had available. Or heck, a closet, I didn't care. Somewhere with a mattress, at least.

I ran my fingers through my hair in a bit of frustration.

Curse bearer...

It was what she'd called me.

I couldn't shake off the feeling that I already knew more than I did about that ominous phrase either.

Maybe it didn't mean 'savior' as much as I'd assumed.

I needed to get my memories back. It was the only way to make sense of any of this. What I was meant for. In this strange, magical land, surely, someone should have some type of mumbo jumbo potion or something that could help recover my memories, and perhaps tell me once and for all what my future holds.

And...I needed to know why I felt this deeply familiar ache in my chest at the mere thought of losing her. As if I'd already lost her once before.

Jumping up to stand, I walked toward the bars, wrapping my fingers around the unyielding, frigid bars. I cast a glance left and right. Empty corridors. I imagined they thought a powerless human didn't need to be watched so closely.

I turned my attention to the heavy wooden door to my cell. I reached over to test the handle for a sec. Locked, of course. Then the door's hinges caught my gaze. It used the kind of hinge plates that were held together by a metal pin.

Huh.

Fun fact about these old doors.

I crouched low, my eyes fixed on the hinge pins. Steadying my hands, I wiggled the top pin loose. The iron groaned in protest, but then clattered to the floor. I jumped at the telltale noise.

Shoot. I shot my gaze left and right again to make sure I hadn't alerted any guards to my escape attempt, but after a moment, everything was still as silent as it was before.

Biting my lip in concentration, I shifted my weight, gripping the edge of the door. I bit back a grunt.

Damn, it's freaking heavy.

I held my breath and lifted slowly, carefully, until the weight pulled free from the loosened hinges, and the door finally tilted with a gap just enough for me to ease through.

Blowing out that breath, I couldn't help a triumphant grin to myself.

I put the door back the way it was, to make my escape less obvious in case guards walked past. I dusted off my hands. With another furtive check up and down the darkened corridors to make sure the coast was clear, I sneaked my way out of the dungeons.

Cool, cool, cool.

2

One Time

The shadowy stone castle stood on top of a hill overlooking a wide expanse of grassy fields, and the lush, green forest surrounding the grounds lent the air its fresh pine and dewy scent.

I tugged my leather jacket closed to stave off the early morning chill. I jumped behind a bush when a pair of armored guards walked past.

I wasn't really planning to 'escape', *per se*. I'd just had enough of being all cooped up in the boring old dungeons. I was sure everyone would agree that I posed them zero threat. What was the harm of my having a nosy around?

This was my first time in this mystical realm.

Or second, I supposed, depending on how one looked at it—*whatever, too confusing.*

This was my *first* time in this mystical realm.

Slipping past the courtyard, through the doors into the main structure, I crept along the edges of the hall, glad at least that my sneakers didn't clip-clop loudly on the marble floors.

I marveled at the tapestries hanging from the walls, breathing history, depicting swirling constellations that shifted ever so slightly when I passed, as if the stars occasionally realigned to some unseen rhythm.

The castle was less gaudy than I'd expected. It was dignified, regal in a way that didn't shout. I ducked behind a pillar as two servants wandered past, their steps steady and purposeful, likely to begin the day.

Pale gold light was starting to filter through stained-glass windows, casting shimmering fragments across the stone corridors like bits of a broken rainbow.

I stopped by a vaulted archway, brushing my fingers along its ornately carved frame. The manicured lawns and flowerbeds outside were turning colors with the daybreak.

Tracing the garden path lines with my eyes up to the courtyard, my heart nearly stopped.

It was her.

She wore a long, simple tunic sleeveless dress, and if her bright hair and violet eyes didn't already make it seem like she was glowing amidst the sunrise, that smile definitely did.

She was accompanying some of the maids carrying baskets and bags of grain up the wide staircase, laughing with them. No hint of anxiety or anger or frustration on her face. Relaxed. Beautiful.

She was such a sight for sore eyes. I had to slap myself to stay alert. I was a fugitive after all. The last thing I needed was to get caught by the guards in a love-struck daze.

I cast another furtive look around before ducking behind a pillar close by so I could be more discreet. I took a deep breath. My pulse was already beginning to race thinking of everything I wanted to tell her, conversations we had left open, questions I wanted to ask—*wait*.

Who the hell is that guy?

The guy, with blond hair and fair features, wearing distinguished garb with a long heavy cape and a seal on his collar, had stopped in the middle of the courtyard to speak to her. None of his clothes disguised his tall, broad stature even a little bit. I thought I could even make out his freakishly well-defined biceps and six-pack through his armor.

Was this the guy she was betrothed to?

I clenched my jaw.

When she'd dropped that admittedly particularly devastating piece of info, I'd still had this ridiculous shred of hope that maybe at least, she didn't like the guy she was betrothed to. Like maybe it was an arranged marriage that she didn't even want, that she was trying to get out of, or something.

But damn, looking at that guy, who the heck wouldn't want to break off a piece of that?

I eyed the huge sword hilted at his side. He was probably also a great warrior.

Oh, wonderful. He had a great smile, too.

How was I supposed to compete with that?

I closed my eyes for a moment in complete dejection and pure green jealousy, before forcibly shaking it all off.

Get a grip, Josh.

I already knew my chances with her were slim to none. It didn't change my mission. I only needed to focus on recovering my lost memories and helping 'save' her world now, whatever that meant.

I sighed before trudging back down the hall.

The two of them had finished speaking, and she was headed back into the castle. Keeping one eye on her, I made my way through the halls so that I could catch her as soon as she was by herself.

When she turned a corner close enough to where I was, I shot out of my hiding place. Clamping my hand over her mouth, I tugged her back through a doorway.

"Mmf—!"

Of course, I should have known better than to surprise my volatile, powerful fairy.

The next thing I knew, I was flung up and over her shoulder, slammed down to the floor—

"Whoa—!"

—before a bright flash of light seared my eyes and I was thrown clear across the room.

"Aahh!" I smacked against the back wall with a hard thump. "Ohh...ow..." I clutched at my very likely bruised shoulder.

Still in a defensive stance, she narrowed her eyes at me in the dim light. "*Josh?*" Her tone carried its usual disbelief and exasperation whenever she said my name.

I liked to think it was endearing.

Although this much closer to her, I couldn't miss the dark circles under her eyes.

Perhaps she wasn't as relaxed as she seemed at first glance.

Uneasy with my scrutiny, her gaze darted away for a moment. Then, straightening up, her chest heaved as she walked over. "What are you—how did you get out of the holding cell?"

Grimacing, I shifted to sit up on the floor. I couldn't quite talk yet.

She rolled her eyes. "What were you even thinking sneaking up on me?"

"Sorry," I croaked with a half-cough, nursing my arm.

"You're not supposed to be wandering around the castle." She bent down to help me up.

I was instantly enveloped in that intoxicating scent—jasmine and cypress. "Um..." It took a bit of effort to clear my head. "What is this place? Am I a prisoner here? That guy you were talking to before, is that the guy you're betrothed to?"

Her mouth opened slightly at the rush of questions, also possibly from the odd combination of my questions. She knew which question I wanted to have answered first. "That guy owns this kingdom, this castle. He's the one you should be thanking for his hospitality—no wait, I meant, for keeping you alive."

I frowned. "So I *am* a prisoner here?"

Her lips pursed. "It's complicated." Grabbing my arm, she led the way to escort me back down toward the dungeons. "Look, this is for your own good." She signaled one of the guards with a meaningful nod, like 'please keep an eye on this random freak', as the heavy door was clanked shut behind me once again.

"What's your name?" I called out before she could leave.

Glancing over her shoulder, her eyes narrowed as if in suspicion. But then she turned and left without another word.

3

All the Ways

The last streaks of sunlight poured through the barred window of my tiny cell. I could imagine those gardens outside the castle would have looked quite picturesque.

I didn't know why I wasn't terrified about being stuck in the dungeons. I wanted to believe she had been telling the truth earlier—it was for my own good. She had told me, in no uncertain terms, that there were people in this realm who would be glad to see me gone. Her people hadn't wanted her to bring me here at all. I wondered if even that guy who owned this kingdom was threatened by me.

I rolled my shoulder, testing where I'd injured my arm when she'd thrown me back earlier. I supposed I'd certainly learned that lesson.

I bit my lip as I absently checked my phone, the only thing I'd managed to bring over from Earth, aside from the clothes on my back.

No signal.

I wasn't really expecting any signal. Miraculously, I had just enough battery charge to turn it on.

Sure, I was missing home. My sister Erin was probably excited to be getting started with wedding preparations. She'd recently gotten engaged to her boyfriend. I was a bit bummed that I would miss it, but at least I was reassured that the only family I had left on Earth would be taken care of with me gone.

I'd lost touch with most of my friends since that time years ago when my memories had been wiped. My jackass boss had recently fired me from that torturous job—good riddance, either way. I really had been living a half-life back on Earth.

There was no going back now. Only forward.

I swiped through the most recent saved photos on my phone.

For nostalgia?

Maybe.

But it sure didn't take long for that young guard guy to be curious enough to crane his neck and look over.

Maybe he didn't receive the directive from upstairs, or he wasn't terribly good at his *one* job—guarding me, the prisoner—because when I offered him my phone in exchange for ten minutes to myself, he totally bought it.

Cool, cool, cool.

Early the next morning, my fairy found me sitting at the balcony overlooking the courtyard, my legs dangling over the railing.

"You didn't really answer my question yesterday. Are you betrothed to that guy?" I prompted with a raise of my eyebrows.

She'd skidded to a stop upon seeing me, her jaw dropping once again. "How the fates are you getting out of the holding cell?"

"Hey, you have your magic, I have mine." I hopped off my seat. "And if you won't tell me your name, I'm not obliged to tell you anything."

A pair of maids walked past us, headed inside the castle. One of them gave me a smile. One of them waved. I'd helped them push the gardening wagon out of a muddy ditch earlier.

"Good day, ladies." I waved back.

My surly fairy shot me a deadpan look before whirling around to walk away.

Jumping in alert, I fell into step beside her. "Do you want me to try to guess your name then?"

She didn't respond.

"Hmm... Is it...Coral? Or Sapphire? Adele? Taylor? Beyoncé?" I rubbed my chin. "Oh, wait. It's one of those tricky Irish names, isn't it? That one spelled like Louise, but is really pronounced as Lisa?"

Another of the uniformed maids walked purposefully up to meet us by the conservatory. She gave a little curtsy before relaying, "My lady, more scrolls have arrived from the archives."

"Thank you, Charlotte." She gave her a smile. "Can you please make sure there are spare candles in the library as well? I think the ones there are nearly spent."

"Certainly, my lady."

I glanced from her to Charlotte in turn. "You're not gonna introduce me? Should I introduce myself? Everyone's aware I'm not gonna hurt you all, right?" I put my hands up in resignation before beaming a big smile at Charlotte.

The maid's cheeks flushed a bit, and she dropped her gaze.

But Miss I'm-So-Nonchalant merely put her hand up. "That will be all, Charlotte."

I followed the departing maid with my gaze before meeting those violet eyes again. "You won't introduce me. You won't even introduce you. Should I keep guessing?"

She didn't oblige my question. She merely led the way through the halls, but I already knew she was escorting me back to the dungeons.

I laced my fingers behind my back as we walked on. "Are you named after a heavenly—er, celestial object? Jupiter has sixty moons—what are all their names again? Io? Callisto? Ah, I should have paid more attention in Science class."

I thought I heard an exasperated huff from her, even though she still didn't reply. I took it as a good sign that she wasn't outright ignoring me. I was at least eliciting some re-action.

"Why won't you tell me your name?" I threw up my hands. "I know it's not 'Freyjn'—that name you made us use on Earth. Who is Freyjn anyway? It sounded like you actually know someone with that name for real. Whose name was it that you borrowed? A friend? Family? Sister?"

It was gone as fast as it came, but I caught that split second when her eyes widened.

Sister, then.

"None of that concerns you," she pointed out.

I furrowed my eyebrows. "Fine. If you won't tell me your name, can you at least tell me what's going to happen to me? Surely, that much concerns me."

There was so much I wanted to talk to her about. Not the least of which was that I likely had some memories that, once unlocked, might be able to shed some light on everything, perhaps even aid in her cause as well.

The air had already turned damp and chilly. I eyed the several guards we walked past, headed downstairs.

I didn't want to reveal my theory in front of the guards or just anyone. It sounded crazy enough in my head—the potential fact that I'd been here before, or that we'd already met, and I just couldn't remember.

I wanted to sit down and have an actual, proper conversation with her.

She yanked on my arm all the way back to my cell. "You should have everything you need right here."

My stomach hollowed at the tension in her face—the taut set of her jaw, the faint tremor at the corners of her mouth. "Are... are you afraid of me?"

A shadow crossed her violet eyes for the briefest of moments, averting her gaze as if she was at odds with herself.

"I... I cannot explain, but... I can assure you, it is better this way."

I clenched my teeth. I could tell something was wrong, but she wouldn't meet my eyes again.

She merely bid the duty guards, "Can you gentlemen please *please* make sure this one doesn't get out again?" before turning on her heel and walking away again.

Tell you what, dungeons were super boring places.

Later on, the older, more 'experienced' guy they'd left to keep an eye on me overnight was already snoozing well into the wee hours, slumped into his chair, even before I fell asleep myself.

When I woke up near the crack of dawn with a fresh surge of motivation, I easily slipped out of the dungeons again. If she didn't want to talk to me, I would have to find some other way to prove that I was more useful than some captive in a cage.

The castle grounds were always bustling. Jumping to lend a hand here and there, it didn't take long for the staff to drop their guard around me. They were all quite hardworking and friendly. Although most of them were still too wary for conversation.

The most I could find out was that the name of this place was the Kingdom of Cephiron, one of the Highland Kingdoms, and that the flowerbeds were seasonal hyacinths.

By the time my fairy found me again, late in the afternoon, I was at the rose garden, helping to pack the fertilizer.

She was crossing the courtyard, right above the wide set of steps where I was helping one of the gardeners. Visibly jerking to a stop, she met my gaze with a glare of exasperation.

She shook her head, clutching a stack of books to her chest. "Are you making friends?"

I pulled off my gloves. Casually wiping the sweat off my forehead, I shot her a triumphant grin. "It seems not everyone is intent on being all surly, like some people I know."

The gardener, Philippe, gave her a little bow in greeting. "M'lady."

"Phil's a real decent guy." I mocked a salute at him as he went on doing his work. "In fact, everyone's real friendly here. I don't understand what harm you're thinking you're keeping me away from by throwing me in the dungeon."

"It's a holding cell."

I scoffed as she marched over to grasp my arm again, no doubt to drag me back. "Holding cell, schmolding cell."

Her forehead creased. "What does that even mean?"

"It means you literally can't keep me locked down here anymore." I paused. "Unless you clap me in chains, and cast spells, and whatnot." My eyes popped wide open in alarm. "I-I mean, *don't* clap me in chains, and cast spells, and whatnot. You didn't hear me suggest any of that at all."

I almost smacked my forehead. This was what happened when I ran my mouth unchecked. I was making even more trouble for myself. I didn't know whether or not those sorts of spells were possible, but shoot, I didn't want to find out.

"I'm really sorry, Josh," was all she said, handing me off to the guards, before she spun on her heel to leave.

4

Darkness

Making friends always pays off.

I gave a short nod to each pair of armored soldiers I walked past. They merely lifted their chin in acknowledgment, but didn't pay me any mind otherwise.

Enough sentries and castle staff had seen me gallivanting about outside the dungeons in the past few days that nobody seemed concerned about me escaping anymore.

Plus, one of the maids I'd helped locate some children she was babysitting, amidst the most challenging round of 'hide and go seek' by the way, had bid her brother—one of the dungeon guards—to be extra nice to me.

Not only had they no longer bothered to lock my cell door, but I'd also managed to ask Charlotte, that other maid from before, to sort me out a full bath in one of the rooms in the back, near the servants' quarters.

The water in the modest metal tub wasn't hot by any means, but there was soap and a proper towel. Charlotte had even found some clean trousers and a long-sleeved shirt for me to change into while my clothes got laundered.

Shaking the water out of my hair, I slipped my leather jacket back on as I strode down the darkened hallways. The castle had turned in once again after the long day.

I was mulling over what tasks I might volunteer for tomorrow in exchange for everyone's kindness when a faint whimper broke the dead silence of the night.

At first, I thought it was one of those weird castle echoes, but then I realized it was moaning.

What were the odds that this castle was haunted?

I bit my lip. Probably high.

I slowed, but found myself not diverting away.

Was I headed closer to where the ghost was? Was I supposed to turn tail and run away? What if the ghost had some sort of unfinished business and was in need of my help? What if it was a poltergeist and ate my face?

I shook my head to clear it again. But as I walked along the hall of chamber doors, I frowned as what I was straining to hear sounded a bit more like...crying.

Approaching a set of chamber doors with ornate carving, I paused with my hand on the knob. *That scent...*

I released the breath I nervously held as soon as I opened the door to peek through to confirm.

Simple wooden furnishings, a faded tapestry of wildflowers above the flickering hearth, a set of padded chairs before a half-read book resting open on the table. A familiar figure was tucked in the elegant four-posted bed, nearly swallowed by a fluffy mountain of blankets.

It *was* her chambers.

A faint sense of déjà vu struck me. Images of the room flashed in my mind—somehow more vibrantly-colored, and yet the same. Dark. Ominous. I had to blink several times to clear my vision. Obviously, there was no way I'd ever been in her room before.

Stepping inside, I carefully shut the door behind me, hoping that even in the stark quiet, I was the only one who could hear my heartbeat pounding so loud in my chest.

Another muffled sound came from the bed.

She was tossing and turning, tangled amidst her sheets, having some sort of nightmare. I moved a bit closer. The moonlight shining through the window was glistening on her sweaty forehead. Her hair matted against her neck.

"NO—!" She clutched at the sheets beside her, her knuckles white.

I had to do something. I had to help her.

Moving to place a tentative hand on her shoulder, I shook her a bit. "Hey, you're having a nightmare."

But she wouldn't wake.

Her face was twisted in pain, as if she wanted to cry out but couldn't.

Bracing both hands on her shoulders, I leaned over her to shake her harder. "Wake up. You're having a nightmare."

"Don't—please—" She gasped, her eyes squeezing shut as if to ward away whatever was haunting her mind.

I was debating whether or not I should do anything more jarring when she sat up in bed with a start.

Her eyes flew open, her face shocked and pale. Then her expression collapsed into anguish again. "No..." Her forehead dropped against my chest, continuously shaking her head, still on the brink of dreaming. "No, no, no..."

My chest was tight. She was always so fearless and stubborn. I couldn't stand seeing her like this.

Dammit.

I shifted to sit on the side of her bed, pulling her closer so I could wrap both arms around her. "Shh... It's okay. It's okay. It's just a dream."

She was trembling all over, curled up, her face buried in my chest. Her skin was cold, clammy. I squeezed a bit tighter to share my warmth. For a few moments, I held her close.

Never mind that it felt like I had never belonged anywhere more than here with her in my arms. I was going to make sure she calmed down and fell back to sleep before I left. Then in the morning, I would make sure to check she'd had enough sleep and get some proper breakfast in her. This much, I could do.

After a while, her trembling subsided. I stroked her hair, hoping to soothe her. "It was just a dream. It's okay. You're safe."

Safe...

The notion seemed to yank her out of her trance. Breaking off, she tilted her face up as if regaining her bearings. Her chest heaving again, she stared up at me with those big, watery violet eyes. "Josh... What...?"

Of course, she didn't look happy to see me.

"Um. I'm so sorry. I...heard something and I..." I swallowed hard. "I wanted to make sure you were okay." I was going to pull away when I noticed her fingers were clutching the fabric of my shirt.

Those eyes were pinned on me again—always in question, in marveling, and I couldn't move.

She took a deep breath, as if to settle herself. I was so relieved I'd just had a real bath. Then somehow, her delicate fingers found the damp ends of my hair, and my breath hitched in my throat.

There went my super loud heartbeat again.

My mouth turned dry.

Her eyes were as wide as mine when I met them.

All at once, she gasped and pushed me away. "You shouldn't be here."

Not resisting at all, I sprang up to stand. "I-I know. I just..." Straightening up beside her bed, I dropped my gaze. "Listen, there were some things I wanted to talk to you about. Important things."

She pulled the covers up to her chin. "Look, if it's about your fleeting human feelings—"

"No. No—" I started to shake my head, but then stopped. "Fleeting, what—? You know what, fine. I guess we also need to clear the air about this." I rubbed my hand over my face in frustration. "Back in my world, that kiss—"

"It meant nothing," she was quick to dismiss.

Frowning, I shot her a sort of indignant look to correct. "To you." I pinched the bridge of my nose. "I have... I obviously have feelings for you, right? To tell you the truth, I don't understand them either. I just—I feel like I can't keep a lid on this anymore."

I put my hand up before she could interrupt. "I don't expect you to do anything. I already know better than to expect anything from you. And I promise, I'm not going to do anything about this either." I stared at the floor again. "I—know you're already with someone else, and I'm really sorry for kissing you. That was, like, 'a moment' thing. I swear it'll never happen again. All I want now is...to help you, okay? Tell me what you need from me and I'll do it. I mean, that's the whole reason I'm here, isn't it? You don't have to avoid me or ignore me. I can keep myself occupied, but please don't lock me in the dungeons anymore. I want—I want to be useful. To you. To this world."

I cringed, trying to stop babbling so I could get to the point. "But more than that, I think... I think I need your help with some memories I've lost. Um...if there was some magic you knew or someone we could talk to about how to recover erased memories, I think it would really help me. Help *us*," I pressed. "I...I want to understand what's going on. Here." I gestured to the quiet chambers around us. "And here." I pointed at my chest.

The glare she gave me hadn't changed since I'd started my somewhat passionate ramble. "How do you keep escaping the holding cell?"

I blinked, my jaw almost dropping.

After my long speech, that was all she could say? Her nonchalance stabbed at my chest. Tamping down my dejection, I heaved a huge sigh and spun to leave. "Fine. Sorry, I'll go back to my cage then."

5

Lance

The mid-morning sun warmed my skin. I dug my fingers into the damp soil, focusing on the cool, yielding sensation and the earthy aroma as I pulled out stubborn weeds. At least, I was certain I wasn't hallucinating all this. But it seemed like all my 'great destiny' was good for was performing menial, everyday work for this kingdom.

I had finished stacking hay bales at the stables earlier. Then I promised Deirdre I would help her with fetching eggs in the chicken coops later. I'd probably look for Philippe or Charlotte next to see if anyone needed any help with anything else. There was always something to do at a castle like this.

I supposed it wasn't too bad. I had proper meals. Maybe later, I would get upgraded to a small servant's quarters instead of the dungeon, waking up behind bars each day. At some point, watch someone finally invent electricity.

"

A commotion near the courtyard was setting quite a few of the groundspeople running.

Looking over, I straightened up to shield my eyes from the sun. "What's going on, Philippe?"

"My Lord is back from the Fae lands. I hope he doesn't need a healer like last time."

"Is there a war going on or something?"

He nodded. "Some of the Fae Isles are in dissent. The Priori regent of the High Fae has asked for assistance from all the nearby territories. However, I believe our intention is not to intervene. The master is trying to negotiate a polite decline to their request." Shifting in his stance, he fiddled with his fingers. "We much value our peace here in the highlands. I imagine it will be a hard bargain to strike since the Priori people are also—"

Philippe cut off, his eyes widening upon glimpsing something over my shoulder.

I should have known that when I turned around, I'd see her again. Her one authoritative eyebrow was already up in warning at Philippe, presumably to shut up.

My pink fairy didn't address me, of course. "Is he back?"

Philippe gave her a bow. "Yes, m'lady."

Acknowledging that with a nod, she hurried across the courtyard.

I was just as curious. I wiped my hands on my pants and followed suit.

A bustle of people streamed in from somewhere, buzzing around that blond guy from the other day as he strode purposefully across the expanse. He spoke to several people at once, giving orders with the confident air of someone who owned this kingdom and knew it.

A smile broke on his face when his gaze landed on the fuchsia figure approaching him. "I trust everything is in order." With a wave of his hand, the rest of his entourage departed with curtsies and bows.

Trying not to be intimidated, I puffed up my chest as I moved to follow, even though I kept my place standing partway behind her. I didn't want to stand right next to him and make a comparison that much easier.

I was sure I'd never met him before, but I already felt this nagging dislike in the back of my mind. I studied her face as they spoke, trying to gauge a mutual affection. They didn't attempt any other display of intimacy, thank goodness, but maybe that was because we were in plain view of pretty much everyone in the kingdom.

If she liked me back though, that wouldn't have stopped me. If I were him, returning from a time away, I would've—

"You haven't been sleeping well." The tall, blond warrior's hand rose up as if to touch her cheek.

I stared at his hand, nearly wide-eyed, but it simply fell away, not making contact.

"I'm fine, Lance."

Her tone was even, but I could tell he wasn't buying it either. Even though he definitely wasn't there to comfort her last night. How many nights had she been struggling to sleep?

Furrowing my eyebrows, I dropped my gaze.

If she was going to end up with someone else, there was nothing I could do to stop it. But I was going to make sure he better damn well deserve her. If not, he was going to have another thing coming.

That steely gaze finally shifted to me. "We haven't had a chance to be properly introduced." He offered his hand. "My name is Lance, of the Heights of Cephiron."

I gave his hand a brief, firm shake. "Hi, I'm Josh Richards. I'm in love with her."

My fairy's eyes popped wide in shock, rendered utterly speechless.

Lance merely raised an eyebrow.

Rolling my eyes, I shot her a pointed look. "Come on. You knew it already. I just figured this guy needs to know it, too. I figure everyone needs to know it. I mean, whatever, I know I have zero chance, but still."

Her face flushed so deep red, a hint of regret prickled at the back of my neck. But I wanted to make sure this guy knew I had a vested interest in seeing that he treated her well.

Lance sort of scoffed. "You were right. He is a bit odd."

Shaking her head, she blew out a breath. "I'm so sorry, Lance. He keeps escaping the holding cell somehow."

"Then perhaps it is a pointless endeavor to keep him contained any longer."

Her eyes bulged again as she stared at Lance, as if that was the most horrific notion ever.

"Oh, yes, please," I piped up, eagerly looking at each of them in turn before meeting Lance's gaze. "Hey, dude. Can you please sort all this out? All I want is a mattress, okay? The smallest bedroom is fine. I don't need much. I just don't want to have to mess with the dungeon door anymore—I mean, that crap is heavy." Pursing my lips, I held my fist up.

Lance didn't oblige my fist bump, but only shot me another strange look. "I think that can be arranged."

Her groan of exasperation felt like my triumph.

Grinning, I dropped my hand. "Thank you. Thank you very much, Mr. Lance."

"Call me Lance."

"Great! I'm Josh. I'm in love with—"

"Yeah, caught that." He took in the grass stains on my pants and the mud caked in places. "Have you been assigned gardening duties in my kingdom?"

My kingdom. The way he said it grated on my nerves, as if it was meant to put me in my place.

"No. Just helping out here and there, taking care of certain things since, you know—" I shrugged, attempting for nonchalant. "You weren't here to take care of them yourself."

I wasn't normally this much of a jerk, but something deep inside me was insisting on hating this guy.

He didn't even flinch. "Alas, some of us must also see to taking care of things that benefit more than just my own kingdom. It is an unmatched weight to bear responsibility for the realms themselves, the entire land of Arcadia. I wouldn't expect someone like you to understand."

"Maybe." I curled my lips. "Or maybe some of us don't need to be born noble to protect what matters."

A sudden gust of wind blew us both staggering back. I didn't even realize I'd moved closer to attempt to make my points right to Lance's face. But he and I both snapped to attention.

The violet mist was already dissipating from her hand even as she tamped down a bored eye roll. Then, completely ignoring me, she turned her attention to Lance. "I need to talk to you about what I've found."

Lance studied her face again, a crease of concern on his forehead. "I was told how many scrolls were sent over last time. You're already staying up late, spending all your time at the library, poring through all those texts by yourself. It would ease my mind if you had help whenever I'm away."

"You know this is a sensitive matter," she reasoned. "I cannot simply ask someone like my maid to help out."

Lance gave her a pointed look. Then he tilted his head in my direction but said nothing.

Leaning closer, she countered him with a glare. "He cannot be involved in this."

Getting more than a little irritated that they were speaking as if I wasn't even there, I strode between them, putting my hands up. "Hey, hey, I'm already involved in whatever this is, okay? If there's something I can do to help, please, let me at it."

Still ignoring me, the two of them continued their staring contest/battle of wills for a bit longer than I was comfortable, before she finally blew out another loud, exasperated groan—likely of resignation.

The half-grin of triumph on his face quirked a bit as Lance gave a distasteful glance up and down my clothes. "Why don't you get cleaned up first before you come back inside my kingdom?"

6

Unknown

My new chambers were smaller than hers, but with the standard bed, closet, sitting area, balcony, and bathing nook, it was definitely comfortable. It was already twice the size of my apartment on Earth. Plus, obviously, any upgrade from the dungeons got my vote.

Tugging uncertainly on the linen tunic I'd been provided to wear after washing up, I gave a nod to the guard right outside my door as I walked out. "Hey, Stannis, if you got time later, I can teach you that ball game I told you about."

"Certainly, sir."

Several servants and maids had helped me set up my new room. I tried to help out, but after a few minutes, it only looked like I was getting in their way, so I stopped. I wasn't sure how comfortable I was being addressed as 'sir' either.

I'd promised Philippe I was going to work in the gardens tomorrow again. With any luck, they'd still let me be as useful as I could. Couldn't say I knew much about what was expected of me here.

Before I could think about how much easier it was when I was an escaped fugitive from the dungeons, Charlotte met up with me halfway down a hallway to tell me my presence was expected at the library, and then led the way.

Once we arrived at a set of double doors, she curtsied before leaving. I almost wanted to ask questions first, but I supposed there was no point since these matters were allegedly 'too sensitive' for the castle staff.

I pushed the heavy wooden doors open. I let out a whistle, marveling at the cavernous space.

Lance's kingdom's library spanned the length of an entire castle wing, its vaulted ceiling supported by arched beams carved with ancient runes. Tall, narrow windows lined the stone walls, letting in light falling across the tapestries and faded rugs. Rows and rows of shelves stacked with books seemingly disappeared further down a dimly lit aisle.

If a library were all a lady longed for in this world, Lance certainly had it in spades.

"Big sword, big library," I mumbled.

Pinching my nose for a moment to adjust to the rich aroma of parchment, wax, and dust, I easily spotted a bright pink figure seated at a large central table beneath a glass skylight across the way. A collection of bundled scrolls sat before her, some with wax seals cracked with age, some lying open on a pile.

Slowing my walk, a huge mural on the wall caught my eye. It was a weathered painting of a map. *Strange...* I traced my fingers across the subtle spots where the paint had clumped, along the lines of the continents depicted on the image, and several points where settlements were indicated.

The Land of Arcadia.

I'd never seen it before, but somehow, I felt as though I was intimately acquainted with it, the landscapes, the towns... My fingers stopped at a settlement to the south, surrounded by a thick forest, a remote village. *There should be a lake...*

My heart started to pound in my ears. I furrowed my eyebrows, straining to remember—something just out of reach, familiar but elusive. But the harder I concentrated, the more it slipped through my grasp, leaving behind only a hollow pressure behind my eyes and a nagging sense that the answer was right there, just beneath the surface, but refusing to be named. Like chasing shadows in fog.

"We are here."

I nearly jumped at my startle when her voice broke through my reverie. I hadn't even noticed she'd walked up and was standing before the map too. Her finger hovered over an area west labelled 'Cephiron Highlands.'

She peered at my face. "That's why you've been staring at it, right? Trying to figure out where we are? This kingdom is of the human realm."

I blinked, starting to nod. "Actually..." I turned to the map again. "Can you tell me what's here?" I pointed to the southern settlement once again.

"The Fae lands."

I bit my lip. "This is...going to sound weird, but I thought there should have been a small lake here. An ice lake...?"

"There are many lakes, some of them ice over." She didn't seem suspicious or curious about my inquiry. Her tone conveyed a steady nonchalance. "I'm not quite sure what you're looking for. Supposedly, these two realms make up the Arcadian continent—Fae, human." She gestured an imaginary line across the map.

"Supposedly?" I echoed.

She pursed her lips and beckoned me over. "Come."

I jumped to follow her. "By the way, thank you for letting me out of the dungeon."

"You can thank Lance for that."

Walking up to the central table, I eyed several scrolls haphazardly strewn across its surface alongside a separate neat pile that had been clearly grouped away. One scrap of paper in particular caught my eye.

"What is this?" I pointed to the bit.

Her forehead creased at my slight movement, as if already envisioning that I would ruin everything. "Please don't mess things up. I still need to have some of these scrolls translated."

But I was more than a little bit confused. "What do you need the nutritional information of fish crackers for?"

She shot me a look. "What?"

I angled my head to read the paper on the table again. "That's what this says. 'Nutritional Information.' 'Fish crackers.'"

Almost slack-jawed, she stared at me. "You can read this text?"

"Yeah, why? You *can't* read this?"

Her eyes narrowed, but I couldn't tell if she was impressed or not. "You really are a being of two worlds. I suppose I hadn't even given it a second thought when you had no trouble communicating with the castle staff either."

I stuffed my hands in my pockets. "Huh. That is so weird. How did something written in my language end up in this world?"

She nodded. "That is the mystery. But this will be perfect. You may be able to help me pick through which of these scrolls are important and which ones are...fish crackers." She blew out a breath. "Now I'm glad Lance insisted that you help out."

I made a face, mumbling, "Sure. Lance is the one who deserves recognition."

She didn't seem to have heard me. She went on, "I told you before some of my people don't even believe your realm exists."

"Yeah, the fourth realm. That's what you called it."

She nodded again. "This is why I had to bring you to this world. The texts say the 'Curse bearer' could only have come from the fourth realm. You're my only proof."

My gaze moved to the other documents on the table. "So these scrolls...we're looking for more proof here?"

Hesitating for a moment, she bit her lip. "Yes."

I caught a hitch in her tone. She wasn't telling me the whole truth. But I was already grateful enough to know whatever she was willing to divulge. I wasn't going to press.

"Cephiron scholars are quite meticulous. This kingdom has the largest collection of books and knowledge all the way back through the ages. I've even liaised with larger libraries across the realm to send me what they have that could be at all relevant. If there's anything to find, we ought to find it here in this room."

"Cool." I slumped back in a chair, ready to get started. I pointed to the scrolls set aside that had caught my attention earlier. "So do you need me to go through those first?"

"No." She snapped her hand over the pile as though protectively. "I've-I've gone through these already. This is just the main text of the prophecy. I-It's been passed down through the ages. It has a lot of vague references, passages that don't make any sense." She waved her hand to dismiss the topic. "You won't need to bother with these."

My eyes lit up at the word prophecy. It was something my dad had apparently struggled with a lot. Back on Earth, he'd revealed that he'd been trying to find a way around this ominous 'prophecy.' I still wasn't too sure what it all really entailed. I tilted my head, studying her expression carefully. "Are you sure I don't need to read those ones, you know, for context?"

"Yes, I'm sure. Just...sort through the others, if you can, please."

"Okay, but you gotta give me something more. Like, what am I supposed to keep an eye out for here anyway?" I rifled absently through the small stack in front of me.

"Any mentions of another realm... possibly references to a 'third' one."

I rapped on the table in late recognition. "Oh, wait—that's right. If there are only two realms, how come mine makes number four?"

"This is the heart of what I've been trying to discover. I believe that a long time ago, there used to be three realms. Fae, human, and... dragon."

Stunned, I nearly sputtered. "Whoa. What?"

She took a deep breath. "The third realm, and indeed these creatures themselves, are now mere legends, folklore. Some of my people have even come to believe they'd never even existed."

My eyes bulged in disbelief as I processed her words.

I stared at her face again, trying to spot the lie, but her expression was dead serious.

I clutched at the corners of the wooden table, almost already at a loss. "Oh-kay... So you're saying...our mission is *basically* trying to prove—" My eyebrows furrowed deeply, I turned to her with a seriously incredulous expression. "That dragons exist?"

This time, there was no hitch whatsoever in her tone.

"Yes."

7

Mythical

The biggest mystery in my life used to be figuring out who was stealing all the dry-erase markers at the office. Or possibly why the orange juice concentrate I usually bought tasted different all of a sudden after the company did a rebrand.

But her expression was completely sober, as though she hadn't said anything that almost blew my mind.

Then again, I shouldn't be too surprised. I'd already recently discovered that magic was real, and that there were, in fact, other worlds out there beyond my own. Considering the existence of these majestic, mythical creatures shouldn't be too much of a leap.

She went on, her tone steady as anything. "Some Fae do believe that dragons used to exist hundreds of years ago. However, the records have so far only ever shown them to be a violent kind, only capable of destruction. Certainly not a type of being civilized enough to govern over their own realm." Her forehead creased somewhat in frustration. "I'd like to find proof that, not only were dragons not an outright danger, but that perhaps they still do exist...somewhere on Arcadia." She dropped her gaze, her last word coming out as a mumble, "Maybe."

I studied the wistful look on her face, easily noting the shadow of pain behind her eyes. "There's something more to it, isn't there? I mean, there must be a reason this means so much to you, or why you're the only one who's working on this."

She didn't answer right away. "That's not important right now." She pushed a stack of papers in my direction, most of the ones she'd indicated needed translating. "Here, why don't you go through these first and weed out irrelevant items?"

I let out a resigned sigh. "Alrighty."

She sat down across the table from me. She pushed her long hair behind her ears and took a deep breath before she smoothed down a page in a leather-bound tome to read it, seemingly carrying on her work as if she'd never even stopped.

The quiet of the library instantly enveloped me, a soothing calm coming over everything. The crackle of the torchlight and pages turning lent a reassuring, peaceful ambiance. The distinct musty smell reminded me that this place was built well over centuries ago.

I couldn't believe I was even here, in a medieval castle's library on a mystical other world. With her. But this was a reality I was most definitely willing to accept.

I'd been dreaming about her for months. A dream that was always too far out of reach. The impossibility of which had always made me ache. As though not being with her rendered me incomplete. As if there was always something missing in my life. And somehow, just sitting here, seeing her, being in the same room, having her close by, filled in some sort of chasmal hole in my soul.

I felt like I could breathe again.

Only half-aware I was doing it, I watched as she read. A soft glow from the candlelight played in her hair, against her smooth skin, those eyes—

Her eyes flicked up at me, already narrowed in suspicion.

I jumped and picked up a scroll of paper to cover my face. My heartbeat pounded in my chest again, even with the thrill shooting up my spine.

I bit my lip, carefully folding down a corner of the scroll to sneak a peek at her again.

She was still glaring at me. Though strangely, not in anger. More like incredulity and exasperation. As per usual.

I couldn't help a self-conscious chuckle. "Sorry." My cheeks warmed. "I'll get to work now. I promise." I sneaked one last glance at her before taking a deep breath, bowing my head to sift through the scrolls before me.

There weren't any more 'fish cracker' tidbits, but what was there was a veritable treasure trove of knowledge. There were all kinds of records, historical data on shifting geographic features across the land, population statistics, a territorial map showing the old boundaries of the kingdom of Cephiron through decades, and its expansions, names of towns that shouldn't be familiar to me but somehow were.

I didn't even realize I was doing it, but before long, I had begun to sort the books and papers I'd gone through into two piles.

Stuff that seemed familiar to me and stuff that didn't. Oddly enough, one stack was growing faster than the other.

I didn't come across anything that referred to any third realm or dragons yet, but I was finding simply learning about Arcadia itself already fascinating.

Among the scrolls about the Fae, someone had meticulously recorded all the types of magic, with each having to do with the four elements and every manner of manifestation. Another scroll inventoried a long list of fantastical creatures, some even with accompanying rough sketches.

I was so absorbed in my reading. I barely noticed when the castle staff came through to bring plates of food. I looked up at the aroma of freshly baked bread as it was plonked beside me on a tray, along with cured meats, slices of cheese, fruits.

"Whoa." My mouth watered.

There was no clock in the library, but it must have been very late afternoon, given the indication of the shadows and the deep orange sky outside. And my complaining stomach.

I gave the brown-haired young woman serving the food a big smile. "This is great. Thank you so much, Miss...?"

"Dora, my lord." She gave me a small curtsy.

"Very nice to meet you. My name is Josh," I offered, before jerking my thumb in the direction of my research partner across the table. "I'm in love with her."

My somber fuchsia fairy's shoulders tensed as she visibly paused from reading, but it seemed she was intent on ignoring me.

The maid simply giggled as she finished up and turned to leave the room, before another uniformed guy came through the doors carrying a tray with pewters of drinks.

Grinning, I waved at him. "Oh, hi, we haven't met yet either. I'm Josh. I'm in love with her."

The guy simply shot me an odd look, making quick work of delivering the tray before hurrying away.

Violet eyes flashing for a split second, she groaned out loud. "Stop saying that."

I rolled my shoulder, popping a piece of fruit in my mouth. "Why does it bother you so much?" I mumbled through my mouthful, casually putting my feet up on the chair beside me.

Maybe I should have relented, but it was true, it felt good to say, and I had a sneaky suspicion that it wasn't entirely unwanted.

"It just does." Her fists clenched on the table, but her cheeks were rosy pink. "Swear to me you won't go around saying that to people anymore."

"Swear to *you*?" I gawked. "There's no way I'm doing any more oaths with you. Not after the last time when you tricked me into that quest, like a scavenger hunt from hell."

"Then please stop saying that."

I raised one eyebrow as a brilliant thought occurred to me. "Tell me your name and maybe I'll consider stopping."

Her eyes widened in annoyance. She pushed her chair back with a loud scrape. "I think that's enough research for today." Straightening up, she quickly whirled around to exit the library.

"Hey, wait!" I downed a cup of water, grabbing some last-minute wedges of cheese, before racing after her. "You know you can't avoid this forever."

She hurried down the hallway, possibly trying to lose me with her fast walking. But I was determined to see this one thing through.

I had no powers to bargain with, no riches to put up, nothing really to my name.

"Come on. It's an easy deal. I'll stop being relentlessly annoying and telling everyone in the kingdom that I'm in love with you. All you need to do is tell me your name."

"No."

I gritted my teeth. How stubborn did she have to be? It wasn't like I was asking for much. "Seriously." I threw my hands up in full disbelief. "What on this *freaky* other world do I have to do to earn the right to know your name?"

She stopped short so fast, the wind rushed past her form. Lips pursed, she tilted her head in consideration.

We were passing by the training courtyard where more than a dozen guards were sparring, and it was like a light bulb came on over her head.

Uh-oh.

Sucking in a breath, I already knew I didn't like the calculating look on her face. I instantly dreaded giving her this opening.

My stomach already gurgled as I spied the great and mighty Lance across the courtyard, too. His fabulous blond hair glinted in the light as he was no doubt leading the training exercises. Either that, or maybe I ate all that cheese too fast.

Dammit. Why did I always insist on making more trouble for myself?

"Oh no..." I moaned, studying her expression. "What?"

Turning to give me a sickeningly sweet smile, the look on her face was nothing short of self-assured. "Tell you what," she proposed, gesturing to the courtyard. "You best Lance at swords, and I'll tell you my name."

My jaw dropped in protest. "What, right now? You *know* he's going to pummel me into the ground!"

She clicked her tongue in mocking. "You don't even know how to use a sword."

"Why on *Earth* would I learn how to use a sword?"

"Because you are no longer on Earth."

Fair point.

Her eyebrows furrowed, eyes darting around like she was trying to choose her words carefully. "You need... You need to be prepared for whatever your destiny entails."

I grimaced. "Like what, sword fighting?"

"Anything!"

I glanced at the training yard where big guys were grunting and heaving as they swung their giant swords around. I was sure I was still cringing.

I ran my fingers through my hair. "Hey, you can't just drop a challenge like that on me. I need—I need time to prepare. You forget the most danger I faced back in my world was like, the random pickpocket on the subway."

She gave me an assessing look up and down. "Fine," she conceded. "Land even *one* strike today, and perhaps I'll consider your request." She folded her arms across her chest. "Surely, you should be able to prove yourself. Prove your potential, at least. Now what do you say? You *are* the 'Curse bearer', aren't you?"

I stuck my tongue out. "I never asked to be your blasted 'Curse bearer', and honestly, I don't think that means what you think it means."

8

Potential

I wasn't surprised when Lance agreed to participate in our little bargain. No doubt he also knew he was going to pummel me into the ground. I was willing to bet good money that he was more than a little eager to show off for his girlfriend and demonstrate just how lacking I was all in one fell swoop.

The warmth of the hot day sizzled off the training yard as shadows began to stretch over the stone tiles. Most of the other guards stepped aside, taking a break from their own training to watch, even as a handful of other soldiers were still training down the other end.

Sucking the insides of my cheeks, I shifted on my feet as I warily watched Lance approaching.

Without any warning, he tossed me his sword—like a complete asshat, assuming that I could possibly ever even catch such a huge pointy thing using my own hands without hurting myself.

"Whoa!" I jumped to one side to avoid it altogether, yelping as though he'd thrown a live snake in my direction instead.

The metal weapon clankity-clanked, skating across the cobblestone floor.

Low chuckles skittered across the crowd of onlookers.

Well, I was glad to bring them all some entertainment.

Ignoring everyone's stares, I bent over to pick up his sword, already groaning. "Okay, that's heavy."

Lance scoffed a chuckle. "Be careful with that. That sword is of the finest craftsmanship. Cephiron blacksmiths are the best across the whole land. If you must know, my kingdom started as a mere blacksmith village. To this day, we produce some of the finest weapons for all the sovereignties across Arcadia."

I gripped the handle, feeling its authoritative weight in my hand. I couldn't help but admire the inlaid jewels gleaming in the light. The sword was definitely as impressive as the man who owned it.

The jackass of a man who was smirking at me, looking entirely too amused. "If you like, you can use a smaller training sword."

I sneered. "Thanks for your concern." I adjusted my grip on the sword, my palm already slick with sweat.

Jeez, was I really going to face down Lance, Lord of this kingdom? He was probably a master of a hundred battlefields, master of sharp, pointy weapons, best and bravest fighter ever. Also, how dare he look so graceful for a man wearing that much armor?

My stubborn fairy stood at the far end of the training ground, her arms still folded across her chest, her expression unreadable.

One of the soldiers tossed another huge sword at Lance as he squared off with me. He caught it effortlessly, of course. "Ready?" He held his blade loosely, almost lazily. His stance wasn't showy—no, he didn't need it to be. Every shift of his weight was precise, every practice parry effortless.

I blew out a breath.

Screw it.

With a loud cry, I rushed at him to strike first, quick and low, only to find his blade deflected with the ease of someone brushing lint from a coat.

I lunged at him again.

Lance didn't counter immediately. Instead, he turned his head slightly to the line of his soldiers who had stopped to observe the match from the clearing's edge. "See that?" His voice was calm but carrying. "He's telegraphing his strikes. Watch the shoulder—tense before the blade moves. That's your warning."

I clenched my jaw. *Know-it-all arrogant piece of—*

Before I could finish that thought, Lance shifted again. I sprang away, lungs heaving slightly, to regroup. I cast a glance toward the bright pink figure across the way once more. I wasn't expecting she would be cheering me on. Maybe a little bit of concern for my welfare was due. But the look on her face was mere incredulity.

My stomach tightened. Wasn't it enough that I had no confidence in myself? She couldn't even muster the smallest hint of any faith in me whatsoever? This was all her idea after all. Besides, if she didn't even believe I could land one strike at Lance, how could she believe I was the one person destined to save her world at all?

I gave my head a brisk shake to focus back on Lance. I was absolutely no match for him. Everyone already knew it. But damn if I was going to give up without a fight—even a tiny one.

Determined, I charged toward him again, my next strike faster, sharper. I was starting to get used to the weight of the sword in my hand.

Lance had to actually step aside to deflect it. For a moment, I caught the faintest twitch of surprise in his eyebrow. I pressed on, ignoring the burn in my arms. He blocked another strike, but instead of retaliating, he held for a beat, steel against steel. "You're rushing your breath," he said, loud enough for me and the onlookers to hear. "Control your breathing, and your blade will follow."

I gritted my teeth. "Thanks for the lesson," I muttered, barely catching my footing after a counter parry. My heart pounding in my ears, I clenched my jaw in tight resolve.

One strike. I just wanted to get *one* strike.

I let out a cry as I swooped closer with my sword once more. Feinting left, I twisted my grip mid-swing, aiming a rising arc toward Lance's exposed shoulder. For a blink—just one—I thought I had it. The tip of my blade nearly touched the fabric of Lance's sleeve.

But Lance moved like wind, fluid, unhurried— *"Oof!"* In the next breath, I found myself flat on the ground, sword knocked aside, Lance's blade resting lightly against my chest. Not cruelly. Not mockingly. Just... decisively.

I stared at the dusky sky, trying to even out my panting. *Shoot.*

Lance pulled back with a curt nod. "Good effort."

I lay there for another second, chest heaving, sweat dripping from the back of my neck into the stone beneath me.

So much for my pride.

Lance held out a hand to help me up, but I didn't take it.

I took my stubborn time to get back up on shaky legs. My muscles screamed. I wanted to fall straight into bed and sleep for the rest of the year.

I leaned against the sword, attempting to stop panting. I was exhausted and sweating like a pig. I lifted my shirt to wipe the perspiration on my face.

"My lady," Lance called.

"What?" she shot out, seeming startled.

I looked over at her to check what was wrong, but her eyes darted around anxiously.

He'd probably caught her red-handed ogling at him. And betrothed or not, why wouldn't she? Lance looked like he had no more taken a casual stroll along the gardens. He took a swig of water, and even I could see those biceps straining against his shirt sleeves.

I tamped down a knowing eyeroll. *Stupid biceps.*

Lance's eyebrows rose in a prompt, "Are you satisfied with the match?"

"Uh, yes...quite." She cleared her throat. Picking up her skirts, she crossed the training grounds to head back into the castle.

I thought she was going to walk past me completely as that intoxicating scent wafted in the air, but then she halted, not even two feet away.

I met those sparkling violet eyes again. Her face tipped up to study mine for a long moment. I frowned in absolute embarrassment, almost looking away. I didn't want to see abject disappointment or regret on her face. I didn't want to see pity either.

Strangely, there was none of that in her solemn gaze.

She bit her lip. "My name is..."

My eyes widened. I seriously stopped breathing as the soft sound of her voice soothed every single ache in my body right at that instant.

"Tala."

9

Dedicated

I strode past the dusty stacks of the library early the next morning to continue with that research. My entire body still felt like I'd been run over by a bulldozer, but a good night's sleep had at least sorted away *some* of the ache.

I stopped in mid-stride just before I arrived at the central table.

The handful of candles strategically arranged along the space had burned overnight, and spent wax drippings pooled around their bases on the wooden table.

And she was there.

Her head nestled within her folded arms upon the table, surrounded by scrolls and open tomes. Her eyes were closed. Her long hair was loosely tied, but delicate wisps still framed her face. She was asleep.

Tala.

My heartbeat started pounding again of its own accord.

I had no idea why she decided to tell me her name. I obviously hadn't landed any strikes anywhere near Lance. That hadn't been the deal, but I wasn't going to complain.

Of course, it was entirely possible—again—that she was lying. That it wasn't her real name.

Granted, it was pretty. One, at least, I was assured I could pronounce properly. But there was a nagging thought in my back of my mind, much like before. That the name didn't click into place, as if I had been expecting something different.

With a small sigh, I leaned my shoulder against the shelf. I didn't want to wake her. She looked so serene and picturesque. I wished I had a camera to capture it, the moment, her beauty.

It really boggled my mind why she was so intent on undertaking all this research, obviously sacrificing sleep and her comfy bed.

A shuffle of boots from behind me made me straighten up. I was only a little bit alerted. I was comfortable enough in the castle to know that nobody here intended me any harm. Spotting Lance step out of the shadows to stand near me, I fixed my posture again.

He could have killed me yesterday if he wanted to. He had to know I was no threat to him. But I was still a little bit stung by how incredibly unmatched we were in terms of skill, in terms of everything.

Although at the moment, our thoughts seemed to match exactly.

Not bothering to give me a greeting, his voice was low and all business already. "She was right regarding your training. It'll serve you well if you know how to handle yourself with a sword."

"Are you saying you're willing to teach me?"

His shoulders lifted almost imperceptibly. "If she wants me to, I will."

I almost scoffed, but a guy like Lance had way more weighty responsibilities than teaching a little scrap like me how to wield a sword. If Tala were awake, she would tell me I should be grateful.

"How about later this afternoon?" he asked.

"Um, how about tomorrow?" I suggested. "At least, let me get the feeling back in my arms first before I try again?"

"No."

I narrowed my eyes at him. It was part self-assuredness and haughtiness on his face. He enjoyed seeing me squirm. He was for sure not going to make this easy for me at all. I could already tell I was going to learn a lot from him.

Besides, Lance and I agreed on this one other thing as well.

If she wants me to, I will.

Lance noticed my gaze move toward the sleeping figure again. He chucked his chin in her direction. "She's been here researching day and night since you got back."

I nodded, a little disconcerted by that fact. "It's important, isn't it?"

"She says it's her duty."

I didn't know why, but I wanted to groan in almost knowing exasperation. I had a sneaking suspicion she was the kind of person who was all about her 'duty.'

"She's trying to save the world... among other things."

I frowned. "By herself? Somehow, I didn't get the feeling that anyone else shared her particular views about your world coming to an end any time soon."

"Some people are content the way it is. The way it's been for a while." He shifted in his stance. "But she knows better. She knows it could be better. Because it used to be better. She believes there must have been a time when magic used to flow across the land freely, when all the realms were at peace. And her parents—" He stopped short. "Well, maybe I should let her tell you about that stuff."

I made a face. "She doesn't seem particularly eager to talk to me."

"Perhaps."

I shot him another narrow-eyed look. What was that even supposed to mean? I was missing something. I'd felt it since arriving, but there were already so many secrets swirling around me, around us. It was difficult to grasp just one.

I swallowed hard. "She's been having nightmares."

Lance's expression didn't even falter. "I know. Do not worry. She's safe here."

"I know."

Because I did. For some reason, I did know that no matter how much Lance annoyed me, he cared about Tala too.

He would do everything in his power to make her happy. Perhaps, he was also deeply in love with her.

I wasn't sure how I felt about that exactly, but it was a small reprieve for a certain portion of my worries. "Gotta say, I'm at least relieved she's going to marry someone like you. I really hate to say this, but...you're checking out okay in my book."

"She's not marrying me."

Stunned, I blinked. "Say what now?"

Lance's tone held no catch. "I am not her betrothed."

My eyebrows furrowed in puzzlement. "But she told me she was betrothed to some guy."

"I know she is." I caught the tiniest hint of displeasure in his tone. "But it's not me."

"Huh."

Great. More questions.

I shot Lance a wary sideways glance. Or was he lying to me, too? I couldn't exactly say I totally trusted the guy yet.

That nagging voice in the back of my mind was telling me I could though. The same one that kept pointing out things in this world that all seemed a tad bit too familiar. Meaning, Lance must have also had something to do with my last visit to this world.

Either way, what did I really have to lose?

I supposed I could trust Lance enough to let him teach me sword fighting. Even if I spent the next few days being battered across the training ground under his instruction, receiving the odd cuts and grazes from some seriously close calls from his giant sword, falling on my face more times than I'd ever had in my entire life, and then getting back up like a glutton for punishment.

I would do it.

For her.

10

Daggers

I liked to say that I had underestimated the punishing tutelage of Lance, possibly the coolest, most competent swordsman dude ever in this realm. After only three straight days of getting my ass handed to me by him, I really couldn't say that. It was like I joined a gym where the coach was intent on seeing me suffer. Then again, maybe all gyms are like that.

Though with all the warm-up exercises, stance positions, footwork, balance, and sword-handling, the only thing I felt I'd grasped so far was how not to drop the training sword. Still, I was proud of my small achievement. I was already way better than when I'd started.

Between my promises to help the staff with the chores around the castle and researching for hours on end at the library with Tala, I was running completely ragged. I'd almost fallen asleep amidst the books and scrolls on the table yesterday, too.

I smothered my face with my hand.

I almost missed being stuck in the boring dungeons.

A faint clang of metal echoing through the still afternoon air grabbed my attention as I walked past a wide lawn bordered by shrubs, lilies, and camellias along the castle gardens. Curious, I went down the lane instead of heading back into the castle.

Fading sunlight spilled over the low stone walls. It was nearing dusk, but this area of the castle grounds was otherwise empty—except for her.

Tala stood at the far end of the green, a blur of controlled movement. Her fuchsia hair fixed in a long braid bounced with each step, twin daggers flashing in her hands as she spun and struck at invisible enemies. Her tunic dress swirled around with every effortless, graceful motion. Each throw landed with a solid thunk into the wooden targets, precise as clockwork.

She didn't see me at first, and for a moment, I watched—almost forgetting how to breathe.

She looked... unstoppable.

Then she turned and caught me staring. "Are you supposed to be here?"

Shrugging, I ambled closer. "If the alternative is getting skewered by Lance again, yes."

Tala tucked loose strands of her hair behind her ear. "Did Lance release you for the day? I hear you're having quite a lot of difficulties with the sword training."

My eyes bulged in instant protest. I'd honestly thought I was getting better. "Is that what that annoying prick told you?"

Her eyes glinting with mischief, she laughed. She was teasing, fully knowing her statement would get a rise out of me.

But the sound of her laughter was sunlight breaking through storm clouds—warm, golden, and impossibly tender, like the world itself paused to listen. It wrapped around me like a promise I hadn't known I was waiting for.

My chest constricted with yearning. I wanted to hear it again.

"Maybe size does matter, and you'd do much better with these smaller blades. What do you say? Want to try?"

Before I could answer, she tossed me a dull training blade. I fumbled the catch and nearly dropped it.

She laughed again.

I struggled to fight off a grin. I swear, the sound was a balm to my soul. "Will you train me at daggers too?"

"Only if you don't annoy me in the process." She waved a signal to get ready. "Come on. Let's see your stance then." Crossing behind me, without warning, she wrapped her arms around mine to adjust my position. "Grip the dagger like this. Elbow loose. Wrist firm."

The warmth of her breath tickled my jaw. My skin tingled where she touched me. I tried very hard not to forget how to hold the dagger. I forcibly shook my head, clearing my throat so I could focus.

She stepped back. "Now aim for the center of that target there."

Sucking in a breath, I threw. The dagger spun wildly and clattered off the edge of the target with a sad little plink.

Tala laughed again.

I shot her a suffering look. "Oh, shut up. It was a warning shot."

"To...the grass?"

My jaw nearly dropped at her quip. She bit her lip, her shoulders shaking, as if she was struggling not to burst out laughing again.

She was usually so serious when we did research in the library. But if this was what it took to get that smile on her face, I didn't mind being the punchline.

When I went to fetch the fallen dagger, she noted the slump in my shoulders.

Her eyebrows rose in a prompt. "Admitting defeat already?"

I gave her an insolent smirk. "A student is only ever as good as his teacher. Are you sure *you're* the best person to teach me?"

The glint in her narrowed eyes turned indignant, challenged. "You know what, just for that, I'm not going to take it easy on you."

"Are you saying you've been taking it easy on me so far?" I couldn't help my mocking question.

As if in response, she reared back and threw three daggers, one after the other, at a row of targets. Each one hit its mark perfectly. She threw me a smug look, but only gave an elaborate wave of her hand for me to take my turn next.

I bit my tongue in concentration, trying to aim my next shot. My dagger ricocheted off the edge of the target board with a louder thump than before. "I got it!" I cried out, already proud of my minuscule improvement.

Not at all impressed, she shook her head at me. Except that glint of exasperation and amusement was layered in the ghost of her smile once again.

She handed me another dagger. I clumsily tried twirling it in my hand. "Hey, how about if I best you at daggers? What do I get?"

"Um, how about your pride intact? Now, come on. Focus." She adjusted my elbow, standing so close to me again, her warmth radiated up and down my side.

A gentle breeze blew her fragrant scent around, and combined with the garden lilies, it was almost intoxicating.

Her tone remained firm, formal. "A learned skill should be a reward in itself. Besides, I already got you out of the holding cells and told you my name. What else could you possibly want from me?"

I almost scoffed.

I didn't even know what I was doing here. She'd basically torn me away from my world. She refused to give me any more information. I'd been killing myself doing everything she wanted me to do, no questions asked. This was the most time I'd spent with her in days. I'd been a giant pent-up ball of frustration for like a week. My patience was strained to the limit.

I wanted to be mad. I turned to fix her with an exasperated glare, but I didn't expect her face to be mere inches away. I almost sucked in a breath.

Against the fading light of sunset, her silhouette was bathed in fire and honey, ethereal light catching in her hair, glimmering against her face. Her cheeks were delicately flushed from the slight drop in outdoor temperature, a rosy pink tinge on that smooth skin. Those luminous violet eyes reflecting the dim light within their arresting depths, even her sharpest glare would cause my pulse to race.

Surely, she already knew.

My gaze dropped to her mouth for a moment.

My stomach stirred at the memory of that 'accidental' kiss from last week, those soft lips against mine, lush, full, curved in such an inviting way that had undone—had *decimated*—my steadiest resolve.

I could have sworn she had almost moaned in my mouth, almost asked for more...

Longing clawed at my insides, a pressure that felt both unbearably heavy and somehow hollow all at once. My chest ached with the weight of everything, the things I was burying deep, this fire curling low in my gut, this desperate hope tightening my throat.

Her gaze lifted to mine, softening as she seemed to read the answer to her question in mine.

For half a second, we stood like that—close enough to feel the heat of each other's breath, the world around us falling strangely quiet.

She blinked, clearing her throat. "You still need more practice." She moved to step back, but I caught her arm, and an obviously redder flush rushed to her cheeks.

Eager anticipation crawled over my skin at her reaction to my touch.

She wasn't betrothed to that guy. There was definitely something between us. I could feel it. It was always in her eyes. The way she looked at me. The way she responded to me. Was she trying to fight it? Was she struggling just as I was?

My chest heaving, I couldn't help the husk in my question. "Tell me why you wouldn't tell me your name, you know...before."

"Because..."

I frowned. "Because why?"

She looked away. "Because it was wrong."

"What?"

"I felt..." She cracked her neck, somewhat in more nervous unease. "Somehow, I felt as though that's not the name you should call me."

My mouth dropped open in marvel. The keening noise in my head nearly blocked out the loud pounding in my ears. I knew it. I wasn't crazy. We had met before—somehow.

I braced both hands on her shoulders to turn her to face me. "Are you...remembering something too?"

She shrugged me off. "No, of course not. How could I be?"

I threw my hands up. "I'm telling you, I keep having this feeling, like certain things are familiar to me. Like the dungeon. And the map. And you. We have met before, right?"

My skin thrummed with eager anticipation. Those memories I'd lost. They were of her. Of this. And if there was a chance that she remembered something too, maybe it could help us both remember. And maybe somewhere in those memories, somehow... maybe she cared about me too.

Turning on her heel, she moved to leave. "I think we'd better head back inside."

"You still don't believe me?" I chased after her as she strode back into the castle. "My dad said my memories were meant to come back on their own eventually. What other explanation could there be?"

"Whatever memories your father spoke of, I am certain they had nothing to do with me. It's just not possible." After an unsettled moment, she cast me a tired glance over her shoulder. "Even if it was, what do you want me to do about it?"

"Well, first, it would be great if you could give me the benefit of the doubt and not dismiss me straight off the bat."

She rubbed her temples in frustration. "You were reading the book about Fae magic last night, right? There isn't any type of magic that could have accomplished what you're talking about."

"What about your magic? Isn't 'portal magic' like the rarest form of magic?"

"Sure, but my magic can't do what you're saying either. All I can do is make holes from one place to another."

Deflated, I blew out a breath. "Well, either way, maybe there's a kind of magic that can help me restore my memories right away. All I'm asking for is, you know, put some feelers out. Maybe tomorrow, we could find someone who can—"

She dismissed with a wave. "I can't. I have somewhere to be tomorrow."

"Where are you going?"

"I have to attend the wedding preparations."

I stopped breathing.

Sucker punch.

What?

For a terrible split second, nothing else mattered.

The words made my stomach lurch.

The way she said it...so nonchalant, so offhand.

I stood frozen. My shoulders slumped.

This was it. I'd known it was going to happen eventually, but I was still holding on to hope that maybe we still had some time. A year. A month. Like it wouldn't be quite so soon.

It was too soon.

She was getting officially hitched. I was finally going to lose her forever.

I couldn't even tell her not to go. There was nothing I could say to stop her. What could I even say?

"Is...is he a good man at least?"

She turned at my question, but my gaze was on the floor now. She stopped walking, her tone vaguely puzzled that I'd fallen behind. "I'm sure he is. Otherwise, the elders would not have approved the match."

I sucked the insides of my cheeks, willing myself to nod.

Was there really nothing else I could do to stop her? For a moment, I considered looking up Fae wedding proceedings in the library. Would it be totally insane if I stowed away to attend the ceremony in case her people did that 'Are there any objections?' part too?

I snapped to attention. "Can I come?"

"No."

"Why not?"

She shot me an odd look. "It will be better if you stay here and continue your training with Lance. Besides, it's got nothing to do with you."

Was she being serious right now? *Nothing* to do with me?

I clenched my fists, feeling utterly helpless and drained.

I didn't miss her point though. She obviously didn't want any crazy people obsessed with her attending her own wedding to ruin things.

In any case, if telling her how I felt could have made a difference, it should have already. It's not like I'd been able to keep my mouth shut about it so far. Or maybe I was being way too forward. Maybe she liked the stoic, more reserved kind of guys, like Lance.

I caught the suspicious, looming shadow out of the corner of my eye—almost too late, right before the glass windows exploded with a thundering crash as a dozen armed soldiers came smashing through.

11

Ghosts

"Whoa—!" I jumped to shield Tala from the shower of glass shards.

"What—?" she squeaked.

Chaos ensued as dozens of soldiers stormed through the conservatory. Black figures carrying long, sophisticated spears, quivers of arrows on their backs, spikes on their armor, and helmets. Some of them gripped torches that flickered light against their sullen faces, yelling whoops and bellows, layered above terrified screams of the castle staff.

The servants cried out, ducking and fleeing, dropping trays of supper service as they got caught in the sudden crossfire. Guards engaged in scuffles near the far hall, protecting the others.

Tala struggled to stand. "What-what's going on? Who are they?" She braced her hand on my arm as we helped each other up.

One of the warriors lunged toward Tala, and I shoved her behind me, raising a broken serving tray like a shield. The blow rattled right through my bones, right as I took another hit square in the ribs, before I was able to kick him in the face.

Hard enough for him to fall, but I grunted, stumbling back myself. "Ow—" Pain blossomed hot and immediate in my side.

A grim-faced man stepped apart from the onslaught. He must have been their leader. He surveyed the commotion with narrowed eyes before pointing a weapon at me. "You." His deep voice rattled the rafters. "I thought I killed you."

I blinked, utterly confused. "What? Who the hell are you?"

His steps, heavy and sure, he stalked closer, the firelight flaring on his face, making him look even more menacing.

Beside me, Tala's hands glowed faintly, fingers trembling as she summoned her magic. "Come on," she hissed through gritted teeth. Her hands sparked, dimmed, sparked again. "Oh, curse it all—"

My eyebrows furrowed. "What's happening?"

Mumbling in annoyance, she wrung her hands out. Instead of answering my question, she asked one, "How do you know this guy?"

"I don't!" My eyes widened in dread as the forbidding figure towered over us.

Guifan…

My chest heaved at an inkling of fractured memories the mere word conjured in my mind, like shards of glass flashing behind my eyes. But what did it mean?

For some reason, this guy's mere presence was indeed triggering an undefined but fairly evident fear that settled low in my gut like a stone.

Crap. *Did I* know this guy?

My palms were clammy, but I clenched my chin. I forced the memories back into the dark corners of my mind where they belonged. It was not the time to be frozen in fear.

The shadowy leader warrior's grim face set off the glint in his armor. His spear pointed at Tala. "We are only here for her."

Scrambling back, I moved to cover her once again. Sticking my chin up, I met his eerily black eyes with my determined gaze. "Leave her alone."

"This is ridiculous." Tala shoved out from behind me in a flash. Pushing up the sleeves of her dress, she braced her feet on the floor, lifting her hands to try summoning again. This time, the wind blew fiercely around her in an instant in response. Her eyes glowed. "Yes."

Bright light seared my eyes for a moment. When I opened them again, the shadowy leader warrior was gone, and so were all his friends. Not 'they were magicked away', but it was as though they simply vanished into thin air.

"Whoa."

Frowning, Tala's eyes darted around in suspicion. "Huh? Where did they all go?"

I shot her a look. "I thought you sent them away?"

She threw her hands up. "I hadn't even done anything yet."

Near silence slammed into the space the ghostly warriors had left behind.

Save perhaps the confused murmurs of the castle staff picking themselves up, the distant crackle of torchlight.

Save that spear that arced through the air, the last remnant of the mysterious battle—silent, deadly—aimed straight for Tala.

Eyes wide, I moved on instinct. I threw myself in front of it, bringing up the already dented tray just in time. The impact rang through me like a bell. The makeshift shield cracked in half, and I hit the floor hard, air driven from my lungs.

My vision swam, darkening at the edges. My limbs felt distant, like they belonged to someone else. "Ouch..."

I woke with a groan.

Streaks of daylight filtered through gauzy curtains, casting warm, dappled light across the whitewashed walls of the large chambers. Potent herbs and clean linen clung to the air, crushed mint and smoke, amidst the soft clinking of glass vials.

That bone-deep aching had gone, my body no longer felt heavy. But several heads were peering down on me in a circle. One blond, one bright-haired, and one elderly, with the only sympathetic eyes in the group.

"He's awake."

"Well, it's about time."

"There may be some lingering soreness. Best he take it easy," the physician remarked before she turned to leave.

Blinking to snap myself out of my sleepy haze, I sat up. I quickly met Tala's gaze. "Are you okay?" I surveyed her up and down for injuries.

Tala gave me a pointed look. "Me? I'm not the one who passed out."

I rubbed my face with my hand. "Is everyone else okay? What happened last night?"

"That's what we've been trying to figure out." Lance folded his arms across his chest. "Fortunately, the staff are at most merely shaken by the incident."

My mind whirled with instant confusion all over again. I took a deep breath. "Were they ghosts?"

Tala made a face. "I don't believe ghosts leave a mess like that. The damage to the conservatory was...quite significant."

"Were those more Fae warriors sent by your uncle again, like the ones who were chasing us on Earth?"

She shook her head. "No. These were human."

"You blew them up with your magic. They just disappeared or something."

"I didn't blow them up. They simply vanished." She shook her head again. "Besides, they were humans. We're not supposed to hurt them."

Lance was deep in thought as well. "Tala said their leader recognized you."

I frowned. "Yeah, that was weird."

"Did you know him? Did any of them seem familiar to you?"

I shook my head, but that ominous dread settled heavily in my stomach once again. I wasn't sure I should bring it up with Lance around. I couldn't put my finger on it, but I had a sneaking suspicion this clue swam alongside all those memories that were veiled in the mist in my mind.

Lance went on, tapping his chin. "They looked somewhat like an army I'd encountered sometime in the past, a small band of a rebellion breaking out of a settlement to the east. However, if memory serves, they were quelled a mere short time afterward."

"Guifan." I couldn't help the certainty in my response.

Lance's sharp eyes turned to me. "How do you know that name?"

I shrugged. "Honestly, I couldn't tell you. But it was the first thing that came to my mind when they broke in."

Lance looked to Tala in bafflement.

She blew out a breath, half in annoyance, half in almost resignation. "Josh is having some memory issues. He thinks he may have been here before, except nobody else remembers."

"Hey, that soldier guy recognized me last night!" I pointed out.

"Who? The *ghost*?" Her tone dripped with mocking.

I grimaced. "Thanks. That doesn't make me sound crazy at all."

Tala's haughty response was wry. "You're welcome." She glanced toward the door with a groan. "I don't have time for this. I have to go. If I'm late today, I'll never hear the end of it."

That hit me like another sucker punch.

Alarmed, my gaze snapped up toward the brightening day outside the windows. Oh shoot, that's right. Today was *tomorrow*. I'd almost forgotten that *other* disaster that was about to happen.

Tala's wedding.

She was already dressed to depart—sturdy boots, thick cloak over a linen tunic, moleskin pants, and a satchel bag hung across her shoulders.

"No," I jumped to protest. "You—you need to stay here and help me. The people here are in danger from whatever those ghosts are, and we need to figure it out before anything else happens."

She met Lance's gaze. "I trust he'll be safe here."

Lance nodded. "Of course."

"If you wouldn't mind continuing his training..."

They were talking about me again, like I wasn't sitting right here. Tala's voice trailed off as the two of them turned to leave the infirmary.

With a slight wince, I forced my body to get up off the bed, hurriedly pulling on my sneakers and jacket, and followed them outside. "Hey! You're not seriously leaving me right now."

Glancing back at my futile chase, Lance offered, "Shall I call for some guards to haul him back?"

Not breaking her gait otherwise, Tala let out an exasperated sigh. "Josh, go back to the infirmary."

Stepping beyond the courtyard grounds, the soft grass yielded beneath my sneakers as we approached the edge of the forest bordering the castle.

Right at their heels, I called out, "Is what I'm saying so unbelievable? You guys have *magic* in this world. Why is it such a stretch to think that I'm telling the truth? I just need to talk to someone who could potentially help me recover my memories faster."

"Being able to restore memories is not the issue." Tala put her hand up. "Stop and think about your story here. Let's say you're telling the truth, and you had been here before, and let's say someone did erase your memories of it. There's no magic that could have possibly erased *you* from the memories of everyone else across the entirety of Arcadia. If you had been to this realm before, surely someone else would remember an obvious outsider like you."

She sighed again, her arms dropping to her sides. "And if I tell anyone what you're saying, *I'm* the one who..." A shadow flitted past her eyes once again. "Let's say, I really don't need any more of that."

I pursed my lips in concern, for the first time struck by considering another possibility. It wasn't that she didn't believe me. There was another reason she was hesitant. She did mention that my mere existence in this world was going to bring her trouble.

"Well then, what do you expect me to do?" I threw up my hands in helpless protest. "Stay here and train forever? Get kicked around by Lance and his awesome soldiers until I'm old and gray?"

Pausing in mid-stride, Lance's face twitched as if something dawned on him. "Oh... You haven't told him yet." He turned to Tala with a prompting look, crossing disbelief with amusement.

I stopped short. "Oh, for god's sake, now what?"

Tala cringed.

His words slow and careful, Lance peered at her face. "Are you sure concealing all this is the best course of action? What if the magic of the Fae lands holds the solution to your problem?"

A flicker of doubt crossed her eyes, her brows drawing tight as she lingered in indecision.

Lance's own forehead creased in thought for a long moment. But then he met her gaze again, a resolve in his brooking no retort. "You know who you need to take him to then." It was more a statement than a question.

Tala groaned again right away. Whatever Lance meant easily crumbled her resolve altogether. She gave an aggressive, resigned shrug. "Fine, fine! I'll take him to the Fae lands."

My eyebrows snapped together in instant irritation at pretty boy's annoyingly unfair sway over her. I looked between each of them again. "Who? What? What are you hiding from me now? And don't tell me it's not relevant to me. I was living a relatively decent life on Earth. You're the one who dragged me here. I mean, I probably should have been asking more questions, and maybe I've been an idiot, but I trusted you."

Dropping my gaze, a bitter heat burned my throat at my own naivety. "I trusted that you knew what was going on and that you'd tell me when you were ready. But were you really not going to tell me anything?"

Her lips still pursed, her gaze shot off to one side.

"How about any information?" I implored. "Anything at all. Like how you're actually expecting me to save your world? That seems like something I ought to know, given that I've travelled all this way to help you." I threw up my hands. "Come on. Something. Anything! Please!"

"You die, Josh."

"What?"

"The Curse bearer...is the sacrifice." Tala bit her lip, watching my reaction. "That's how you save my world."

Ah.

This time, it hit me like a knockout punch—one clean, devastating blow, and I stood there half-convinced I'd actually blacked out for a heartbeat.

I could have sworn time froze in that instant.

"You...want me to die?" I almost mumbled the words.

Everything drained from me. As if I were standing as a mere hollow shell, with the rest of my being having sunk away at the devastation. As if I were only half here. As if I were gone already.

She shook her head. "Josh, I'm so so—"

But the rest of her words muted in my head in the crazy din.

Curse bearer.

Not savior.

Sacrifice.

No wonder my father had been so adamantly against my coming to this realm. Had been so adamantly *against* fulfilling this prophecy.

My father had also said I had a knack for always seeing the best of any situation. Maybe I was only finally getting unnerved by the notion that the length of my remaining life was almost at its end. This time, I couldn't muster any more optimism.

The pounding in my ears drowned everything else out. My chest constricted, I almost couldn't breathe. I wanted to slump to my knees on the grass, squeeze my eyes shut, pretend none of this was happening.

Somewhere in my periphery, a brilliant spark of light ignited as Tala summoned her portal to take us away.

I'd long known I was headed for heartbreak with her, but I never expected this.

She had brought me here to die.

Well, shoot.

* * *

PART TWO

- TALA -

12

Portal

Tala

The magic started in my core—deep beneath my sternum, where breath met being. It tugged, thrummed, demanding focus, and I obliged, drawing it up like lifting a weightless, volatile thread through my chest, into my shoulders, down my arms. My fingertips tingled, hot and cold at once, the kind of sting you get from grabbing snow bare-handed for too long, but charged with lightning.

The air around me thickened, like the moment before a summer storm breaks, and I reached into the weave—the invisible threads that connected everything in this realm—and twisted. The strain pulsed through my veins like a river current. Not painful, exactly. But alive. The kind of power that reminded me, unflinchingly, that I was only borrowing it.

Light exploded outward in a sudden whoosh, bluish-white and blinding. The portal spiraled into being before us, like someone peeling back the fabric of the world to reveal something behind it. It wasn't transparent—at least, not entirely. The surface shimmered like opalescent glass submerged in water, an undulating wall of light with the suggestion of depth.

Then it flickered.

Just once—a sputter in the light, like a candle guttering in wind—and the edges of the portal wavered.

I winced.

Oh, no. Why was this happening again?

I tightened my grip on the magic instinctively, adjusting the threads, steadying the spell. It stabilized quickly.

Glitches, I rationalized. Both of them. Last night, during the ghostly battle, when I couldn't summon my magic either, I was too surprised. That was all. That's all they were. *That's all they must be.* I let out a breath, tamping down the faint nagging unease lingering in my chest.

Through the haze of magic was the rim of a forest valley, drenched in mid-morning sun, verdant trees swaying gently, and wildflowers glowing along the ridge. The clean, earthy scent wafted through, faint but distinct.

Home.

I exhaled, shoulders trembling slightly from the toll.

Glancing back across the grassy expanse, I signaled a curt nod of acknowledgment to Lance. He stood amidst the backdrop of his majestic castle of Cephiron, where the everyday morning bustle was going on as usual.

He gave me a mock salute. "I'll ride out and join you again as soon as I can."

I shook my head. "You don't have to. I can handle things from here."

"I don't *have* to. I want to," Lance reassured with a smile.

I gave him a grateful one right back.

Lance's friendship was one I'd relied on for years. His hospitality never failed, and his library was the best ever in the land. I often wished I could do more to repay his kindness over the years, but he'd never asked for anything in return. My only hope was that he knew he could also count on my help if he ever needed it.

I turned to Josh.

He was ashen, stock still.

I couldn't even blame him.

I tried not to let the acute desolation on his face bother me as I secured my grip around his wrist and tugged him through the portal.

The village of Ipera sprawled like a secret, cradled in the arms of the Fae lands forest, hugged on all sides by towering green sentinels that swayed with the wind. The fresh air tickled my nose as we stepped through. Cypress and pine, sweet and sharp, mingling with the faint tang of river water that threaded beyond the western edge of the valley, and the soft rain that regularly fell to keep everything lush and blooming.

I rarely summoned portals within our village. I supposed that's why it never failed to become a spectacle.

As soon as Josh and I stepped through the bluish-white watery sphere, a small crowd had already gathered on the main thoroughfare.

Some Fae smiled politely. Others didn't.

Of course, there was often another reason everyone stared at me.

I'd always flinched at the attention. I never wanted it. All I'd ever wanted was to be the same as everyone else. Unnoticed. Looked past. But it was rare in a day when there wouldn't be someone whispering in awe, or indeed in fear, of me.

Even here. In my home. I was different.

I kept my chin high.

I was the only portal summoner in a generation—just like my mother had been. Portal summoning was the rarest form of magic across the realms. But it was the fact that I might be more like my father that had everyone in the village on edge.

Out of the corner of my eye, Josh's eyebrows furrowed as he surveyed our surroundings and the crowd that had gathered as the portal closed behind us with a crackle. No doubt, he noticed the stares as well.

Then again, perhaps the odd stares today were not entirely aimed in my direction. I was, after all, dragging along someone who was a spectacle enough on his own. Josh, with his shiny leather jacket and odd squeaky shoes from the fourth realm. His round, non-pointed, non-Fae human ears.

Although Josh's expression was unusually still. That spark—the sarcastic smirk, the restless commentary—had vanished since we crossed into the valley. I could tell he hadn't heard a word of my half-hearted explanations back at Cephiron. Not really. My latest bombshell revelation sat behind his eyes. A shadow refusing to leave.

You...want me to die?

The despondent look on Josh's face made my heart ache. That usual charming smile on his mischievous face was gone, replaced by a sad emptiness.

I couldn't help my stupid-as-heck question. "Are you okay?"

His livid gaze met mine. "Seriously?"

I bit my lip in helpless remorse. His dark aura was itself a heavy weight pressing down on me as well, lodging in my hollow ribs, tightening everything until even breathing felt like a conscious, useless effort.

I had no words of comfort. All I had was something I knew to be true. Something that was also a constant struggle for me. "Sometimes...we can't help our destiny."

I'd said it so quietly, I thought he didn't hear. But the stark animosity in his expression faded for a moment. That was, until I kept babbling on. "And I swear, I'll do everything I can to protect you. Until..."

His eyes narrowed. We both knew my argument was ridiculous. "Until you need to kill me, is that it?" He feigned a wistful clutch at his chest. "Gosh, I can't tell you how great a comfort that is."

I met his glare with a scoff. Couldn't he tell I was already trying my best? I wished I could explain further. I'd only found out about the devastating extra detail right as we'd gotten back from the fourth realm. I hadn't wanted to hide the truth from him back in Cephiron, but it seemed pertinent.

Also, perhaps because I didn't want to believe it myself. For days, I had been desperate to find something else, new information, during our research that might contradict what I'd found—something, any little hope. But it was all in vain.

However, today, instead of doing more reading, I had to be here.

Things were bad enough already.

Above us, streamers fluttered—bright silks in blues, golds, and deep violets strung from rafter to rafter like a sky-bound celebration, tugged occasionally by an errant breeze. Lanterns, paper chimes, and multi-colored banners hung across the lamp posts, which lined the streets.

I didn't often see the village looking so festive.

But it was one of the reasons I had tried to delay my return.

I led the way down the main road, past wooden houses with sloped roofs, bearing the same gentle craftsmanship that had built this village generations ago. Elegant in their simplicity, with ivy climbing the beams and sunflowers nodding from window boxes.

The stalls lining the road brimmed with greens still wet from morning dew, carts of apples, and baskets of fresh loaves that nearly made my stomach audibly protest.

Fae villagers bustled by in clothes dyed with forest hues. It was true that Fae aged differently from humans. We would come of age, stop aging, and often live for centuries. Most Fae were elegant, possessing beauty that easily bewitched others. Sharp eyes, long hair, and pointed ears.

I tugged my cloak hood closer over my own head.

Several cheerily dressed young women were staring as we walked past. All doe-eyed, they whispered to themselves, not so discreetly pointing at my rogue human companion, and then covering their mouths to giggle in delight or something.

Josh stood out like a sore thumb in our Fae village. With that unusual sullen frown as he stalked down the road, hands stuffed in his pockets, he was a genuine brooding hunk. Tall, lean, his stupid leather jacket making his shoulders appear so broad. Deep green eyes, that strong jawline, even clenched in tension as it was. Thick, dark hair always tousled in a way that looked intentional. Softer than I'd imagined against my fingertips...

A shiver almost shot up my spine from remembering the feeling of those arms tight around me when he'd held me in bed the other night in Cephiron. I could never help but always feel so safe around Josh.

How could he be so strong, but so weak at the same time? How could he be so adorable, yet be so annoying?

I'm really sorry for kissing you. I swear it'll never happen again.

I wanted to smack myself upside the head. I should have never let that kiss happen either. I knew it was my own fault for sending mixed signals. But I would challenge anyone to resist getting so easily lost within those brilliant green depths. And the decisive way he'd taken charge when he couldn't help but finally give in to that desperate need...

Never happen again?

I briskly shook my head before the flush in my cheeks spread elsewhere altogether. I'd already resolved to keep my distance. I had to focus on my mission. There absolutely were going to be no more unguarded moments with Josh.

Absolutely.

Another titter of giggles came from the group of flighty women.

I clenched my teeth, tamping down the urge to growl.

Mine.

A wave of annoyance washed over me. I bit my lip. Well, technically, no. Josh wasn't mine. He was the 'sacrifice' that would save my world.

I was the one who found him. He was bound to me. He said he loved *me*. And I brought him here to kill him.

Now he wouldn't even look at me.

That's just great, Tala.

Josh had left his home. He followed me to this strange land. He faced unimaginable threats head-on when most humans would have run away. He was willing to endure, insisted on seeing the best in every situation. He used to always look at me with such light in those beautiful, shimmering green eyes. So much faith. So much trust.

Used to...

I supposed it was a little too much to hope that he could still love me anyway. Even if there was little much either of us could do about it. Even if he shouldn't. Getting any more involved with me was dangerous. I *needed* to make him hate me to keep him safe. And pushing people away was something I was very good at. And why shouldn't I? It was better this way.

Who would ever care for a half-breed outcast orphan whose father was a Deathbringer?

13

Lineage

A symphony of wind chimes indicated we were almost at my uncle's house. Approaching the modest-sized house with the thatched roof and wooden porch, one wouldn't think it belonged to the highest-ranking Fae family among the Priori.

My uncle Stellan was the strongest warrior in our clan. His wife, Caelina, had been the strongest mage. They had governed peacefully over all the Fae for years until the great battle that had claimed my aunt's life.

Stellan currently held the regent position until his first-born daughter could ascend as the rightful High Fae mage leader of our people. Just like her mother. The ascension ceremony was already being planned. It was scheduled to follow soon after the wedding.

I certainly didn't envy my cousin's position. Even though I was aware that many Fae thought I did.

The buzzing that came was faint at first—like a distant swarm or the flutter of wings—but in the next breath, a flurry of glowing sprites zipped straight at me, tiny things with flitting wings and mischievous, shimmering eyes. They dove into my hair, tugging at strands and yanking at my clothes, giggling in high, silvery tones as they wove themselves into a whirlwind of chaos.

I yelped and tried to swat them off, batting at my cloak, but they only danced faster, gleeful in their torment.

"What the hell is this?" Josh tried to shoo some away, but they circled back and tugged on his jacket for good measure.

"Oh, come on," I growled, flicking one off my shoulder and stomping as another tried to tangle itself in the laces of my tunic. With a hiss through my teeth, I narrowed my focus, let the magic bloom in my palms, and released a pulse of energy. Not violent—just sharp enough. The sprites scattered like smoke in the wind, blinking out of existence with startled pops of light.

A burst of giggles exploded from behind a nearby tree.

My stomach churned.

Of course, it was them.

Mead was the first to step forward, her honey-blonde curls arranged in flawless spirals that didn't dare move in the breeze. Her sheer blue gown clung delicately to her figure and matched the subtle glitter dusted across her collarbones. Mead's smile was as sharp as ever. She let out a breathless, delighted laugh. "Oh, relax, Tala. It was just a joke."

Behind her, Brynn barely contained her laughter. With dark hair pulled into an elegant braid and a pretty sneer, her fingers glowed faintly with the telltale shimmer of sprite-binding magic.

I straightened my shoulders. "Funny. Guess your sense of humor hasn't changed at all."

Neither had they. Not one bit.

We had all grown up together, gone to school together. And when we were all much younger, I'd imagined these girls considered me a friend. They had dared me to climb down the old stone well at the edge of the village—the one ringed by crooked benches. They laughed when I'd panicked as the darkness pressed in too fast. I'd screamed loud enough to bring three elders running.

I shoved the memory aside like I always did.

Also, Mead was eyeing Josh with interest, and a prickling fire sizzled beneath my skin.

"Hello," she purred as she crept closer to him. "My name is Mead. What's yours?"

He shifted on his feet, his forehead creased. "Um, Josh."

"Joshhh..." Mead fluttered her eyelids as she elongated the sound. Perhaps she thought it was attractive. It was not.

"Tala, you're back!"

I turned to the other young woman stepping out of my uncle's house's front door behind us. Her eyes were crinkled as she met my gaze.

Alys—freckled, slight, with an ever-so-slightly crooked nose from one too many falls during her reckless climbs—had always tried, once or twice, to be kind to me. But she never pushed past Brynn or Mead's sway.

"Alys!" I was going to smile at her when, past her shoulder, a Fae male shut the door behind them.

"Holten!" Brynn cried out in glee as she flew across the way to drape herself on his arm.

My jaw tightened the moment Holten tilted his head.

He hadn't changed either. Still all charm and cheekbones, his grin tilted lazily the moment he saw me. He looked me over like I was some long-lost secret worth remembering. Unlike the rest of them who treated me like a malady they were afraid to catch, Holten had always fancied himself drawn to the different, shiny thing. Though I never encouraged his advances, he never stopped trying—something which Brynn obviously found annoying.

Brynn's hand tightened on Holten's arm as his gaze lingered too long on me. "You're not actually staying though, right?"

"Oh, trust me, Brynn." I gave her a suffering look. "I would rather be anywhere else but here."

"Right," Brynn said. "And we should take comfort in that because your glorious lineage is known for—oh, how shall I put it, *not* burning everything down to the ground and killing everyone around you?"

I narrowed my eyes at her, struggling against the urge to smack her across the face with magic.

Leave it to Brynn's rudeness to bring it up.

People didn't often speak of my mysterious lineage, or indeed about the true nature of my father, in open company. It was more whispered in huddles amidst layers of ever-evolving rumors. Monster. Demon. Deathbringer. Nobody had proof one way or another.

I'd stopped bothering to correct them. Everyone was intent on believing the worst of me anyway.

Mead was still focused on Josh, staring fascinatedly at his ears. She twirled her hair around her finger. "We don't often get humans visiting here. Are you here to attend the wedding festivities later on, too? Would you like to accompany me? I would really love to get to know you better."

I thought I caught Josh wince. "Um. I think Tala needs me."

Despite the burning in my stomach, I scoffed, "Of course not. Why would I need you?"

Mead let out a snorting laugh. "Exactly. Tala doesn't need anything, except maybe a nice jump off a high cliff."

"Mead!" Alys was aghast. Of course, they didn't pay her any mind.

I didn't want Mead to sense my fury, my frustration. As a Fae mage, she was an expert at manipulation, especially with emotions. She could practically smell someone's weakness from across the village. She'd always known how to use my own thoughts and fears against me. If she even caught a hint that I was interested in Josh at all, she wasn't going to let it go.

I tried an offhand chuck of my chin, meeting Josh's gaze for a moment. "You should go with Mead. Have a good time at the festivities. I know I will."

I thought I caught something flash in Josh's green eyes, but he turned to Mead. His entire face brightened, his demeanor flipping an instant one-eighty. "You know what, on second thought, I think I would really love to get to know you better too," he replied with a disarmingly charming smile.

So disarmingly charming, Mead startled. She tipped to one side, so disoriented she'd lost her balance altogether—but not before Josh caught her arm, of course.

"Oh, hey, be careful," Josh said smoothly. "I'm sure you wouldn't want to ruin such a pretty dress."

Glancing from one of them to the other, Brynn squealed. "This is so great! We should all go together." She tugged on Holten's arm once again. "I mean, the four of us," she amended quickly, giving Alys a pointed look.

"There's an idea." Josh's eyes lit up. "I haven't been in such good company for a while. I'd like to make the most of my time here. I've been told I won't be around for much longer." He tilted his head to give me a dull, pointed look.

Still clinging to Josh, Mead fussed with his leather jacket. "I love this material," she cooed. "Is this type of cloak all the rage in the human realm?"

Ignoring the lump forming in my throat, I blew out a breath to move past them, heading into the house.

Brynn stepped in my way. "Your cousin's busy right now."

I gawked at her. "Are you blocking me from going inside my own house?"

"You haven't been living here though," she reminded me. "From what I heard, you've been vacationing in the human kingdoms, too busy digging into dumb old lore, buried in stinky books." She flashed a grin. "Lucky for the future leader of our people, she has us girls to keep her company, people she can always count on."

Despite the fact that Brynn and Mead had made my life miserable when we were younger—not that they'd really stopped—these girls worshipped Freyjn. They would bend over backward to earn her favor. To them, Freyjn was nice and kind, a delicate flower, the smartest, prettiest, most perfect Fae mage ever.

And I was the black sheep.

"How does it feel to be always second-rate?" Mead smirked.

I rolled my eyes. "I guess I'm lucky, because I don't care."

Mead's lips curled in revulsion. "Lucky? That's the last thing I would call you, a non-Fae half-breed with your strange hair and deformed ears—"

"Yes, *thank you.*" Cutting her off, I gave her a flat look. "That must be it. Anyone who's different must be scary and dangerous. You're so clever to have figured that out."

She hissed, lunging forward as if to pounce at me, but Brynn held her back.

Holten beckoned them away, even as he gave me a half-smirk. "Come along, girls. I'm sure you'd rather enjoy this extra time to prepare for the evening's festivities."

As he passed me to leave, Holten caught my arm. He leaned close to my ear before I could pull away. "Glad to have you back, Tala." His breath against my neck sent shivers down my spine.

I shot him a suffering look, shrugging him off.

Suddenly, Josh was right between us. He stood so close to me, the heat of his body warmed me like an instant wave of comfort. His face was even darker than before as he set his glare on Holten. "You don't touch her again." His voice was unusually low and deep, I almost missed the words of warning.

My pulse raced anyway. I didn't need to hide behind Josh, even as he stood before me like a shield against the vile Fae. But I struggled against the urge to clutch at his arm to pull him closer.

Mead still shot me a mischievous, scheming glance. She bid Josh a cute little wave. "Looking forward to seeing more of you later, Josh."

And with that, Mead walked on, the rest of them following suit. Alys gave me a tiny nod, barely visible. An apology in a glance. Even as I could still feel Holten's eyes on me and Brynn's jealousy like a prickling heat in the air.

14

Freyjn

Crossing the threshold into the cozy house, I savored the wood smoke mingled with the aroma of cinnamon and green tea, and stepped into the familiar old living area that currently looked like a dressmaker's salon.

Freyjn was standing amidst rolls of fancy fabric. Her bright blue eyes lit up upon catching sight of me. "Tala!" She hurried over to throw her arms around me, despite her dress being unfinished, fabric spilling all over the floor.

"Hey—" I couldn't help a smile as her warmth enveloped me.

I didn't even realize how much I needed a hug right then. Admittedly, after my encounter with the mean Fae girls, I was a bit raw. But for everything I hated about being back in the Fae lands, Freyjn was everything I missed.

Freyjn was a few years older than I was, and infinitely more accomplished. Naturally, since she was being groomed to lead all our people someday. On all counts, I agreed with

Brynn and Mead. I also believed Freyjn was the most capable, most talented, most effortlessly beautiful Fae mage across the Land of Arcadia. She was the best of us.

But more than that, Freyn had always been kind to me—perhaps too kind. She helped me train to hone my Fae magic. She and I would laugh when girls like Brynn and Mead would snipe at each other behind their backs. Freyjn encouraged me to speak my mind, to not be afraid of being different. She supported me in whatever endeavor I undertook. She never failed to stick up for me whenever we got into all sorts of trouble when we were younger. One time, I was too sick to go to school, Freyjn faked being sick too, so we could stay home together.

She was more than my cousin. She was my sister.

Freyjn was giddy, jumping. "Why are you only arriving today? We've missed you."

I pulled back a bit to give her a look. "Missed me? Is that why your father sent a horde of Fae shadow warriors all the way to the other realm to chase me down?"

"A horde? You're exaggerating." She waved dismissively. "You know we only wanted you back home safe and sound." Her voice lowered to a hush. "Besides, it's not like we could tell anyone else where you went and what you were doing."

"Well, it's about time, Tala." Another deep male voice came from behind Freyjn.

"Auric." I gave the tall Fae warrior entering the room a smile. I assessed his embroidered ceremonial cloak, woven in regal Priori colors. "You look nice today."

As the Fae warrior the elders had chosen to be Freyjn's betrothed, Auric was likely the most powerful warrior in Ipera. He had a strong warrior's build, broad shoulders, a well-muscled, bulky physique, sharp brown eyes, and a handsome face beneath his shaggy, black hair.

I'd met him before but hadn't had the opportunity to get to know him all that well, since I spent most of my time away from the village.

Seeming unbothered with pleasantries, Auric's suspicious gaze landed on Josh. "Who is this?"

Hovering partway behind me, Josh's dark glare had found a new target in Auric.

Freyjn's attention slid over to Josh, belatedly realizing I had brought someone else into the house. "Oh, hello."

Josh let out a deep sigh. "I suppose Tala's not going to introduce me again." He gave everyone a dull shrug. "I'm Josh. The 'Curse bearer', apparently."

The lump in my throat was back.

I took a deep breath.

Here goes nothing.

I turned to Freyjn with a meaningful glance. "I've found him. Josh is the one the legends foretold."

Her jaw dropped. "What?"

I couldn't tell if she was shocked, upset, or afraid.

"Curse bearer. That old bedtime story?" Auric asked. "That's ridiculous. That would mean that you'd have to have gone all the way to—"

I met his gaze evenly, already nodding.

"The fourth realm?" Wide-eyed, Auric's mouth hung agape, his eyebrows furrowed almost in a bewildered rage.

Biting her lip, Freyn put her hand up as if to hold Auric back. "Auric, that's where Tala had gone a few weeks ago. I'm sure you understand why I couldn't tell you at the time, but—"

"He's a demon! He's not of this land." Auric pushed Freyjn behind his forbidding form.

Josh's eyebrows snapped together in mocking. "I'm not a demon." He put up his hands. "Look, I only came here to figure out why I have memories of this place. I think I might have already been here before."

My eyes bulged. How could he drop a bomb like that right now? I'd still been mulling over how to break it to Freyjn gently, and certainly in a much calmer, more receptive situation than this.

"Surely not," Auric scoffed. "If a demon from the fourth realm were spotted on this land, you would have already been captured and killed."

Josh's lips thinned. "But so many things here seem familiar to me, it can't be a coincidence. I know it sounds crazy, but—"

"Don't listen to his lies. Back away from him, both of you." Auric tugged on my arm before he called out, "Malik! Payten!" In seconds flat, a couple of big, beefy warriors stormed through the door, ready to take his instruction. "Take this demon to the dungeon."

"Auric, for the love of—" Exasperated, I threw my hands up. "You know what, sure. Try that, why don't you?"

"Tala!" Josh protested, trying to shrug away from their grasp.

Freyjn shot me a surprised look. "Tala?"

Unconcerned, I let out a sigh and let the two men drag him off. I was willing to bet Josh would be out of that dungeon in five minutes. If not, at least I would be assured of his safety. There was no telling what any of the Fae dead set against fulfilling the prophecy would do to him if he was discovered.

Besides, there was already too much going on. I still had to suffer through the wedding ceremony, get that all over with, then go back to Cephiron to finish my research. It was better if Josh was more or less contained, away from the festivities, away from the villagers—specifically Mead, and also away from me.

Auric had the same notion. As soon as Josh and the warriors were out of sight, he whirled around to face me. "Why would you bring such a dangerous creature to the village? Today of all days?"

I shot him an incredulous look. "Josh is *not* dangerous. Are you kidding me? He wouldn't hurt a Uquix. He's like a fluffy, little—" I broke off to gesture to Auric's figure. "And anyway, what about you? He's probably harmless compared to you. You're so big, how do you not knock everything over whenever you walk into a room?"

"What?" Auric's jaw dropped at my insolent, completely irrelevant retort.

Always the peacemaker, Freyjn stepped between us. "Hey, you two, can we please defer whatever this is until after tomorrow? You know, something pretty important is going on today."

I immediately backed down. "Oh, of course. I'm so sorry!"

Eyes still narrowed in displeasure, Auric looked away with a deep sigh. "Very well." Folding his arms across his chest, he moved to leave. "I'll be taking care of things at the venue."

I watched his retreating back until he was out the door. "He's fun." I couldn't help my amused quip. "He's almost as particular about perfection as you."

Freyjn smacked my arm. "Oh, leave him alone. Auric's a little bit strict, that's all. But he's a good man."

I rolled my eyes. "Whatever. As long as you're happy." I nudged her shoulder. "You are, right?"

I thought I caught a twitch in Freyjn's expression before she broke a big smile. "Of course!"

Okay... Convinced I'd imagined that odd note, I beamed at her. "Then I am really happy for you."

"Enough of that." Cheeks flushed, Freyjn waved the topic away. "I'd like to hear more about what you've found. It sounds like you had quite an exciting few weeks."

"Not exciting." I fidgeted in my stance. "You know, you guys should really cut Josh some slack. I've already dragged him to this world against his will. He's suffered enough. Besides, he's a really nice guy. He's absolutely not a dangerous demon."

Freyjn gave me a scrutinizing, narrow-eyed look. "Are you in some type of relationship with this human?"

I almost choked on my spit. "What? No!"

She tilted her head in rationalization. "Your hand has already been promised to—"

"I know, I know!" I cut her off, rubbing my forehead. "That's not even—" I broke off. "I mean, I didn't want to worry you this close to your wedding, but...there's something I need to help him with, some business outside the village afterward."

"Alright." Freyjn's pout was disappointed. "As long as you promise to stay for the celebration first."

"Fine. You know I'd do anything for you."

When the door creaked open, we both looked over.

Rosa, the elderly Fae dressmaker, had returned with a couple more rolls of shiny fabric. With silver hair coiled high like spun thread and eyes sharp as a tailor's needle, Rosa had been making dresses longer than I'd known her. Though she'd somewhat slowed down with age, her face crinkled with her smile. "Oh, Tala, I am glad you are here."

"It's good to see you again, Rosa."

"I remember every dress I've ever made for your family." Rosa gestured to Freyjn, standing in the middle of the room. "Doesn't she look so much like her mother?"

My smile faded. I had never met my aunt, but I'd been told stories that Caelina had been a great beauty—long, brown hair, ice blue eyes. She was kind and clever. A powerful Fae mage. A great leader. Just like Freyjn.

I'd also been told that my mother, Soleia, Caelina's younger sister, shared those exact same physical features, as most women in our family did.

I peered at a small oval looking glass perched above a set of wooden drawers. I tugged at my own weird, bright fuchsia hair, staring at my strange violet eyes. I knew I looked nothing like my mother.

"Now, Tala, for your dress, what do you think of these?" Rosa held out some gorgeous rolls of fabric. "These colors are beautiful."

I was still somewhat deep in my own melancholy reverie. I almost didn't hear her question until her next prompt.

"A deeper pink or lighter violet, perhaps... magenta?"

"Yes?" I snapped to attention, an undefined thrill shooting up my spine.

"Do you like this color?" Rosa repeated her question, holding up the silky roll of fabric. "It matches your hair quite well."

I blinked. "Oh." I had to shake my head briskly to clear my confusion. "Yes, of course, it's a lovely shade."

15

Wedding

"Days like today, I miss my mother more." Freyjn's eyes were wide with her wistful smile.

I couldn't quite tell if she was nervous, excited, or anxious. Otherwise, she was the picture of a perfect Fae bride standing at the dais in her ceremonial gown—with its dark crimson trim, hand-stitched intricate patterns, beads of onyx and shimmering quartz adorning the neckline, while delicate embroidery wound its way across the bodice like whispers of magic.

I gave her a knowing smile anyway. "I'm sure she's very proud of you."

She gripped my hands like a vise. "I'm glad you are here." Tears shone in her eyes. "And I cannot wait for your own special day."

My smile turning tentative, I cast a glance out at the forest Theatron. Everything pulsed with life as guests in embroidered robes and glittering crystal circlets whispered, laughed, and toasted with fluted glasses.

Afternoon sunlight filtered through the canopy in golden shafts, casting a dreamlike shimmer over the event. Vines of silver blossoms curled along the carved wooden arches, and soft harp music drifted from an unseen corner. The ceremonial dais was draped in silk and petals that danced in the breeze. Everything smelled of honey cakes, fresh moss, and anticipation.

It made sense—for Freyjn.

It was difficult to imagine this many people celebrating me, the black sheep of our family. Not to mention, it was likely an event that was far, far into the future.

My uncle, Stellan, was by the far edge of the dais. Tall, with a warrior's broad frame and uncommonly handsome, I heard he still made women's hearts flutter across the Fae lands. Although he never did seek another mate after Caelina passed away. His life's focus was solely on Freyjn. And while he was technically my guardian, he knew better than to breathe down my neck with expectations. I appreciated him for that.

Arms crossed over his chest, his head cocked slightly to one side as he oversaw Auric speaking quite authoritatively to a group of Fae elders, including the officiant.

I could only imagine Auric was giving everyone a very detailed set of instructions on how he liked the proceedings to go.

I hid my amusement.

Yes, I certainly could not imagine anything like this for myself.

Then the birds screamed.

It started with a single, frantic flutter, then a sudden cacophony of wings, as flocks of ash-winged birds burst from the trees in a swarm, spiraling through the open air.

Heads turned upward. Confused murmurs rippled. A scream of fright that pierced the air next seemingly triggered everyone's panic.

Freyjn's eyes narrowed in alert.

"What in the—?" I instinctively clasped my hands to prepare my magic.

Guests scattered, shrieking, silk robes tangled in chair legs, a flute shattered underfoot. All around us, mages and warriors ducked and scrambled, some summoning weak shields, others simply running.

Rosa, who had been sitting in the front row, had gotten up, but she was struggling against the mob of retreating Fae who weren't paying attention as they fled.

Alarmed, I ran to help her. Taking her arm, I led her to the back of the dais. "Are you okay, Rosa?"

Relieved, she gave me a nod.

"Tala!" Freyjn's voice rang out.

I whipped my head around.

Freyjn was already getting organized. Eyebrows furrowed in determination, she conjured a shield of magic covering the elderly and vulnerable, while effortlessly directing the other Fae to deal with the chaos. She signaled me with a nod.

"I got it!" After making sure Rosa was safe, I bolted back into the fray to take care of the creatures. With my air magic, I sent a flock of birds sailing across the way before they crashed into the banner.

I missed a second wave of birds, swooping like trained messengers, diving straight at me.

"Get out of the way!"

I'd barely braced myself when someone tackled me to the ground. We landed with a crash—narrowly avoiding the sudden onslaught of strange birds. Sputtering my hair out of my face, I recognized his face instantly—dark hair, green eyes—and my bewilderment was overridden by annoyance. "Was that absolutely necessary?"

Out of breath, brow furrowed, Josh helped me up. "I'm sorry."

Another group of birds was circling to swoop back our way, and I yanked on his arm. "Watch out!"

Little winged creatures were landing on the fancy food spread out on the elegant tables, feasting on all the things. There was a great commotion as people jumped up to shoo them away, wildly waving their arms.

A beastly snort rumbled from behind.

I turned to see a massive, glimmering bull with two curved horns protruding from its massive head, come crashing through the underbrush. Its entire body appeared to be wrapped in smoke as if it weren't quite solid. That was, except for when it roared and charged headlong straight through some chairs, some tables, those flower arrangements...

Eyes alight with flame, it bellowed—deep and unnatural—before barreling into the food table with an explosion of pastries and berry glaze.

The bull snorted steam and charged again, overturning chairs and sending a startled usher scrambling into the hedgerow.

My eyebrows snapped together. "What in the Fae lands is that?"

Josh bit his lip. "Um...it looks like a Dreadtaur."

"A what?"

Overhearing, Freyjn yelled out from across the way, even whilst she herded more elders to safety. "Who cares what it is? Just get rid of it!" Her hands glowed with magic as she sent some creatures back, yelling out instructions to the others.

The Theatron was a whirl of fabric and shrieks. Fae scattered like startled deer as the rampaging bull let out another guttural roar, steam puffing from its nostrils in angry bursts. Iridescent birds dive-bombed through the air, leaving trails of shimmering feathers in their wake.

I darted to the center of the clearing, skirt hitched above my boots, dodging fallen decor and tumbling platters.

Around me, several of the older Fae guests had rallied—hands glowing, murmuring containment spells that sparked like lightning in the golden afternoon light. A few of the stronger Fae warriors, clad in embroidered armor, moved with lethal grace, circling the bull. Blades flashed, but they couldn't quite get close enough to slow the beast.

I threw up a hand, channeling a tether of binding magic toward the bull's hooves—only for it to flow right through, the creature's hide phasing out of a solid state. "It passed right through it!"

"Another ghost?" Josh's tone was bewildered, too. "Like what happened at Cephiron?"

I nodded, thrusting my palms forward to try again. This time, part of the ghostly bull caught in the ripple of magic, and it stumbled with a deep bellow, crashing onto the arch of flowers behind the dais.

Josh leapt onto a table to get a better view.

Exasperated, I narrowed my eyes at the strange stampede of animals. They seemed to be variations of certain creatures from Arcadia. "Josh, what the fates is going on?"

"Um, those are—" He paused, as if straining to recall. "Tangler hornets! Water—water repels them!"

My mind whirled as I tried to keep up, but I cast my magic, streams of water shooting from my hands.

How could Josh possibly know about these things? How was he doing all this? But I resolved to yell at him later, once everything was dealt with.

Out of the corner of my eye, another swarm of wasps was headed straight for Freyjn and Auric.

"Freyjn, stay back!" With a flick of my fingers, I attempt to cast a small wind spell.

It didn't work.

Oh no.

I wrung my hands out. It was happening again. I shot an alarmed look back up at the wasps. At the last moment, another Fae mage struck up a shield of wind, sending the creatures splintering off in chaos.

Frustrated, I bit my lip. No. This was dangerous. If I couldn't rely on my magic, I was more likely to get someone hurt instead.

I met Freyjn's puzzled gaze for a brief moment before she whirled around to cast another spell, arresting the fall of part of the arched ceiling.

Casting a bewildered once-over at the devastation, I tossed Josh an accusing look. "Someone must be summoning these creatures. Is it you?"

He winced. "I'm not summoning them. Maybe you are!"

"I'm not the one who seems to know exactly what the hell they all are and what to do with them!"

Most of the distinguished affair's guests had scattered away, running down the road, ducking away for shelter, or going home, leaving only a handful of Fae trying to deal with the pandemonium. A symphony of screams mingled with chaos as the Dreadtaur crashed through a decorative marquee. The other Fae warriors moved in unison, blades catching the light as they helped to redirect the rampaging beast creature toward the perimeter.

Josh's eyes lit up. "Hey! Corral the Sallows—those black birds—together and lead them away to the forest. They're what the Dreadtaur wants. It should follow them and leave us alone."

I didn't hesitate. Gesturing with my hands, I conjured a whorl of magic to gather all the birds in a flow of wind to whisk them away from the clearing, toward the thick cover of the forest.

With a huff and a growl, the Dreadtaur reared back on its hind legs, digging into the ground, getting ready to charge. Fortunately, it took the bait. Its attention focused solely on the flock of birds drifting away on the sharp breeze, the Dreadtaur let out a final cry as it bolted.

Not before one of its horns snagged on a trail of streamers, attached to a handful of fireworks, triggering a cacophony of crackling, brilliant flashes, and then dragging the sparkly trail across the Theatron, clotheslining everything in its path—including Josh.

"Whoops—!" He tumbled back, crashing into a heap of flowers and other debris.

The beast's final cry reverberated throughout the village as it disappeared into the forest, hoof beats and rattling trailing off, fading in the distance until the only sound that remained was the hush of disbelief across the upturned crowd of Fae.

I stood panting, hands glowing faintly, even as I did a quick scan around for injuries or further potential threats.

All the ghostly creatures had gone.

It was over.

Except, a different type of animal rage had overcome Auric.

"YOU!" His darkest of glares were pinned on Josh as he stalked toward him. "You ruined everything!"

Attempting to scramble back on the ground, Josh threw me a panicked glance. "Uh...help?"

I couldn't help an inward groan. For someone so amiable, Josh was certainly accumulating enemies faster than even I ever could.

Without warning, Auric leapt forward to tackle Josh head-on.

You gotta be kidding me— I blew out an exasperated breath before throwing up both hands to summon the wind again to shove them both apart.

Auric skidded back, landing on his feet, still growling.

Josh scrambled up, dusting off his clothes. "That's right, you big, beefy—" He stopped short of his sneer when his gaze landed on me again. Then he glanced up toward Freyjn, approaching to help Auric straighten. He watched the two of them for a moment, scrutinizing their appearance or their clothes.

Despite the ruckus, Freyjn and Auric still looked elegantly regal in their matching ceremonial outfits.

Josh's eyes darted from me to Freyjn and then back again. He was confused as heck. "What...?"

"What?" I prompted in incredulity. "What have you got to say for yourself?"

He looked lost, his tone flat. "You...said you came here for the wedding."

"Yes." I nodded emphatically. "Today is Freyjn's wedding. What about it?"

Upon hearing my words, Josh's shoulders visibly slacked as if in relief. He blew out a huge breath.

I stared at him. "What is the matter with you?"

Josh shook his head, staring at his feet. As though he'd just had an epiphany. He cleared his throat. "Uh, nothing. Nothing at all." When he met my gaze, there was a wide, disarming smile on his face.

I couldn't help my heart skipping a beat.

Josh hadn't smiled at me since we left Cephiron.

But like a magical gust of wind, it was gone in a flash.

Josh's face darkened once again, his forehead creasing with a brisk shake of his head. Except this time, it seemed more of annoyance, instead of despair like before. A reprimand. As if he'd shown more than he intended.

My eyes widened in concern at the trail of blood trickling down the side of Josh's temple. "Oh, you're hurt." I reached up to brush his hair back.

Josh swatted my hand away. "Don't touch me."

Startled, I almost gasped. I instantly dropped my hand. "I'm-I'm sorry." I swallowed hard. He really did hate me now.

Auric was stalking over. "Tala, why in all the realms isn't he in the dungeon?" His face was red with fury. Steam almost came out of his ears. "Malik! Payten!"

I blocked their way before Auric's Fae warrior minions could get closer. "Oh, would you give it a rest, Auric? He was trying to help." I put my hands on my hips. "Besides, I'm responsible for him. I'll run him out of the village myself."

I flashed Freyjn an apology. "I'm so sorry, Freyjn." I beckoned for Josh to follow me. "Come on, Josh."

16

Aftermath

Dodging the trail of disorder and Fae running amok as we hurried down the road, I glanced back at my odd, human 'trouble magnet' companion. "Now, can you tell me exactly what just happened?"

Josh's eyebrows snapped together, annoyed right away again. "Well, I was minding my own business, locked in the dungeon—you know, as I do so often in this world, apparently," he drawled. "Then I saw a bunch of birds across the street. They were strange and swerving all over the place, knocking down apple carts and stalls of—"

I shot him a suspicious look. "You saw all that from inside the dungeon?"

"Whatever, you already know I escaped in like ten minutes." He rolled his eyes. "The birds were familiar to me, so I followed them, and that's when I saw the Dreadtaur tearing down the street, headed straight for that fancy amphitheater." He cast his glance to one side, scoffing. "I mean, I certainly didn't think it was perfect timing for a stampede of animals to disrupt your little ceremony. It didn't even cross my mind at all to just let them crash the party, maybe burn everything down."

Even though I caught the sarcasm dripping off his mumbling, I already knew Josh wasn't the kind of guy who would ever let that happen. Not if he could do anything about it.

My own stomach squirmed as throngs of people also headed to the infirmary. I could imagine an animal stampede of that sort resulted in a few injuries. But I didn't want to call any more undue attention to us.

Sneaking around to the back of the structure, I knew exactly where to poke my head in to find the only other Fae in the village I could tolerate.

With tousled copper curls, mismatched earrings, Renn bustled around a few cots of injured Fae with bandages and herbs. He moved through the infirmary with a dancer's grace and a sharp-tongued wit, his healing hands as quick as his comebacks.

An outcast in his own right, Renn and I were thrown together a lot when we were younger. Except, since he had grown into the best healer mage in Ipera, he'd earned the respect of many Fae, and really, the only other person I could trust to tend to Josh's injuries.

Always one for details, Renn easily spotted me creeping past the curtained area. "Well, I'll be..." His eyebrows shot up as Josh and I approached the isolated exam corner. "How did I know that a ruckus of this sort could only have been accompanied by your return to Ipera, my dear Tala?"

"Technically, it wasn't me this time." I put my hand up. "And last time, I still stand by what I said—that elder officiant only has himself to blame for being so intoxicated at Mead's affirmation."

"Of course. His blessed goblet of water fermented and turned to Fae wine all by itself," Renn mocked. He tossed Josh a pointed look. "Can you believe the balls on this one?"

Josh almost sputtered out a chuckle.

I gestured to Josh's head. "Can you please just help him?"

"Fine." Renn let out a sigh of helpless resignation. "You know you owe me."

"I know, I know." I waved them away.

Renn motioned Josh to come along. Having easily broken the ice with him, Josh yielded without apprehension.

Backing out of the corner to let Renn work, I kept to the sidelines to stay out of everyone else's way. Surveying the hustle around the infirmary, I was relieved that most of the injuries seemed minor.

It didn't take long for Renn to finish and step back out of the curtained area by himself. "All done." He disinfected his hands with a cloth as he walked up to me, waiting by the triage desk in the middle of the room. "I told him to sit and settle his head for a moment, in case he has a concussion."

"Thanks, Renn."

He grinned. "Did I say welcome back yet?"

"Not sure anyone else shares the same sentiment, especially after, you know." I gestured around us to the room full of injured Fae.

Renn's eyes widened, but it was absolutely in amusement. "Oh, is *he* what happened to Freyjn's wedding ceremony?"

"Him and then some." I rubbed the bridge of my nose. "I'm afraid he might be summoning the ghost of chaos everywhere he goes. He's...not exactly from around here. I mean, did you sense anything—anything off with him?"

"Anything off?"

"Come on, Renn. You're a Fae mage and a healer. What do you really think?"

A glint of mischief layered over his perpetual smirk. "I think he's cute."

I rolled my eyes. "Oh, is that your professional opinion?"

"Professionally? Most Fae would kill to have those broad, firm shoulders," Renn quipped under his breath. "Personally, I'd like to have a go at tugging on that thick hair. You know me, those are my top two." He nudged me with his elbow, his voice lowering. "Have you seen what's beneath that shirt yet? You have, haven't you? I mean, I only treated his head. I bet his abs are sculpted like marble."

Heat rushed to my cheeks. "Oh gods, Renn. I meant about his well-being." I willed my pulse to stop racing from the very vivid images of Josh's body that Renn's words were conjuring unbidden in my head.

"Oh." He blinked, stopping short before throwing up his hands. "Relax, Tala. I've patched up his injury. I think...physically, he's in perfect health." He pursed his lips. "Other than that, I'll admit I could sense the fringes of some type of powerful magic, possibly mind magic. But whatever it is, it's way over my head." His eyes lit up. "Oh, you know who you should take him to then, right?"

I blew out another breath in resignation. "Yes, yes. Why do you think I brought him to the Fae lands to begin with?"

When Renn's eyes widened again, it was with apprehension as he gazed past my shoulder. "Oh dear, here comes the cavalry."

It would have been a storm cloud with the matching sullen faces of Stellan and Auric, who were stalking through the infirmary from the front door, if Freyjn's kind smile and bright countenance weren't leading the group. She moved through the roomful of cots with gracious greetings and words of comfort to everyone she passed.

Renn gave them all an acknowledging nod, then backed away to tend to the other patients.

As soon as Freyjn came up to me, she took my hands in hers. "I'm so glad we caught up to you before you left." Her tone was all reassurance. "I know it's a mess, but it's going to be okay. It's not like we haven't been through worse, right?"

I almost laughed, but the weight pressing on my chest did lighten immediately. I totally ruined her precious wedding ceremony, but Freyjn was the one trying to make me feel better.

On the other hand, Auric's arms were crossed. He wasn't inclined to comment any further.

Glancing up, I gave Stellan a tentative smile. "Hello, sir."

Stellan's thoughts, however, seemed far and away from our small village of disrupted weddings. "Has Lance changed his mind about offering assistance?"

I blinked, surprised at the abrupt change in topic. "Um, I don't think so."

His forehead creased. "I would have thought your friendship with him should convince him fairly quickly."

A bit puzzled that Stellan thought I might use my relationship with Lance to sway him, I made sure my tone was even. "The people of Cephiron value peace."

"There won't be peace for much longer if the dissident Fae isles decide to invade us or the human realm."

Freyjn put a calming hand on her father's arm. "The magic wanes all across the land. The weather has been chaotic. Crops are dying, rivers running dry. Every remedy we've conjured so far has only worked temporarily." Her eyes were rueful, despite her matter-of-fact statement. "The Fae Isles have always endured much more than we do here. We must be firm and keep them in line. I am certain we cannot afford another war."

The finality of her statement fell into a tense void of silence. Each of us already knew too well the cost of what the previous war had been. But it was also true that things could not go on as they were much longer.

I was acutely aware it wasn't the right time to bring it up, but I did anyway. "But what if the prophecy can prevent war?"

That prompted a groan from Auric. "Are we wasting time with this ridiculous myth again?"

Stellan leveled me with a look. "Tala, you of all people already know the risks of using the rare magicks. Had I known your portal summoning skills had advanced as far as to let you travel to the fourth realm, I would have persuaded you to pick a different path."

"I *am* sorry. But after all my research and training, I couldn't pass on the opportunity to, for once, be of use. Especially after everything you've already done for me." I dropped my gaze for a moment. "Freyjn will be a great leader for our people, but this—this is the only thing I can contribute."

Stellan's shoulders slacked with a heavy sigh. "You should consider yourself lucky. You are the only natural portal wielder among our people. We could have depleted our stores of magic with the few trusted warriors I'd sent to escort you back."

"A few?" My jaw almost dropped. There had been dozens of shadow Fae warriors pursuing me all across the fourth realm.

My eyes narrowed at the conflicting information. Then again, I should have realized earlier how much such conjuring would have borrowed from what little magic we had left. Given how Stellan knew the strain on our resources, it indeed didn't seem rational for him to have sent dozens of warriors to retrieve me.

Stellan's stern scolding continued. "Or what if your powers had faltered at any time while you were in that dangerous realm? You could have been stranded there altogether."

I shook off my confusion for the moment. I clasped my hands together, eager to show my work. "But I wasn't. My mission was a success. I have found the 'Curse bearer' and brought him back."

At my fervent declaration, Stellan met his daughter's gaze with a narrow-eyed look as if to seek confirmation first.

Freyjn gave him a pointed nod.

Stellan lifted his chin. "I'd like to meet this 'Curse bearer'."

17

Sealed

Motioning with my hand, I led them back to the corner. I drew the curtain back so we could all step in.

Surprised, Josh jerked in his seat at the sudden group of people looking in on him with increasing curiosity. "Oh, hi." He hopped off the cot to straighten up. Running his hands through his hair, he gave everyone a sort of guilty shrug. "Is everyone from the ceremony okay?"

Freyjn's nod was almost appreciative. "I assure you it looks worse than it is."

As soon as he set eyes on Josh, a strange look passed over Stellan's face. It was gone too fast, but for a crazy second, I almost wondered if it could have been the ghost of a memory. Could Stellan be one of the people Josh had memories of? If so, did Stellan have memories of him, too?

But Josh was watching me, his eyebrows raised in expectation.

"What?"

Exasperated, he sighed. "Fine. I'll do the introductions again, shall I?" He lifted his hand in a wave. "My name is Josh. It's nice to meet you all."

Freyjn rose to the task with a smile. "This is my father, Stellan. This is Auric. And I am Freyjn, Tala's cousin."

I didn't like the way Auric was still glaring at Josh. I also didn't like the way Josh was studying Freyjn. His eyes were soft, like he was entranced by her.

Jeez.

Before I threw up in my mouth, I cleared my throat. "We have to show them the seal."

Josh shot me a questioning look. "The what?"

My gaze dropped below his neck. "The mark on your um, chest. Take... take off your shirt."

His eyes bulged. "Seriously?"

"This is why I brought you here," I reminded him. "You are my proof."

With a self-conscious groan, Josh shot the closed curtains a glance as if to make sure they were drawn properly, then he shrugged off his leather jacket.

I couldn't help my heart race when he tugged his shirt up and off altogether. Renn's comment about Josh's physique stirred something inside me again.

But there it was.

A mystical golden swirling mark of a shimmering dragon spewing out a potent fire hovered about an inch or so from the middle of his torso.

I didn't tell Renn before, but I had been exposed to Josh's bare chest one too many times already, being that was where the mythical seal was located. It was how I'd found him. Still, I couldn't look away. I was hoping my cheeks weren't flushed. *Were* his abs sculpted like marble?

Josh had only been training with Lance in Cephiron for a few days, but it already looked like he'd gotten bigger than before, his biceps more toned, his muscles more well-defined.

Oh gods. I had to stop staring.

Josh's cheeks were tinged pink, his gaze off to one side.

Eyes wide, Freyjn's gasp lodged in her throat. "It's true."

Auric's eyes were also wide, but it seemed he still didn't want to believe what he was seeing.

Almost in marveling, Stellan shook his head. "I was wondering if this would happen in my lifetime."

Auric finally sobered enough to speak. He gave Stellan a bewildered look. "You knew about this?"

Stellan made a small nod. "My apologies, Auric. Only the rare few families in Ipera have been privy to this information. It has been essential to carefully preserve the secret that dragons once truly existed. While many Fae have long dismissed them as nothing more than myth, the High Fae chose to guard this truth, believing that concealing it was necessary to maintain stability among our people. Besides, it's been centuries since dragons have roamed the Land of Arcadia."

"But their return is foretold to replenish the magic of the land once and for all. It's going to fix everything." I was unable to keep the eagerness out of my voice as I turned to each of them. Then my gaze distracted toward Josh's bare chest.

With a brisk shake of my head, I reached for his shirt to toss at him. "You can put your shirt back on now."

Josh stuck an insolent tongue out at me and spun to get dressed, offering the privileged view of him from the back, of those shoulders...

I forcibly snapped myself back to attention, toward Stellan and Freyjn again. "I need to take Josh to Sylvara. There is...some powerful magic we're hoping to untangle first." I couldn't help my fists clench in ardent resolve. "Please. I know I am close to the solution."

A ghost of a smile was on Stellan's face. He shook his head. "You are so much like your mother. So headstrong, strong-willed. So determined, to the point of recklessness."

A thrill shot up my spine.

Stellan didn't say it disparagingly, but more matter-of-fact, perhaps almost amused. It almost seemed like a lifetime of memories flashed past his eyes as he added, "But I suppose that's also how she won over your father."

Auric's tone was ominous. "That means the rumor about Tala's father is true. He was a real Deathbringer." His glare turned wary, as though alarmed a monstrous creature might explode out of my skin at any moment.

I almost hissed at the venom that accompanied his words. I would have pounced on him, too, if not for the hand that briefly touched my elbow. Josh had moved to stand beside me again, much like he had before with Mead, Brynn, and Holten, and I was easily enveloped in warmth, in calm. My fury dissipated in an instant.

Freyjn corrected Auric herself. "Tala is still Fae. Her *father* was a dragon. That doesn't mean Tala is a danger to anyone."

"If Soleia's love was anything to go by, I am assured your father was a good man," Stellan said, more for Auric's benefit than mine. "I only met him once. We thought him to be a demon at first."

Josh snorted. I almost thought I heard him think, *Typical.* But he didn't say anything out loud.

Taking a step closer, Stellan peered at my face. "Your parents entrusted you to me. I considered it a great honor and a privilege." He braced his hands on my shoulders. "I didn't hide any of this from you because you deserve the truth, but it certainly had not been my wish for you to journey to dangerous realms and put yourself at risk in service of this prophecy."

I shrugged. "It's too late now."

"Indeed." Stellan sighed again. "I only ever wanted to make sure you are safe." Dropping his hands, he looked from me to Freyjn. "But I know you girls are all grown-up now. You can make your own decisions, fight your own battles, and help our people fight our battles as well."

Auric was still frowning, eyes still narrowed. "It will be difficult to convince people about something that fundamentally changes the way they view history, the world."

Stellan took a deep breath in thought. "It's true. Dragons were a valid threat to this land at one point. Unfortunately, this is the only part of the legend that lingers in people's minds."

My chest tightened as I also knew this to be true, but I had not worked this hard for so long only to give up now. I was determined to see it through to the end. "If the prophecy comes to pass, that should be proof enough for everyone."

"I believe in our people," Freyjn began. "Remember that at one point, everyone had believed the northern forests' wraith infestation was a natural phenomenon, when in truth the creatures were allowed to propagate there to hide yet another curse. Instigated by our great-grandmother, no less."

Stellan shifted in his stance. "Some secrets we must keep."

I frowned, catching a shadow crossing his face. It was entirely possible that Caelina, as the leader of our people, had kept a few things from him as well before he'd ascended as her partner. Perhaps, he felt regret at how certain things seemed out of his hands. Then again, to bear the weight of such things for all the Fae was a great responsibility. I wanted to believe they had only done what they thought was best at the time.

"Let us hope that this next world-altering secret does not culminate in another war." Auric's statement was dry, but his tone was resigned.

"Then you must let me go and do this," I urged. "Myth or prophecy, shouldn't we try to do everything we can?"

Freyjn gave me an assessing look. "Are you feeling any adverse effects from your venture to the fourth realm? I thought I saw your magic faltering earlier at the wedding ceremony. Has that happened before?"

I bit my lip. "Well...it's flickered maybe once or twice."

Stellan's forehead creased. "I shall send some warriors to accompany you to Sylvara. It could be a risk for you to travel right now. What if your magic fails altogether at the worst possible moment?"

"No," I argued. "I know your warriors are needed elsewhere. I wouldn't want to disrupt their assignments. Please."

Stellan spoke again, his tone brooking no argument, "In that case, it will be dangerous for you to summon portals right now. It's the rare magicks that tend to be particularly vulnerable to these types of instabilities."

Willing to comply, I nodded. "Horses then. We need horses." I turned to Josh with a dubious look. "Can you ride?"

Josh grimaced. "I can hold on, how's that?"

Freyjn met Auric's gaze. "I would come along, but with the wedding being rescheduled, Auric and I must take care of the arrangements here."

I shook my head. "You don't need to worry. I can take care of myself. I have to do this."

Freyjn gave me a wan smile. "I know." She pulled me into a hug. "You're the only one who can do this."

18

Quest

"These people seriously need to get a life."

I glanced over at Josh's wry statement. He was eyeing the staggered crowd of Fae watching us ride out of the village.

Nearly everyone had turned out to Freyjn's wedding ceremony. They had all witnessed the strange occurrences with the ghostly creatures. And whoever hadn't been at the event itself had, by this time, already heard about it.

Auric, to his credit, had not revealed Josh's true origins to anyone. But given the spectacle we'd unintentionally put on and the damage that ensued, everyone was now in full suspicion of Josh. We passed Mead and Alys along the road, and even they were looking on in wary curiosity.

As we left Ipera and its gawking throng of onlookers, heading for the deep forest, the wind and pounding hooves left little room for conversation. I peeked at Josh to make sure he was indeed 'holding on.'

Josh shifted in the saddle, gripping the reins with the uncertainty of someone unused to the task, but there was a natural ease in the way he moved with the animal. The horse tossed its head and sped up, but instead of fumbling, he adjusted smoothly, as though instinct carried him where training had not.

I couldn't help my stare. His dark hair ruffled by the wind, sharp green eyes narrowed with focus, his tall frame striking against the strength of the mount beneath him.

The breeze cooled the fire in my cheeks, though it did nothing to steady the racing of my heart. I rubbed my sweaty hands on my pants. I'd changed into my travel clothes again and packed up some supplies before heading to the stables for our departure.

"Last two," the Fae apprentice had told me, lugging over the saddles. "The stable hand said you almost had to share one horse."

My stomach stirred again at the notion of having to be so close to Josh for an extended period of time. I tried not to imagine having to ride behind him on a horse all the way to Sylvara. To share his warmth, to be bathed in that minty scent... I would have to hold on to him, my arms wrapped around his—

Stop it.

I cleared my throat in an attempt to clear my head. I needed to focus.

The road was narrowing before us, and we slowed to a trot. The forest paths were worn, with roots twisting like traps beneath our horses' hooves. The lateness of the day through the tall trees cast long shadows across the trail.

Despite the world unfolding around us in a cascade of emerald hills, the valley below shimmering like a painted dream, every creak of the branches overhead and rustle in the underbrush kept me on alert.

Outside the protection of Ipera, there was no telling what dangers we would encounter in the woods. News of the conflict with the Fae Isles reached as far as even Cephiron. Enough to know they weren't idle gossip—of dissident Fae raiding outlying villages, of convoys ambushed in the cover of night, acts made in protest of which grew bolder by the day.

"Be wary of everyone we pass," I told Josh in passing. "Dissident Fae are clever enough to disguise themselves as ordinary travelers until the moment they strike. The conflict is getting worse by the day as the magic of the land keeps dissipating, and will only continue unless we fulfil this prophecy and heal the land."

He was silent for a while as if absorbing that. When he spoke, his response was muted. "Your cousin said she was looking forward to having a chat with me about the fourth realm when this is all over. She doesn't know I'm marked for death, does she?"

That constriction was back in my chest. Dropping my gaze, I pursed my lips. I didn't need to reply out loud.

"Does anyone?"

"Just Lance."

Josh chewed on his bottom lip. "Do you know... by any chance, do you know how it will happen?"

I hid my grimace. I hadn't wanted to ponder it myself. "There might be a test. You may have to prove yourself worthy first." I shifted in my seat with unease. "That was what my research had uncovered. Test and sacrifice."

His eyebrows furrowed. "This is why you were nagging me about learning to fight, to use a sword."

Rueful, I shook my head. "Josh, you are the realm's only hope. The only way for a peaceful resolution for all this is for you to undertake whatever the test requires."

"What is a Deathbringer?"

I winced at his sudden question.

"What Auric called your father." He turned his gaze to me, his eyes gently tracing across my features. "Your ears aren't pointed. I didn't even think of it. You're only half-Fae."

I took a deep breath. "Deathbringer... is a bad name that the Fae used to call his kind—my kind. My father was a dragon shifter."

He nodded. "No wonder you're so invested in all this. Did nobody else know about him in your village?"

I shook my head again. "Stellan and the High Fae have tried to keep it quiet, but there are always rumors. And the problem with rumors is that eventually, they grow too unwieldy until the truth is barely recognizable."

Josh's face was dark, the outrage in his tone thinly veiled. "How could they have let you grow up like that? Letting Mead and Brynn treat you that way, with everyone thinking the worst of your father, all for the sake of some—secret."

"I suppose they thought it was for the best."

"For everyone else, sure." He seemed almost as upset as I was. His eyebrows were drawn, his lips pursed. "I should give all those High Fae a piece of my mind."

The notion of Josh going against the High Fae almost made me chuckle. "Fae have never had a brilliant track record for honesty. They—or I suppose I should say, we can be quite tricky."

He gave me a pointed look. "You don't have to remind me."

I bit back my grin. "Oh. You're talking about that thing again."

"That *thing*," he echoed in mocking. "You mean when you manipulated me into doing your bidding using some kind of Fae bargain back on Earth?"

I rolled my eyes. "I released you right away. You don't have to keep complaining about it."

"Ugh, that feels like forever ago." Groaning, he rubbed his hand over his face. "This whole thing hasn't gone at all how I was hoping."

Guilt washed over me all over again. That prophecy was like the gift that kept on giving. I thought it had already ruined my life the first time I discovered it, but every single day, it kept bringing all that ruin.

We passed beneath mossy archways of twisted trees and wound our way down into a quiet glade where the world hushed.

Suddenly, Josh slowed his pace.

Frowning, I glanced back as his horse came to a full stop. Before I could ask what he was doing, Josh dismounted without warning. His gaze was pinned somewhere in the distance, and then he was off.

"Hey! Where are you going?" Hopping off my horse, I grabbed the reins from Josh's horse as well so I could secure them around a nearby tree, then broke into a jog before I could lose sight of him.

If Josh got lost in the woods, it would be very much my problem.

Wading through the brush, I squinted to attempt to see what Josh could possibly be seeing or looking for under the dim cover of the thick forest.

Josh had stopped at the edge of a small lake framed by towering pines.

I stopped to stand beside him, rubbing my hands over my arms. The shade of the trees barely permitted any warmth from the sun to seep through. "It's cold here."

"What is this place?" Josh murmured, brow furrowing.

I cast a curious survey around, but the place was deserted. "Nothing. It's just a forest. Just a lake. I suppose Fae hunt for game here." I peered up to study his expression. "What are you seeing?"

"At Cephiron, remember when I asked you about that place on the map? You said it was in the Fae lands. Is this that place?"

Tilting my head in momentary thought, I blinked in astonishment at the realization. "Yes. How did you know that?"

"I feel..." Josh clutched at his chest. "I feel as though this place is very important to me. I've been here before."

He wasn't looking at me, but the intensity in his eyes was making me breathless anyway—and it hit me.

I believed him.

19

Mystic Lake

A gust of wind blew through the reeds on the shore, through the long, wild grass. The lake's surface itself was glassy, serene, still—that was, until a fallen leaf twirled in the air only to land on it, the ripples disturbing its mirror-like smoothness.

Standing beside Josh, I could feel the ache in him as he took everything in. There was no denying the wistfulness in his entire being. Everything he'd said before. The things that felt familiar. The memories he'd lost. They were of this. This place.

Josh had been to Arcadia before.

Somehow.

A breeze stirred the air, the lush fragrance of nature swirled about, as if the forest itself breathed—branches shifting, leaves rustling as though the trees exhaled in unison.

I let out a slow breath. "What else do you remember?"

Those brilliant green eyes turned to me. I couldn't look away from the intense light in them. "I remember you. The past is full of fog, but you are the one distinct thing that's always been crystal clear to me." His soft gaze on my face felt like a whisper of a touch. "You've been in my head for so long it feels like I've known you forever. In my dreams, before we even met, you were always out of reach. But being in this special place, with you, finally—I can't even explain how much this means to me."

His solemn tone sent shivers up my spine. An unseen weight pressed in. As if something in this forest remembered us, even if we did not. The tension was its own storm, a thousand unsaid words straining to be let loose. It tugged at me to cross the warmth of the space between us.

Almost involuntarily, I lifted my hand to touch his face.

Josh shrugged me off, stepping back. "Don't."

His rejection stung my chest again. "Sorry." I dropped my hand.

His mask of annoyance shook back into place. "Don't feel sorry for me," he snapped, overwhelmed by the silent battle raging in his mind. He knew he should keep his distance from me. I'd done nothing but treat him badly so far. But it seems he couldn't help it. He both wanted *and* didn't want my touch.

"I wasn't. I—" I blew out my own frustration, mortified at my lack of control. Neither of us could help wanting to be closer. "I just wanted to say thank you."

Josh flashed me a look of pure disbelief. "What?"

I looked away. "For coming with me. For being here. For your help at the wedding ceremony, earlier today."

"What else did you expect me to do? Run away in the other direction?"

"You could have." Frowning, I had to meet his gaze again. "You know you could have run away. Every time you escaped the dungeon, even back at Cephiron. You could have run away and saved yourself, especially now knowing what destiny has in store for you."

He pursed his lips. "Shut up. You know I wouldn't do that. I came here to help you."

Remorse weighed heavily on my chest once again. I wasn't sure he heard my soft response, "Thank you."

Except, somehow, my gratitude triggered his rant instead.

Josh ran his fingers through his hair with a hiss. He paced on the grass. "You know, I really should have just run away. I mean, why the hell would I want to stay here? Why would I even want to help you?"

It didn't seem like the question was directed at me.

"You've done nothing but keep secrets and lie to me right from the start," he said. "You've been dragging me around this land like I'm a piece of luggage. You've made it perfectly clear what I'm here for. You don't care about me. You were pimping me out to those mean Fae women. You were going to let your monster of a brother-in-law pound me into the ground. Throwing me in the dungeons every chance you get."

My eyes widened in indignation. "I told you! You should have waited for me to bring up the discussion of your memories with Freyjn at a better time. If you had let me explain the situation to them myself, Auric wouldn't have snapped like that."

He stopped pacing, his eyebrows snapping together. "I had to tell them. It had to come from me. I'm sure they would have locked me up regardless, so let them hate me. Let them think I'm the one who's lying, that I'm causing all the trouble. That way..." He trailed off, his eyes widening as though he hadn't meant to reveal that.

My mouth nearly dropped open as it struck me again—the real reason he had done that. "What...?"

I'd mentioned that I was already under fire for believing the legends, for having a suspect reputation among the Fae. He'd seen for himself that my relations with my own people were not entirely congenial. He was trying to spare me more grief.

Josh was trying to protect me.

Despite my lying to him, pushing him away all this time, treating him like 'luggage', he was still looking out for my best interests. I couldn't help the warmth building in my chest. If it wasn't so preposterous—not to mention, pointless—I would have laughed. "You're such an idiot."

"Stop it." He let out a loud, exasperated groan. "Stop looking at me like that."

"Like what?"

Still frowning, he averted his gaze. "Stop looking at me like I put the stars in the sky. It makes me think you like me too, when I know you don't. When I know you're betrothed to someone else and there's not one damn thing I can do about it."

A flush of heat rushed through me once again, of trepidation, of near embarrassment. Was I looking at him like he put the stars in the sky? I was toeing a dangerous line. Especially with Josh being so open about his own feelings. I couldn't tell him the real reason I was specifically trying to keep him away from me.

Because he was absolutely right.

Yes, of course, it was to ensure his safety for the prophecy.

But also... I couldn't tell him how incredibly, inexplicably drawn to him I already was. How much I admired his courage, his caring, his unfailing good nature. How every time I thought about fulfilling the prophecy, my insides felt desperately hollow. How I would give anything else across all the realms if it meant he would be safe, if it meant I didn't have to cause his demise. How much I wanted him to know that if I had any choice in my betrothed at all, I might be persuaded to choose someone else.

But I already knew. None of this was bound to end well for us at all. It was safer never to take that step. If I gave in to these feelings, Josh would eventually end up getting hurt. I couldn't bear it if I were the cause of any more of his suffering.

I swallowed past the lump in my throat. "Stop interpreting my looks in your favor." I kept my tone firm, unaffected. "You're only seeing what you want to see because of your own human feelings. And I already told you, you can't do that."

Those sharp green eyes flashed with something akin to hurt, remorse, dismay. His brows knitted at the faint tremor in his breath—as though frustration had hollowed him out and left him aching for some impossible release. His jaws were clenched tight, his expression burning with a raw, restless fury that had nowhere to go.

"Well, you don't have to worry. I'm over it," he declared, his tone lower, darker. "After everything, I thought at least we were friends. But you know what? You don't have to pretend anymore. Look, I don't even want to be around you—since you obviously don't want me around either. When we get back, I'd rather sleep in the dungeon again. Just... just call me when it's time for me to die."

His words stabbed at my chest, but this was exactly what I wanted.

For him to hate me. For him to push me away.

I felt like absolute crap.

I nodded. "Good."

20

Closer

Sylvara was a small village tucked between forested slopes, with its cobblestone paths, ivy-cloaked cottages with thick thatched roofs, and sweet smoke curling from chimneys. Wind chimes tinkled softly from eaves, and a few lanterns had already begun to glow as evening settled in.

Firewood, wild herbs, and sweet tarts tickled my nose as we entered the inn, a sturdy timber-framed building, the warmth of the hearth meeting us like an embrace.

Approaching the front desk, I gave the stout Fae woman tending it a polite nod. "We're here to see the caretaker."

Tugging on her woolen apron with silver-threaded cuffs, her crinkled eyes lit up despite her regretful smile. "Ah, loves, you just missed her. The caretaker's locked up for the evening. Keeps a tight schedule, she does. You'd need to come back in the morning, and she'll see you properly."

"Oh." I'd forgotten how much longer things took when I couldn't travel using portals.

Josh let out a small grumble beside me.

"I'm sure you'll find her bright and early tomorrow." The lady reached for the guest ledger. "Shall I check you in for the night then? Best to rest after a long journey."

I met Josh's wary gaze for a moment. I was really hoping this little sojourn would be quick. We would meet with the caretaker. Josh would get his memories back. We would return to Ipera. I could finally safely leave Josh's company once again. To the dungeons or otherwise.

I supposed we didn't have much choice.

She snapped her fingers, and a young man came over, only to skip away to follow her bidding. "Felix, why don't you make sure their horses are taken care of?" She gave me a warm smile as she leafed through her book. "I made some berry tarts, freshly baked today. I'll be sure to conjure some up in your room."

"Thank you."

Glancing down again, she stopped short at the open page of the book. "Oh, it's been a busy day today." Her eyebrows rose. "It looks like we only have one room left for the night."

My eyes widened in trepidation.

"Hmm...and only one bed—"

"What did you say?"

Josh's eyes were even wider than mine.

My heart pounded in my chest—hard.

It was bad enough that we almost had to share one horse earlier. Our argument by the lake newly solidified that resolve we were supposed to keep our distance from each other. Were we supposed to sleep in the same bed tonight? All night long?

I couldn't help my entire body flush as the mere notion blazed hot in my mind. I turned a horrified glare at Josh.

He took it as accusatory, putting his hands up. "What? I didn't do anything!"

The lady tapped on the page. "Oh, wait, sorry, my mistake," she cheered. "We do have one last room with two beds."

Sucking in a deep breath, I almost collapsed against the counter in relief. "Oh, good." I almost couldn't get the words out.

Josh's gaze was on the floor. I didn't even want to imagine what could have been running through his mind either.

"Splendid!" The lady reached for the keys from the wooden cubby with a jingle before beckoning the two of us to follow her up the stairs. She hummed happily to herself. As if she hadn't almost given us a heart attack.

She led us to the modest-sized room at the end of the hall, opening the door while magically producing a plate of berry tarts in her hand. She handed it to me with another warm smile and a "Have a good evening" before she turned to leave.

Peering into the room, I noted in relief the two sturdy wooden beds standing side by side against the far wall, each dressed with thick woolen blankets and embroidered coverlets that bore faint patterns of ivy and stars.

After we stepped inside, Josh shut the door behind us—not suddenly, but I still jumped. The room was too quiet, despite the faint crackle of fire from the small stone hearth in the corner, filling the room with a soft glow and the scent of pine logs.

I set the plate of tarts on the small table between the beds. I let out a shaky breath. The tension in the air was still thick, the unsettling notion of the two of us sharing a bed still fresh.

Josh cleared his throat.

But when I met his wary gaze, a hint of a smirk played on his lips.

"And here you thought it would be awkward."

Despite everything, I almost snorted in mirth.

***

For all its creaking beams and rustic charm, the inn offered adequate amenities for washing up—a steaming basin, neatly folded linens, and fragrant herbs laid out. After our long journey, it wasn't hard to succumb to the heavy cloak of weariness.

Sleep claimed Josh quickly and without resistance.

It claimed me too, except a lot less peacefully.

Much as it had always done.

Darkness pressed in on me from every side. It was thick, suffocating. Like stone walls closing tighter with every breath. My lungs ached as if the air itself was being stolen. Each gasp felt thinner than the last as it scraped down my throat in ragged desperation.

I knew it was only a dream, that none of it could touch me. But this certainty was slippery, sliding from my grasp no matter how hard I tried to cling to it.

I clawed at unseen walls, my nails raking over nothing, my hands trembling as panic surged hotter, faster, through my chest. The void swallowed even the sound of my own cries, leaving me small and silent and terribly alone. My heartbeat thundered in my ears, frantic, uneven, as though it was trying to hammer its way out of me. The struggle inside me useless as the dark crept closer, pressing against my skin until it felt like I was drowning in shadow.

I thrashed in the void, arms flailing as I sank deeper.

I grabbed at the dark, but there would be nothing to steady me, nothing to quell my panic. My body trembling, my mind screaming, I would sink deeper and deeper, my hopelessly reaching hands only meeting endless emptiness, again and again—

Until I grasped a hand in the darkness. Real, strong, the hand closed around mine. Solid where everything else had been nothing. I clung to it, the only anchor in my nightmare's abyss.

It held on to me firm. And I knew it wasn't going to let go.

I woke with a gasp, blinking a few times in the dim light to clear my vision.

Green eyes were gazing down at me as Josh hovered over my bed, his hand on my shoulder, his voice low. "Are you okay?"

Sitting up, I tried to even out my breathing. "S-sorry..."

Out the window, the calm, night sky showed off a scattering of stars, sharp and silver. Faint embers in the hearth glowed low, painting the walls in a soft, flickering haze, with only the faint chirp of crickets drifting through the wooden shutters against the hushed stillness of the rest of the inn.

Josh was standing by my bed, his hair rumpled from sleep, a slight crease on his forehead. I had obviously woken him up.

I ran the back of my hand across my damp forehead. "It's late. I didn't mean to disturb you."

His frown deepened, but not in annoyance. Looking me over, his gaze was concerned. "Nightmare again?"

I looked away.

It was my usual nightmare—already become familiar to me in waking as in sleep. Night after night, I would drown in suffocating darkness.

Endless. Hopeless.

Until tonight.

I took a deep breath. That strong, calming aura from my nightmare was still vivid, reassuring. I'd have to be a fool not to know what it meant. "I'm sorry for waking you up."

"It's fine." Josh started to pull away, but I caught his arm.

The nightmare clung to me even after I woke, the darkness in the corners of the room heavy and watching, my bed far too cold and empty. I curled my other hand in my blankets. I shouldn't need him like this, shouldn't want the safety of his warmth. But after struggling with the shadows for so long on my own, the temptation of his reassuring presence was a revelation.

His forehead creased again. He studied my face for a moment, waiting expectantly for a question, an invitation.

Crap. I couldn't ask. My tongue was stuck to the roof of my mouth.

Closing his eyes for a moment, he blew out a resigned sigh. Not at all gently, he pushed me to move over on the bed so he could climb in. "Whatever. Tell me to leave if you don't want me here."

My heart pounded in my chest again—not in fear this time.

"Don't."

He froze. "What?"

"Don't leave."

I didn't meet his gaze, but at my words, the tension left his shoulders.

Shaking his head above mine as he settled back, he gently slipped his arm around me to ease me against his chest. "Fine. I'll stay." He was quick to amend, "Not because I want to, by the way. I just want to make sure you fall asleep and don't disturb me anymore."

I bit back my smirk. He tightened his arms around me, and gods help me, I all but melted against him.

Perhaps I could rely on the simple comfort of his closeness, the steady warmth of knowing I wasn't alone in the dark. Just this once, perhaps it was okay to let it all go—the prophecy, the impossible choices, the shadow of doom hanging over us, and the worlds we were meant to save, of letting myself feel something selfish instead of shouldering destiny's endless burden.

I shouldn't want this. But for one night, perhaps we could sit here and forget everything else, to breathe in the quiet and believe that nothing existed beyond the steady rhythm of each other's presence.

Perhaps Josh was thinking the exact same thing.

The back of my neck prickled when gentle, tentative fingers stroked my hair.

"Tala..." he whispered near my ear.

I closed my eyes at the shiver that shot through me from the reverent way he said my name.

Oh, this was so bad.

I swallowed hard. "Yes?"

"Why are you still awake? You should get some rest." His chiding felt playful.

"Why are *you* still awake?" I countered, tamping down a grin.

His nearness, the warmth of his body, was a quiet shield. The shadows in the room softened until they no longer looked like they meant to swallow me whole. The silence of the night shifted from suffocating to steady.

Josh gave my shoulders a brief squeeze. "Tell me a story."

"What story?"

"Any story. Maybe a bedtime story, one you were told when you were a child."

A different sort of quiet came over me.

There was one story. One that Stellan would tell Freyjn and me all the time when we were younger. I still knew it by heart.

With Josh's grounding presence wrapped around me, perhaps I could tell this story for once without the desolation that often greeted me upon its end.

Focusing on the faint glowing embers in the hearth across the room, I took a deep breath. "Many years ago, a great war ravaged the Land of Arcadia, across all the realms—Fae, human, and dragon."

I felt Josh's startle as he realized what story it was, but I didn't stop. I wanted to share this with him. With the 'Curse bearer' having wholly accepted his destiny, it was only fair for him to know.

"The High Fae of Ipera led our warriors to battle, with their strongest leaders at the helm—Caelina and Stellan. The High Fae mage Caelina's magic was the strongest anyone had ever seen."

Josh didn't cut in to interrupt. He didn't argue. He didn't offer any snide commentary. He merely listened intently, his steady breathing a constant reassurance as I wove through the epic story, little known to even some of my people.

"In the end, the High Fae and our allies defeated the forces of evil rogues, and there was cheering everywhere. The war was won, gaining us victory over our treacherous foes. However, our losses were also many. Sadly, the great High Fae mage Caelina lived only long enough to taste her triumph, and a great many others perished on all sides. Some say the dragons perpetrated the war, but in truth, the leaders of the High Fae, Caelina and Stellan, saved all the realms by working together with the leaders of the dragons—the king and his powerful Fae bride, who made the ultimate sacrifice for all the realms."

I felt Josh's quiet gasp at my shattering conclusion. I couldn't see the reaction on his face. He didn't pester me with questions. He only held me tighter, waiting for me to finish.

"And the mystical land of the dragons sank into the ocean, disappearing forever..."

The silence of the night consumed my words as I trailed off.

When he finally spoke, his knowing tone was loaded with sympathy. "Your parents."

"They both perished during the war. My uncle Stellan raised me. He and Freyjn are my only family. I know they love me as their own, and I'm grateful. But some days, it's tough to be only somewhat adjacent to their official noble positions."

"Wait a minute. Your parents were the king of the dragons and his Fae bride. That means you're a princess."

I let out a rueful sigh. "A princess with no kingdom. A royal with no throne. I don't even know where I belong. I'm the last of my people. I was hoping that in my research, with this prophecy... I just—" I shrugged, that familiar cloak of heaviness settling over me. "I don't want to be alone anymore."

"You're not alone."

I winced at the pity in his tone. Clearing my throat quickly, I straightened in my seat. I'd never told anyone else that part of the story. Not even Lance.

"I mean, of course not," I dismissed, smoothing my hands over my lap. I forced a steady breath to hide the sting of my weakness, pretending the ache in my chest wasn't there from the truth I'd let slip. "It's not too bad. I've dealt with worse. I do well enough on my own anyway."

Josh peered at my face. "You don't have to act strong in front of me. I'm nobody. I'm just Josh. I'm the weakest one here."

I turned to meet his gaze, with half a protest for his own sake in my conviction. "You're not weak."

But I hadn't realized how close we already were until the space between us vanished, until his face was right there, his mouth only a whisper away from mine.

I caught the subtle hitch in his breath again, the way his chest tightened as if even the nearness of my mouth to his was enough to steal the air from him. The change in his breathing was instant—shallow, uneven, like the air itself had betrayed him—the warmth of it ghosted across my lips.

The longing to draw nearer tugged at me with a strength I couldn't ignore. I lifted a tentative hand to press against his chest. His heartbeat hammered against my palm, through the fabric of his shirt. The warm, solid strength of his body beneath my touch was hard, unyielding.

My own heart lurched in my chest, every nerve in me alight with the awareness of him.

His green eyes shone down on me despite the deep crease in his forehead. There was no mistaking the husk in the words rumbled deep from his throat, "If you do that, it'll make me want you again."

I was already breathless. I had to stop touching him. I had to push away. But I couldn't. I furrowed my eyebrows. "We can't do this."

His eyes narrowed on me as if trying to decipher what my words really meant. "But do you want to?" His gaze dropped to my mouth and stayed there. "How do you really feel about me?"

My mouth was dry. I licked my lips. "I feel... I feel comfortable when I'm with you."

Wincing, he pulled away a bit. "What am I, a security blanket? You shouldn't be comfortable." He looked to the ceiling with a scoff. "God, my every nerve is aware of you, is alive because of you. Am *I* comfortable right now? Hell, no!"

His reaction made me chuckle. "I mean...you make me feel safe."

A despondent shadow crossed his features. "But that's all, isn't it?"

I dropped my hand. "It's complicated."

Josh took a slow, deep breath. "I'm...trying to understand. I respect your decision. I know I'm not good enough for you anyway, and I'm doing my best to accept my fate. To stay away. Except...I'm slowly realizing that my fate also seems to be wanting to give you whatever you need. You don't even have to ask. I'll always be here for you." He lifted his shoulders in a shrug. "I mean, you know, until..."

I couldn't help the twinge in my chest at his precious words, but all I could say was, "I appreciate that."

Josh let out a helplessly resigned half-groan, half-sigh. He shifted his hold on me carefully, making sure I was comfortable. "Now, time to get some rest," he ordered with a surprisingly firm tone. "If I'm going to help you save the world, you have to be awake enough to keep me from dying until then."

I couldn't help a smile. "I shall do my utmost."

As I closed my eyes, the solemn words murmured near my ear sent me off straight into the most restful sleep I'd had in quite a while.

"That's my girl."

21

Breathe

The fine weather felt stark. The light of day cast a blatant glare on all the things I really shouldn't have said or done last night. I'd worked so hard to build walls, to keep Josh at arm's length. Only to be undone by a moment of weakness. Perhaps it had been too much to hope that destiny would allow a short reprieve.

Josh said nothing either, his wariness clear in the way his eyes flitted toward me and away again during breakfast, as if one wrong word might shatter whatever fragile balance we'd stumbled into.

The innkeeper lady offered a quiet warning as she put away our plates. "Be careful around these parts whilst you're wearing Priori colors. Felix says he's seen some warriors from the Fae Isles going around. I've no quarrel with either side, but I've an aim to keep the peace around these parts. Conflict is never good for my business."

I bid her our thanks and went on the way she indicated, the caretaker's domain being a vigorous walk down the road, through the forest.

I tried to keep my attention on the way ahead, as the path narrowed between roots and stones, on the danger that might lurk in hidden brushes, but my gaze strayed to Josh more often than I cared to admit.

He strode beside me, deep in tentative thought. Then he shifted closer. His hand flexing, his jaw worked as if he was gathering something to say.

I braced for words that might drag last night's events out into reality. My heart raced with the memory of his heartbeat under my palm, the heat of his nearness.

But then he glanced at me, green eyes flicking over mine for an instant, and I saw the restraint there. He swallowed whatever it was and turned back to the path. The air between us grew heavier for it, like a storm cloud overhead.

Perhaps it was better this way, for what had passed between us to linger unspoken, suspended like a secret neither of us could bring ourselves to name.

We crossed wooden bridges over babbling brooks, but even as the crisp scent of pine clung to the air, the birds chirping in the high branches, the awkwardness between us was palpable.

Focus on your mission, Tala.

Clearing my throat, I steadied my voice. "We're not far. It seems the caretaker lives just beyond that ridge. Her grove is shielded, hidden from most."

Josh nodded, his gaze flicking over the woods. "Do you often ask her for help?"

"I've never met her, but her magic is legendary." I tilted my head in consideration. "It's old, deep-rooted magic. A tricky sort as it seeks to fathom the mysteries of the mind."

The trail thinned into a winding footpath between thick, towering trunks.

The faint crunch of movement up ahead, not belonging to us, set my pulse spiking instantly. I backed up against a tree. I motioned for Josh to do the same, my hand drifting toward the dagger at my belt.

As I peered through the trees, at least half a dozen Fae emerged clad in dark leathers, weapons slung across their backs as they marched down the worn path. They hadn't spotted us yet.

"Are they from the Fae Isles?" he murmured, low enough that only I could hear.

I nodded. "They shouldn't see us." I didn't want to waste time engaging them. Not to mention, I would have to watch out for Josh, too. I beckoned for him to follow me as I crept along the forest, dodging roots and ducking branches.

"Couldn't you just talk to them? Explain we're not here to fight?"

I shot Josh a flat look.

Always the optimist.

"I'm not going to risk that. I have to keep you alive, remember?"

He rolled his eyes. "Yeah, so you can kill me off later."

Not dignifying his remark with a response, I pulled on his arm to move faster.

We turned left, nearly landing in a thicket of thorny brambles. Josh stumbled over a log, but the warriors stayed on their path, with the occasional boisterous laughter amidst their low chatter.

After what felt like an eternity, the forest grew quiet again. My gaze darted around to make sure we were safe as we moved along. "I think they didn't see us."

"That's a relie—*whoa*—"

The ground vanished beneath our feet.

Dirt and leaves gave way to darkness as we fell into a pit carved into the forest floor.

"Ow!" I squeaked, landing hard on the ground. Josh fell with a thud, his figure bent awkwardly by my side. The hole barely fit both of us standing up, but it was dug well deep.

Josh sputtered out dirt. "What the hell is this?"

I swallowed hard, my pulse already beginning to race. "An-animal trap...it must be—" I gritted my teeth, pressing one hand to my aching side as I stared up at the rim of the hole. Roots clawed down like gnarled fingers. The daylight above seemed impossibly far.

Josh shifted beside me, brushing off dirt from his clothes, wincing.

Black spots danced in my vision. I clutched at my throat, my chest heaving erratically.

His eyes widened. "What's—what's going on?"

"I'm—I'm—" Struggling to breathe, I squeezed my eyes shut. "I can't breathe—it's too dark—"

Josh jerked as if a realization struck him. "You're claustrophobic. We have to get out of here right now." He cast a desperate, hopeless glance upward. The pit walls were too steep and slick with damp earth. "Of course, I should have known. You hate enclosed spaces, aquariums, cages."

I pressed my hands on either side of my head. I was in my nightmare all over again. Thick, suffocating shadows pressed in all around me as I sank into an abyss of darkness. "No... no..." I moaned in despair, my body falling slack.

He caught me in his arms, hissing in frustration. "Oh crap. You have to focus, Tala. If I yell out for help, the wrong people might hear me." He brushed my hair back from my face. "You need to do magic. Magic us out of here. I know you can do it."

I shook my head. It was too dark. There was nothing but fear, emptiness, and loneliness in my void. Much like it's always had.

"It's okay." He stroked my back. "It's okay, Tala. Listen, focus on my voice. Focus on me. I'm right here. Imagine...imagine—" His tone brightened. "The forest. Imagine you're on top of the tallest tree in the forest. It's all yours. The trees. The sky. You own all of it. Can you smell that?"

He leaned closer, his breath brushing my cheek as he spoke, "It's pine and fresh air. The wind's blowing all around you. You're standing on a sturdy branch. If you lift your hand up, you can almost touch the sky. The sun is setting, the clouds are all pink, purple, just like your hair. Can you see it?" His lips ghosted across my eyelids, so soft it was barely more than a whisper. "I can see you. Standing on top of your favorite tree, with the wind pulling at your hair."

The pounding in my head eased the slightest bit. Josh's picture was somehow a very easy image to conjure in my head. Almost as though it was part of a memory. As though I had done it for hundreds of years. As though *this* was home.

And I could breathe again.

I know you can do it.

I focused on Josh's words, his encouragement, his warmth, on the strength in his arms as he folded me tight against his chest. Struggling to claw free from the shadows in my mind, I clasped my hands together.

The air around us shimmered faintly before it sparked—a flicker of gold against the brown—and burst upward in a narrow column of force, like a reverse whirlpool of wind and light.

With a rush of energy, we ejected from the pit, weightless and whirling, before we landed face down on the forest floor.

"Oof—" I spat grass out of my mouth.

Josh coughed beside me.

When a shadow fell across us, I looked up in alert.

A slightly older woman towered over us. "Well, if it isn't the one who's marked for death." She leaned against her walking stick, her lips quirked in amusement. "We have been expecting your arrival."

22

Gazen

The strange woman kept a brisk pace as she led us through the forest. "Name's Gazen, the caretaker. Pleased to meet you." Her hair was short, cropped, a smattering of wrinkles on her face, wisdom in her glassy eyes. Her brown vest covered in thistles, beads, and feathers, jangled as she strode on, her walking stick tapping a steady rhythm against root and stone, every step measured.

I peered at her face.

Gazen's eyes never fixed on what lay ahead, and yet she adjusted seamlessly to the uneven ground. Despite her limitations, she was quite easily plowing through the forest, sidestepping gnarled roots and ducking beneath low boughs as if she saw them before they came.

Josh almost had to jump to keep up. "Cool, I'm Josh—hey, just curious, how did you know about the 'marked for death' thing?"

"I saw it."

He frowned. "But how? Aren't you blin—?"

Eyes widening in alarm, I smacked him across the back to shut him up.

"Ow!" he yelped, half more surprised than hurt, rubbing the spot with a dramatic wince. "Sorry."

Gazen merely cracked a smile. She gestured her hand out as we crossed a narrow ridge where the path opened into a sun-drenched glade, golden and green under the afternoon light. "With their help, of course."

I caught my breath at the herd of magnificent creatures grazing on the wide field that stretched before us.

With their massive leonine bodies, the griffin's feathered heads gleamed, eyes intelligent and alert. Some of the creatures moved lazily in the distance, catching the sunlight in ripples of bronze. Some flapped their powerful wings as we wandered near.

"Whoa." Josh stepped closer with no apprehension whatsoever. "They're beautiful. I didn't know you had griffins in this world."

One of the creatures approached him, its huge beak dipping curiously as Josh extended his hand, and the beast rumbled softly in approval.

"I believe Gazen is training with the creatures for their rare gift of sight," I said to Josh before giving her a prompt. "Is that correct?"

"Yes." Gazen nodded. "Though my eyes see only darkness, they've gifted me with a kind of seeing. Through them, I perceive the world—not with sight as others know it, but with a clarity born of bond and magic." She waved her hand to add,

"But more than that, these majestic creatures see things often beyond our own limited comprehension, past or future. They can read someone's innermost being with a look, with a particular penchant in magicks of the mind."

I couldn't help but be awestruck. Gazen certainly lived up to her reputation among the Fae lands. We'd certainly come to the right place.

As a tawny griffin approached Gazen, she moved to pet the creature with the ease of someone walking among old friends. It lowered its head so she could rub beneath its feathered crest. "They don't sense any fear in you," she told Josh. "Often, humans are too wary to come any closer, and without my presence as a signal, the beast would likely toss you halfway across the valley."

Josh's eyes bulged. "Whoa, what?"

I almost chuckled at his endless positivity. He had been stroking the giant creature for quite a while. Did Josh not even consider at all that they might harm him?

His hand was frozen on the griffin's neck, but it let out a harrumph and nudged his hand to keep going. He jumped. "Oh, sorry." And continued to scratch. He grinned, much too curious to be embarrassed. "Have you had them long? What do they eat?"

Gazen glanced in his direction, the faintest smirk forming. "They eat a special grain blend most days, with raw meat once a week. Some like fruit as a treat. I've been working with this herd for three hundred years."

"Three hundred years?"

My eyebrows rose. "That's almost older than me."

moment it touched his tongue, he jerked. The next
he took was sharp. His eyes went wide. He stiffened,
buckling as he collapsed. The cup clattered to the

Whoa. What just happened?" I dove to his side. "Josh?" I
k his shoulders. "Josh!"

His eyes were closed. He didn't move. His skin had gone
. He didn't look like he was breathing.

turned my blazing gaze up to the old witch. "What did
do to him?"

Gazen stood over her apothecary table, calm, too calm,
hands still dusted with herbs. "I did what I do."

Her nonchalant words triggered a molten fury of
thing in me. What the fates did she mean by that? She
asn't even concerned at all that her dangerous potions
ight have killed someone. My blood roared. Before I even
ought it through, my hand flew to the dagger at my belt.

In one motion, I was on my feet as I pounced on Gazen,
knocking her back, staggering against the counter. Several
vials and jars tumbled over, a couple falling to the floor with
a loud crash.

I didn't care. I pressed my blade hard against her throat,
my voice shaking with rage. "Tell me what you did to him.
Was it poison? Did you poison him? Who sent you? Who are
you working for?"

Gazen's lined face remained maddeningly serene. "Lower
your blade, child."

"Tell me the truth—now!"

Josh's gaze shot to me. "What?" His question nearly came
out as a high-pitched squeak, as his eyes darted up and down
me, as if he couldn't fathom what I'd just said.

I bit back a smile as Josh's mouth opened, then closed,
struggling to wrap his head around that notion. But he
merely shook his head briskly as though to clear it, focusing
back on Gazen, looking fully impressed. "Uh, well... That's
incredible. You must have a solid bond with them."

"We do." Gazen stroked the griffin's neck. "Without it, no
magic in the world would keep them loyal."

I reached out to a silver-feathered griffin nearby, my
palm brushing its warm side. A pulse of quiet strength and
trust flowed through me—echoes of Gazen's bond with the
herd.

Josh couldn't keep his eagerness contained. "Hey, so...can
they fly with people? You know, like—"

"Are you thinking about riding them?" I gave him a look
half in mirth. "Did you actually forget what we are here for?"

His cheeks colored. "Oh, right."

Gazen didn't seem bothered at all. "They could carry you,
if trained. Riding them is not for the unskilled—or the faint
of heart. But perhaps we can revisit that a bit later on? I believe you are indeed on some urgent business." She clicked
her tongue as though a signal to the creatures, then beckoned us away.

"Yes, thank you." I gave her an appreciative nod, falling
into step beside her.

With a reluctant purse of his lips, Josh withdrew his hand
from the creature's flank to follow suit.

The caretaker's cottage stood at the edge of the field, nestled under the roots of a great, ancient tree. Smoke curled lazily from the crooked chimney, and wild herbs grew in tangled rows near the doorway.

Gazen led us through the doorway, her hand brushing the frame for the briefest moment before she crossed into the room.

Stepping inside, the scent of earth, spice, and old magic wafted over me. An apothecary dominated the corner space tucked neatly by the hearth, its orderly shelves laden with jars of crushed leaves, roots, and powders.

The caretaker moved with unhurried certainty, counting steps in a rhythm that seemed second nature, her staff tapping softly once before she leaned it against the wall. "So, tell me more about why you've come all this way."

I cast Josh a brief assessing look. "Well, Josh here believes he's had some powerful magic done on him. Some of his memories have been erased. Yours was the only name that came to anyone's mind for help with a problem of this nature."

"Hmm... that sounds like a potion I haven't made in a long while." Stepping past the kitchen, Gazen tilted her head slightly, listening for the faintest echo of where jars rested on the shelves, then let her fingers trail along the wood until they found the smooth curve of clay and the familiar texture of dried herbs bundled with twine.

"It will require old magic," she went on, gathering ingredients in carved wooden bowls. Each motion was careful but practiced—no wasted steps, no searching longer than a

breath. Her eyes never fixed on what s way her hands moved, precise and stea memory guiding her instead of sight. "I c be dangerous. A mind that's not ready can... break."

I shot Josh a tentative look. "Break?"

"Memories are tricky things to meddle w times, they like to stay buried for a reason. lifting, she crushed the leaves in a mortar wit as someone who could see every detail, des turn of her ear toward the sound of the grindi

Josh stepped forward. "If getting my m means I can help Tala, I'll take that risk."

I almost winced at the twinge in my chest. *Tala...*

Was he really doing all this for me? Josh alw so eager to take on things or do almost anythin reservation, without fail. He was already resigne the sacrifice and giving up his life—all because I a to.

Uneasy, I folded my arms across my chest as if ward myself from feeling. I focused on Gazen mix paste into a watery solution. I was eager to get it with. "Let's get on with it then."

When she was done, Gazen poured the potion i small stone cup, the liquid glowing faintly, before offeri to Josh. "If you're ready."

Josh didn't hesitate. He took the cup, drained it in onds.

But her glazed eyes were steady, as if my dagger meant nothing at all.

Incensed that she didn't even care for my threat at all, I shoved away from her. I sheathed my blade. What mattered more right then was Josh. I wasn't a healer, but maybe there was something else I could do.

I tossed Gazen a dagger with my eyes instead. "Tell me. Is he dead?"

Her shoulders lifted. "Why don't you check?"

My knees hit the ground beside him before I even realized I'd moved. I pressed two fingers to his neck, desperate for the steady thrum of a pulse—nothing. My hand hovered over his mouth, waiting for the faintest brush of air—still nothing.

"No—no, no, no—" I shook his shoulders, searching him for any signs of life. My throat burned, panic clawing up my chest. My fingers dug into his shirt, clutching at him like I could anchor him here by sheer force of will.

I shook him again, harder. "Wake up, you stubborn idiot!"

He lay so still. Too still.

My chest tightened, and a rush of heat pounded in my ears. My heartbeat was a wild, unsteady drum in my chest, my breathing sharp and shallow, the only sound in the room. A hard lump swelled in my throat. I stared down at Josh, willing his chest to move.

His eyes were still closed. His expression empty. His face was ghostly pale. That usual light, that mischievous smile, was gone.

I would never see that smile again.

This wasn't how it was supposed to happen. Not here. Not like this. He was supposed to save my world. He was supposed to stand beside me no matter how bad it got.

I slumped to the floor, the fight draining out of me, leaving nothing but the hollow ache spreading in my insides.

Looking up at Gazen again, this time, there was only a plea in mine. "Do something? Please?" My voice cracked, my anger and fear ebbing out into despair.

Gazen didn't so much as twitch. She only spoke with the same infuriating calm. "This is the will of the gods."

The words hit like a blow.

I stared at Josh's ashen face as the silence pressed in. Each dreadful moment bled into another, the world narrowing, grinding me down until the edges of my panic dulled into something worse—acceptance. I hated how quickly my self-assurance was slipping.

Josh was the one who saw the bright side of things. He was the one who always saw the best in any situation. He was my hope.

And without him, everything just—

Josh's chest rose in a faint breath.

"What...?" I gasped at the smallest movement from his pale body.

Then he drew in another, longer breath.

Wide-eyed, I whipped my head toward Gazen, my pulse surging all over again.

A ghost of a smile was on the caretaker's face, grave, knowing. "He is a being of two worlds. This is a powerful potion. Perhaps it demanded he lose something of himself first. If it is his old life that has been forgotten, perhaps he needed a new life."

I took Josh's cold hand in mine, torn between wanting to scream and the overwhelming rush of relief flooding through me.

A sound stirred in the distance. It was faint but sharp enough to pull me from my thoughts. The rhythmic pounding of hooves.

Gazen's eyes narrowed. She lifted her head, straining to hear. "Fae warriors." Her following observation was taut, foreboding. "But not from the Isles."

23

Agenda

"What?" Getting up, I crossed to the front window, pulling the curtain back just enough to peek out, and my stomach turned to ice.

Among the advancing warriors, gleaming armor catching the light, was Brynn. Her golden hair was pulled into her usual intricate braid, her expression sharp with smug satisfaction. They were shadow warriors from our own village.

What the fates was Brynn doing here?

My mind whirled in confusion, but it wasn't the time to untangle that mystery. I turned to Josh, still sprawled on the floor, breathing steadily but unmoving. I glanced back out the window. There were easily a dozen Fae warriors, armed, menacing.

I would fight them, but my powers might glitch out again. And Josh was even more vulnerable now.

My pulse spiked. "We have to go. We have to run. Josh, wake up!" I shook his shoulder, then his arm harder. "Come on, now's not the time to be annoying—"

Outside, the hoofbeats grew louder, joined by the metallic clank of weapons and the sharp bark of orders.

"Josh!" My voice pitched higher, panic flaring again. I slapped my hand against his cheek—not gently—and his eyelids finally fluttered open. "Wow, I should have tried that earlier."

A low groan slipped from Josh, his brow furrowing. His eyes fluttered open halfway, unfocused. "Wha—"

Boots crunched on gravel outside—more than a few pairs.

"We're out of time." Gazen's voice cut through, calm but urgent. She swept toward the back door to lead the way. "Outside. Now."

Following behind her, I dragged Josh to his feet, his weight half on me, his steps clumsy but moving. He was dead weight for a moment before his legs found themselves.

Somewhere deep inside, my nerves screamed that this was impossible, that we couldn't possibly outrun them. The front door to the cottage shuddered under a hard impact, splinters raining from the frame as the Fae warriors thundered through.

As we burst through the back door, the cold air bit my cheeks. The grassy field opened before us, along with Gazen's herd of majestic griffins. But we didn't make it three steps beyond the covered shed before shadows moved in from both sides. Warriors surged toward us, their leathers dark, their blades sharp.

A forceful hand seized my arm, wrenching me back. "No!"

Another warrior caught Gazen to pull her to one side.

Josh, still half-conscious, staggered against me—only for two warriors to grab him by the shoulders and shove him to the ground so hard it knocked the breath from him. He groaned again, struggling weakly.

"Stop it! You're hurting him!" I tried to lunge toward him, but rough rope was already biting into my wrists. "He can't even stand, leave him alone!"

The warriors ignored me, yanking Josh's arms behind his back, as he slumped forward.

We were dragged across the grass and shoved onto the dirt floor of the barn. The musty smell of hay and fertilizer pressed in. Josh was half-propped up beside me, wrists bound, eyes still half-shut and unfocused.

"Make sure their hands are tied so they cannot do magic."

I turned my molten gaze onto Brynn as she sashayed closer. "What in all the realms are you doing here, Brynn?"

Her mouth twitched into a smirk. "What do you think? We're here for the Curse bearer, of course."

Eyes wide, my blood chilled. "What? What do you know about that?"

She let out a giggle as light as air, as though we were having a casual conversation about dresses and hairstyles, instead of ancient prophecies under duress. "Aren't you re-lieved? We're not after you, Spawn of Deathbringer."

Several of the shadow warriors took their posts to guard the door back into the cottage and the wide-open gate leading to the field.

Toying with the links on her armor, Brynn gave me a sly smile. "After that display at the wedding, you couldn't really believe that we would let you fulfil that dumb prophecy, did you?" She gave me a mocking look. "We know the High Fae have been colluding with the Deathbringers all these centuries. The stories have been passed down through our family lines. When it mattered most, your family chose the welfare of our enemies and risked the lives of our own people."

Her eyes blazed as though a lifetime of agony flashed through her mind. "And they did this despite knowing that we have already suffered great losses because of them. My people won't let it pass this time, and you better believe we've been waiting a long time for this."

My mouth had dropped open in disbelief. No wonder Brynn had always had such a vile hate for me, over and beyond her jealousy. I supposed it might have been naïve to believe that *all* of the Fae had dismissed the legends as just that—stories, myths.

I studied the armor she was wearing with a vague nagging in the back of my mind. Upon closer inspection, they were Priori colors but had a distinct, darker shade. I'd seen them before.

"The shadow warriors, when I was in the fourth realm..." I mumbled in realization.

Brynn clutched her stomach with her mirth. "Oh, did you just figure that out?" She clicked her tongue. "Stellan and his secret plans. Of course, when we heard you were in pursuit of the Curse bearer in the fourth realm, we had to go and try to catch him first." She sighed, despite the wicked glint in her eye. "But you already know how that turned out."

I let out an overwhelmed breath. Freyjn and Stellan had claimed they had only sent a trusted few. Brynn's horde of shadow warriors were the ones who had chased me down in the fourth realm.

Looking up, I leveled my gaze with hers again. "Come on, Brynn. I know you hate me more. Take me. Leave Josh alone."

Her laugh was brittle, mocking. "You? You're not worth the trouble. Not even good enough to use as a bargaining chip."

I bit back my retort. "But the prophecy—don't you care at all that Arcadia is dying? Josh can change everything. We're trying to fix the—"

"If restoring the magic of the land means bringing back the Deathbringers, I think you'll find not everyone is happy to merely sit back and let it happen."

"So, what?" I jerked in my seat. "You're just going to kill us?"

"No, silly," Brynn cooed sweetly, her gaze flicking to the warriors around us. "We're going to wait here for our Fae mage to arrive. They'll remove the legend's seal from your little human pet—and *then* we'll kill him. Don't worry. We'll let *you* go right after." Her cold smile lingered long enough to burn before she turned away, leaving me staring after her, my heart a tight, furious knot.

Brynn's people probably also had an inkling that Josh's death might inadvertently fulfil the prophecy. And even if they did manage to de-curse Josh and kill him, not one soul on Arcadia would care much one way or another. It was well planned.

I blew out a frustrated groan, helplessly pulling at the ropes, digging in my wrists. It was tied too well. I couldn't quite reach close enough to call on my magic.

Gazen sat on the other side of Josh, her countenance still as calm as ever. She probably knew they didn't plan to harm her either. Even as her eyes were still unfocused, I was certain she could perceive everything around us. She didn't offer any words of support or otherwise. She was likely also certain they wouldn't make much difference in our situation.

Furrowing my eyebrows, I tamped down the fire of my rage enough so I could focus on thinking about how to escape.

Tilting my head, I assessed the ropes binding Josh's hands behind his back. I'd already seen Josh escape from traps worse than a double-knot rope. Surely, this should be no different.

He just had to wake up first.

"Josh, hey. Hey, wake up." I wasn't sitting close enough to nudge him or kick his leg. I hissed louder, "Josh!"

One of the Fae guards assigned to keep an eye on us glanced over at the noise, but neither he nor the others seemed to care. Most of the shadow warriors, including Brynn, had gone closer to the road by the barn entry, waiting to meet their mage.

"Mm..." Josh moaned, blinking slowly a few times.

"Josh, are you awake?"

He took a deep breath, collecting his bearings. His head lolled to one side before his eyes opened to survey our surroundings, our predicament. "Hmm..." His forehead creased in question. He was snapping out of it.

"Josh!"

He winced at the harshness of my tone before looking up. A groggy haze remained on his face for a moment. When the mist in his eyes finally cleared, his eyes lit up upon recognizing me.

A warm rush shot through my entire being when his gaze softened as he met mine. I bit back a relieved smile, my pulse racing as those sparkling green eyes focused intently on me. The color was back in his face.

Josh was alive. Josh was okay.

He jerked up in his seat. "Mag—I mean, uh, Tala." His surprised expression collapsed into a frown. He wriggled his bound hands behind his back. "What's going on now?"

I didn't bother asking if he was still feeling ill. I pursed my lips. "Shadow warriors grabbed us. They're waiting for their mage before they come and kill you."

"Huh," was all he said. He glanced over to see Gazen sitting at his other side, likewise bound. "Oh, hey." He jerked up in his seat again, his eyes lighting up once more as if an epiphany struck him. "Gazen! It's you!"

Gazen's eyebrows merely rose in amusement, but she didn't seem to catch on. "Yes. It's me."

Josh dropped his gaze. "Ah, of course." He averted his gaze for a moment, as if he was suddenly far away. He released a short laugh. "Of course, you don't remember we've met before. Holy crap, I remember."

My eyes widened. "The potion worked. You got all your memories back?"

Gazen wrinkled her nose in thought. "We've met before?"

"Yep," Josh said, before turning to me.

I narrowed my eyes at him. "And I suppose you think we've also met before?"

He let out a shout of laughter. "Oh, yes, we have. I'm sure of it now." A bright smile spread on his face. "I used to call you..." Taking a breath, he paused as if he needed to highlight the moment. "Magenta."

That inexplicable thrill shot up my spine again. Except this time, I finally knew the reason for it. Whatever memories Josh had of this realm, in that time, in that world, that was the name he called me.

At the same time, there was an uneasy stir in my stomach at the look on his face. It was fondness, overwhelmingly, but somehow, it felt as though it was not entirely directed at me. Curious at the lifetime that likely flashed before his eyes, I couldn't help but wonder something else.

I turned to Gazen. "Is this possible? How can he remember me when I don't remember him? Could it be I have erased memories as well?"

Gazen's eyes narrowed for a moment. "No. I don't sense any forgotten memories in your being. Deliberately hidden or not. There is nothing for me to restore."

Josh was chewing on the inside of his cheeks, his mind seeming to race with possibly a deluge of memories. "Nona and Naomi probably haven't been born yet. Hmm...odd, then I would have thought Lance shouldn't have been born yet either."

I blinked. "Lance? You've met Lance before, too?"

He shot me a curious look. "Do you know anyone named Dantilian?"

I wrinkled my nose. "No."

"Huh."

I couldn't help but chuckle at the light in his face.

Despite being all tied up, his life in mortal peril, Josh's motivation felt freshly renewed. His energy, his bright, sunny aura, was emanating right off him. He was zinging with eager excitement. It was almost infectious.

"What else do you remember?"

Josh met my gaze again. This time, a slow, wistful look came over his face. "Everything."

Grimacing, I tilted my head, lowering my voice. "Well, do you by any chance remember how to escape from being tied up with ropes?"

That glint of ridiculously adorable mischief was back in those brilliant green eyes. Shifting to one side, he discreetly lifted one free hand to wave at me. "You mean like this?"

24

Escape

"This way—now," Gazen ordered, her voice low but urgent.

We had to keep our movements slow and discreet until Josh could untie Gazen and me. But even with Josh still unsteady from the potion, he somehow kept pace as the three of us hopped over the wooden fencing to break out of the barn.

The shadow warriors spotted us as soon as we bolted, shouts ringing out, boots pounding after us.

My heart hammered in my chest, but we didn't slow.

Gazen led us straight into the griffin field. She sprinted to the nearest creature, murmuring something in its ear before vaulting onto its massive back with the grace of someone who'd done this a hundred times. She yelled out to us, "Get on!"

I shoved Josh up behind her, then swung myself on.

From the barn, the door slammed open—more shouts, footsteps, the clatter of weapons.

Gazen let out a sharp, trilling whistle that cut across the field, and every griffin's head snapped toward her. In unison, the herd broke into motion, talons digging into the earth as they leapt skyward, wings beating in a flurry of gold and white.

"On!" Gazen called, patting the creature we were riding as a signal to move.

All around us, the rest of the herd launched into the air.

I glanced back as we lifted off the ground.

Yelling alarms and strings of curses, the shadow warriors tried to give chase, shooting arrows amidst sparks of sharper magic attempts, but by the time they reached the edge of the field, there was nothing left for them to seize. Only empty grass and the fading thunder of wings as we and the entire herd vanished into the sky.

Josh's exhilaration was more than evident. "Woohoo! I knew we'd get to ride one of these."

I couldn't help the small, breathless smile that pulled at my lips.

Gazen turned her head a bit. "Where would you folks like to go?"

I furrowed my eyebrows as I considered a few possibilities.

Cephiron was too far. I wasn't sure if we could go back to Ipera yet, since Brynn and her faction had likely already infiltrated the village. Likely to get to Freyjn.

I bit my lip in worry. I needed to get a message to her somehow.

"Can we set down somewhere to regroup first?" I called out over the noise of the wind.

Gazen signaled a short nod. "Looks like we're just east of the old wraith forest."

With another whistle, Gazen directed some of the griffins to scatter.

I imagined she was intending to hide our real destination in case the shadow warriors were able to track us. The airborne flock disbanded in graceful dips and turns as each creature went its own way.

The wind rushed past my ears, cool and sweet with the scent of open sky, tugging at my hair until it whipped in wild streams behind me. My arms were looped firmly around Josh's waist, his warmth seeping through my skin, grounding me even as we soared higher.

He held on to me tight—steady, protective—his solid frame absorbing each shift of the griffin's powerful muscles beneath us.

Below, the world stretched out in a breathtaking sweep of emerald forests, winding rivers glinting like silver threads, and lush valleys. The clouds hung so close I could almost reach out and brush my fingers through them.

I pressed my cheek against Josh's back. I'd never ridden a griffin before, never felt this kind of freedom, as if the air itself might carry me anywhere. But wrapped in Josh's strength and security, for the moment, it was an insignificant triviality where we would land.

Coming up above a verdant forest, Gazen led ours and a few other griffins to circle before landing in a clearing surrounded by ancient trees, with gnarled roots and hanging vines.

Gazen pushed off the griffin easily.

Josh hopped to follow.

I didn't move yet.

Beneath the still canopy, each creak of branches and distant rustling echo carried the sense of an unseen witness. Faint traces of spent magic hung in the air even after several hundred years. As though, despite the world having moved on, it still clung stubbornly, whispering that what was lost was never truly gone.

I cast my gaze upward, squinting at the scant sunlight filtering through the towering trees that rose like pillars.

This forest used to be overrun by monstrous wraiths, planted here to hide where my father had been sealed away with his curse for decades, until my mother found and freed him.

I breathed in, settling within the eerie murmurs of wind until it was as though the woods themselves acknowledged my presence.

The occurrence of wraiths nowadays was few and far between, and my parents long gone, as was their legend.

I almost didn't notice Josh standing to one side. Lifting his arms, he reached for me, intending to assist me to come down off the griffin.

I didn't need his help, but I braced my hands on his shoulders anyway, swung my leg around, and let him catch my waist. The strength in his hands, the firmness of his sturdy frame brushing beneath me, shot a shiver up my spine.

He set me down before him, lingering so close I could feel his warmth.

When I looked up, I met a dark green storm in his eyes, the intensity nearly taking my breath away.

You're not alone... How do you really feel about me?

I swallowed hard, but before I could say anything, he spun away.

I respect your decision.

A cold unease settled over my skin, a hollow in my stomach.

Josh seemed to shake it off easily. He had grown accustomed to my brushing him off. His mood shifting, he patted the satchels of supplies on the griffin's harness with a low whistle. "Oh, hey, was this griffin pre-packed for a quick escape?"

Gazen was tending the other creatures across the way. She turned to wink. "Of course. One must always be prepared for any eventuality."

"Awesome." Josh grinned. He started to untie the bags. When he stretched up to do so, I caught him wince. It was slight, but I still frowned. Was he still weak from the memory potion? Did Brynn's warriors handle him too roughly when he was unconscious?

My chest tightened.

When I considered him to be the sacrifice given by prophecy, I had convinced myself that it was an acceptable exchange. His life, to save all the realms.

But after this morning, when I'd almost seen it first hand, the mere idea of Josh dying, of him being gone, of his brilliant soul being snuffed out, was an agonizingly unacceptable option.

I'll always be here for you. I'm slowly realizing that my fate also seems to be wanting to give you whatever you need.

I struggled to steady my quickening breathing. What I needed was a world where Josh was alive.

Gazen brushed off her pants, heading toward the forest. "I'll check the area, have a bit of a nosy, make sure there isn't anything suspicious."

"Sure." Josh gave her a mock salute, not caring that she couldn't see it. He continued unloading the supplies, latching some satchels on his shoulder. He peered inside a small bag, and his eyes lit up. "Hey, I think there's biscuits in here!"

Walking across the clearing, he noticed my ominous stillness. He slowed his pace to give me a curious look up and down. "What's up with you?" His eyebrows snapped together. "Those goons didn't hurt you, did they?"

I almost scoffed in disbelief. I wanted to smack him. He was concerned about *me* instead—again. That lump in my throat was back. Did he even care how grave his situation had been? How easy it could have been for everything to take a wrong turn?

Clenching my fists, I shot him an incensed glare. "I thought you died! I thought you died before—with the potion. Oh, gods." I paced across the grass. "I didn't even think twice when I let you drink it. I didn't even consider the risks. I was so stupid!"

Josh put his hands up in defeat right away. "Whoa, whoa. Is it your fault now? I'm the one who insisted on recovering my memories faster. It's not like you forced me to take the potion."

I tossed him a pointed look. "I was being so cavalier with your life. What if you had died back at the cottage? What if those shadow warriors had decided to kill you right away? What if I didn't even get to—" I stopped short with a loud, frustrated groan.

Josh's jaw had dropped. He stared at me across the way—likely in complete disbelief.

The dread stinging in my chest from everything that had happened today was still fresh. From everything that had been happening for the last few days.

With a bitter frown, I averted my gaze. "I know you despise me. It's too late now. I've been a real jerk. I lied to you, betrayed you. It was the only way to make you stop liking me. Can't you see? You are—good and brave. You deserve better than some orphan daughter of a Deathbringer. I'm—I'm dangerous!" I threw up my hands. "You'd only end up getting hurt. So, yes, I wanted you to hate me—but then, at the same time, I *didn't* want you to hate me. I'm a complete mess!"

I closed my eyes for a moment. "And I can't believe I brought you to this realm to sacrifice you. Even though I pored through all that research night after night, reading through all those scrolls to find some way around the prophecy to save you—I... I'm sick to my stomach that I couldn't find another solution!"

His eyes widened—stunned, or possibly he was horrified at my spectacular failure.

The fight draining out of my limbs, I stopped pacing and heaved a long sigh. "I wanted to tear Mead's eyes out for batting her eyelashes at you." I almost growled in fury all over again. "But of course, I had to make it like I didn't like you at all. For god's sake, I kept you in the dungeons at Cephiron for days on end, so no matter how tempted I was to see you, I knew I wouldn't be able to stand it down there for too long, and maybe these strange feelings would go away, but it didn't work."

"Holding cell."

I rolled my eyes. "Whatever."

Josh still didn't say anything.

I didn't even want to guess how crazy I seemed to him right then, but when I dared to look at him again, my stomach lurched.

It was like the sun had risen in those sparkling green eyes. The ghost of a smile on his face as he absorbed my words wasn't scandalized at all.

Josh was...pleased.

He carefully set down the bag of biscuits, dropped the two satchels from his shoulder, and unhooked the skins of water from around his neck.

My pulse racing in anticipation, I furrowed my eyebrows. "What are—what you doing?"

Josh tilted his head, his jaw clenched in determination. "I'm going to kiss you now." He crossed the clearing, stalking forward, hands already reaching for my face, and before I could even gasp in surprise, his mouth was on mine.

As soon as our lips touched, a surge of warmth blazed through me—fierce, certain. My eyes fluttered closed. His kiss was confident, consuming, heartbreakingly tender all at once.

As though it belonged to me all along, waiting for me to finally claim it.

Inevitable.

Kissing Josh was like stepping into a place I'd been searching for all my life, but at the same time, something that had always been with me—as sure as I knew myself. Tinged with incredible relief, it filled me with a deep resolve, the finality of a foregone conclusion. Every doubt I carried fell away, replaced by a quiet truth.

Josh was home—solid, steady, the answer to a question I'd been asking all my life without knowing the words. I didn't need to fight it. It simply fit. A missing piece sliding quietly into place, leaving me whole in a way I hadn't dared to imagine.

I had felt that inkling in our last kiss too, but I had been too afraid to acknowledge it. Too overwhelmed. It felt big and impossible. I had never felt that way about anyone before, never felt *this* way. My chest almost burst with the burgeoning fullness of it.

His fingers slid into my hair and tugged just enough to make my breath hitch, sending a molten shiver right down my spine. Pulling me closer, his strong arms slid around my back to press my body against his. I wound my arms around his neck in response, a rush of heat curling in my belly.

I knew there were a million reasons why we shouldn't be doing this. But if all the realms were threatening to collapse around us, at least we would have this. If fate wanted to come and take Josh from me, it would find me standing in its way.

And I would not yield.

Josh broke off for a moment, those brilliant green eyes shining down, sending flutters inside me everywhere. Cradling my cheek in his gentle hand, he gave me a soft smile. "I missed you, Maggie," he murmured before taking my mouth in his once again.

25

Armies

A very loud clearing of one's throat rumbled behind us.
Startled, I pulled away from Josh with a gasp. Looking over, my eyes nearly popped out when the filtered sunlight glimmered off his armor and part of his blond hair. "Lance!"

Turning toward the new arrival, Josh dropped his arms with a groan. "Oh, great. This guy again."

Lance stepped out of the forest shadows into our clearing. His hand propped casually on the pommel of the sword sheathed at his side, an amused, knowing grin already on his face.

Still catching my breath, I smoothed down my clothes. I tucked my wild hair behind my ear, clearing my throat to compose myself. "Um, how did you...find us?"

"I found him." Gazen's boots crunched over the dry brush as she stepped past Lance. "My lord's sharp eyes spotted the griffins soaring about the Cephiron marshlands. He and his men decided to investigate all the way to the cursed forest."

Lance gave me a dazzling smile. "We were halfway to the Fae lands. I did tell you I would join you as soon as I can."

I beamed my appreciation. "Thank you."

Josh's storm cloud refused not to be noticed. His eyebrows were furrowed, his glare dark, blatantly focused on Lance.

I cleared my throat again. "Oh, uh..." I started to Lance with a carefully even tone. "What Josh was telling us before, it seems he was right. With Gazen's help, Josh has recovered his memories. I still don't understand exactly what it all means, but he said he's met all of us before. Even you." I met Josh's gaze with a prompt. "Josh?"

Josh's gaze narrowed on Lance. "Do *you* know anyone named Dantilian?"

Blinking in surprise, Lance shot me a look instead. "How does he know my middle name?"

"Oh, jeez." Josh smacked his palm on his forehead. "You are Dantilian."

Lance's eyes flicked to me, but he looked about as confused as I was.

"How did you even meet Dantilian—" Josh corrected, "I mean, Lance?"

"We were part of the diplomatic delegations some time ago. It's been essential for ensuring peace across the Fae and human realms." I tapped my chin in thought. "It's quite fascinating how you've run into the same people on your journeys to these realms." I met Lance's gaze for a moment. "Lance always does say life is not a mere series of accidents."

Josh's cringe deepened. He shot Lance another suffering look, his tone dripping with sarcasm. "How very wise of him."

I couldn't help my shoulders shake in mirth at the displeasure on Josh's face, but then I winced at the first drop of precipitation landing on my nose.

Gazen tilted her face up. "Looks like we'd better head for shelter right about now. You folks decide where to go yet?"

"Yes," Josh said. "We're gonna need a big boat." He turned to Lance, as if already in expectation.

Lance's forehead creased. "Of course. I own some ships off the eastern coast of the continent."

"Great." Josh's tone was surprisingly authoritative. "Last time, we had to sail across the ocean to find a really important place. I have a feeling that's where we need to go." He shot me a look. "But first, I want to go back to Cephiron to fetch your research. I want to read through those scrolls again. Now that I remember things, I'll actually have context, and the information could be more useful to us."

Lance nodded. "My men are standing by with horses. I'll accompany you."

Josh crossed the clearing, his strides urgent, confident. "Gazen, why don't you and Tala go somewhere safe first? Maybe Brynn and her people won't go back to your cottage looking for you so soon after what just happened."

Watching him, I blinked. "Whoa, hey, who put you in charge? Since when do you decide what we're supposed to do?"

His response was short. "I'm trying to complete my mission."

I gawked. "I'm sorry, what? You're not even from this realm."

Tilting his head, he gave me a mocking look. "Do *you* know where we're supposed to go?"

I frowned. "No, but—"

"Then it's *my* mission." He turned to dismiss me outright.

My jaw dropped. If it wasn't so ridiculously unbelievable, I would have burst into indignant protest. I would have gotten right in his face to list all the reasons why a mere human like him had no business telling any of us what to do.

The drizzle turned to a steady fall, soaking cloaks and dampening the ground beneath our boots. But I couldn't stop staring at Josh as he went around getting ready. This was not the easy-going, weak human I'd met a couple of weeks ago.

Josh's sharp, green eyes burned with new determination, his every step purposeful. He no longer looked lost and confused. Rather, his manner was more self-assured, resolved.

He knew exactly what we needed to do. He knew exactly where we needed to go. With his restored memories, I could imagine he'd regained an incredible range of knowledge about all the realms.

Could it be he knew more about Arcadia than any of us now?

The rain fell harder in grey sheets, turning the forest around us into a shifting mirage.

An ominous uproar rumbled from the deep woods.

What...? My stomach stirred in dread at the foreboding in the air.

Lance's keen eyes snapped to attention as he strained to see.

Nearly blending in with the trees, a horde of shadowy men marched forward from the darkness. Clad in mismatched armor, faces hidden by helms, and their weapons glinting. Torch lights flickering despite the rain, spears and swords clanking, arrows all bristled toward us like a single wall of death amidst the boots scuffing on the forest floor.

Already breathless, Josh's eyes were wide as he looked around. "Are they from the Fae Isles?"

Lance stood at the ready, bracing himself in a defensive stance. "No."

"Shadow Fae warriors?"

"No."

"Ghost army?"

Lance nodded. "Yes."

"Oh, great." Josh clicked his tongue, stepping back. "I'm being chased by several armies across Arcadia again. Good times."

A battle cry prompted a wave of fiends to come pouring out of the forest. Arrows hissed overhead like angry serpents, striking the ground in deadly thuds.

"Tala, look out!" Josh jumped forward as if to shield me.

My eyebrow snapped together in indignation. I yanked his arm to shove him behind me instead. "*You* look out. I'm the one with powerful magic. I'm supposed to protect you."

"No! I'm supposed to protect you."

Gazen whistled. "How about we divert all that enthusiasm over to attacking the actual enemy?"

A shriek tore through the air. Answering Gazen's call, one of the griffins had launched itself into the fray, plucking one soldier from the ground and hurling him into the trees.

Steeling myself, I woke my magic and thrust both hands forward. A surge of blue light shot from my palms, sweeping through the front line of soldiers. Spears clattered uselessly to the mud, and a half-dozen men staggered back, shouting in confusion.

Lance was across the way, his sword clashing with another dark warrior's spear. His blond head visibly ducked when an arrow whistled close.

"Watch out for those arrows!" Josh called out. "Those are lethal."

"Got it!" Lance gave a forceful shove and effectively subdued his opponent.

I barely felt Josh's hand slip to my side, and in a flash, he was darting around the clearing. I hadn't realized he'd swiped one of my daggers until he met another soldier head-on, steel ringing against steel. With a grunt, he twisted, disarming his foe and driving the hilt of his blade into the man's leg, sending him sprawling.

I gathered my magic again and sent a blast outward that shattered another line of spears, their fragments spinning harmlessly into the mud. Triumph bloomed hot in my chest—until the power wavered once again, sparks of my magic crackling at my fingertips.

With a groan, I wrung my hands out in frustration. "What the—?" Why did this always have to happen at the perfectly wrong times? My light faltered, guttering like a flame in the rain—and in that heartbeat of weakness, an arrow streaked straight toward me.

Josh lunged, tackling me to the ground and rolling us behind a fallen tree.

My breath caught at the weight of him over me, his body a shield, before he jerked his head toward the battle.

His body pressed against mine, solid and unyielding, his breath hot against my ear. "Are you okay?"

I could only nod.

Grabbing my hand, he pulled me up to crouch behind the cover of the tree. "Wait." His forehead was creased in deep thought. "Do you think...your magic glitches every time these ghosts show up?" He shot me a look. "Remember? It happened in Cephiron with these guys, and then again at the wedding ceremony with those animals."

I frowned. "What does it mean?"

Josh's face crumpled as he strained to think for a moment. But he cursed under his breath in frustration. "I don't know yet." He peeked out over the log before ducking back down with a groan. "Yep, they definitely are goons from Guifan. Except, I still don't understand what they're doing here. Lance said their faction dissolved some time ago."

"How do you know them?"

"Let's say I frequented their dungeons too, that last time I was here in this world. Though I suppose I should say this seems like a slightly different world than what I'd visited. When I'd crossed paths with them, they dominated an entire region of the human realm."

"What did they want from you?"

He pinned me with a look. "You."

My wide-eyed gaze met his stormy green one.

Josh swallowed hard. "They poisoned you. You almost died."

My heart pounded in my chest at the terror in his eyes. It was as though he was already reliving it. If it was anything like what I'd felt when I'd thought he had almost died from the Gazen's potion, I intimately understood the dark shadow that crossed his features.

His chest heaved with an almost devastating intensity he couldn't voice. He lifted his hand to stroke my cheek. As if he needed to check that I was real, needed that reassurance I was here. Despite the rain, his solemn touch warmed me.

I gritted my teeth.

Josh was alive.

I was alive.

We were together.

If these ghosts thought they could break us, they had another thing coming.

Lance was still fighting with several soldiers with yells and groans. Gazen stood at the edge of the clearing, under a griffin's protection, her voice calm as she commanded her flock.

"That's it. I'm putting an end to this." I pushed up with a renewed resolve. "I'm still the strongest Fae here. We have a mission to get on with. Damn the fates if I'm sitting this one out."

The sparkle in Josh's eyes looked like pride. He wore that same unfailing faith in his smile, despite the hint of worry creasing his forehead. "What if your magic glitches again?"

Pushing my sleeves up my arms, I clenched my jaw in determination as I marched straight out. "I'll show them some glitches."

I caught Lance's eye from across the way, his jaw dropping in alarm. "Tala, wait!"

I didn't stop.

I charged against the dark tide of ghostly soldiers, headlong into the storm.

***

PART THREE

- JOSH & TALA -

26

Mission

Josh

Rain pelted down in sheets, plastering my hair to my forehead and turning the forest floor to a sucking mire of mud.

The ghostly army pressed in on all sides, their armor glinting dully beneath the storm. Steel clanged against steel, griffins shrieked overhead, and Tala's magic lit the woods in pulses of blue fire.

Lance jumped across the fallen tree in front of me. He shot me an expectant glance, his eyebrows quirked up.

"What?" I blinked at him.

He gestured toward the throng of fighting in near incredulity. "You just let Tala dive right into the throng of bloodthirsty warrior ghosts."

"Sure."

"You're not worried she went in there all alone?"

I gave him a mocking look. "Have you met Tala? I'm more worried about *them*."

Lance followed my gaze, pinned on the whirling blur of color.

With a fiercely determined look in her eyes and a swish of fuchsia hair, Tala somersaulted past one soldier, threw a magical gust of wind to deter another, and in the same breath hurled a dagger through the air with deadly accuracy.

She was so magnificent. I almost had to shake myself from simply staring.

"Fair point." Lance shrugged before he shot off to rejoin the fighting.

Every time Tala flung her hand forward and light erupted, my heart still pounded in a mix of worry and relief. My instinct screamed to shield her, to take the blows for her. But watching her disarm half a dozen soldiers with a single sweep, it only filled me with pride and confidence in her strength.

She didn't need me to keep her safe. But god help me, I still wanted to.

This thing between us had been waiting, simmering, aching for way too long—desperate to be given form, to be given release. That kiss just now had been everything I had been yearning for.

Having her in my arms, feeling those soft, sweet lips against mine, filled a distinct hole in my soul. Especially with my having recovered almost a year's worth of memories of her, of wanting her. One kiss was nowhere near enough. I wasn't sure I would ever have enough of her.

Regardless of what my destiny had in store for me, even if she still pushed me away, I was determined to stay by her side...right up to the end.

I faltered for a split second, overwhelmed—not by the fight, but by the flood of memories still unraveling inside me. Faces, voices, an entire lifetime I'd lost had come crashing back to me. I'd nearly staggered under the weight of them at Gazen's field earlier today.

But something had shifted inside me, too. Relief surging like a tide—I remembered who I was, who I'd been. I wasn't stumbling blind anymore.

Across the way, a soldier was about to lunge at Tala's flank.

With a yell, I charged out of the fallen tree's shelter and threw myself between them, a well-aimed kick driving the fiend back.

Tala shot me a glare, strands of wet hair clinging to her face. "I can handle myself!"

"I know," I shouted back over the rain, parrying a blow.

For once, it wasn't ignorance or naivety that pushed me forward. It was responsibility. I knew the stakes now, the danger looming over not only this realm, but all of them. Knowledge weighed like lead in my chest, but it steadied me too, gave my every strike purpose.

I swiped another dagger from Tala, blocking against a soldier's strike, before lunging away.

My mind whirled. These soldiers were indeed menacing goons from Guifan. Certain things clicked—the shape of their formation, the way their weapons angled, the details on their armor.

A spear came, and I dodged it with newfound certainty. My body remembered what my mind had only caught up to.

During my forgotten year when I'd been stranded in Arcadia—the *last* time I was here, I had picked up more than enough to fend for myself—defensive instincts not just learned, but ingrained. I wasn't the same boy who had tripped through this world. I was sharper, stronger, surer.

Even though something still felt off. It was subtle but definitely there. A few misaligned pieces, like echoes from a world *almost* but not exactly like this.

Breathing heavily, Tala backed up against me. "They're not disappearing like last time."

Another weight pressed in at my other shoulder—Lance, sliding into place with a grunt while still facing off with one of the ghost warriors behind us. "Should I call for my army?"

I shook my head. "Let's just get out of here."

Breaking away, I rushed to Gazen's side. "I'm so sorry, Gazen, but we need to borrow one of your griffins again. You've already given us more than we could ask. I won't force you into another fight. You can take the rest of your flock back home and look after them in peace. You have our gratitude."

For a moment, Gazen said nothing, only listening to the rain spatter against the hood of her cloak, her griffins shifting behind her. Her response carried weight enough to cut through the downpour.

"I will join your quest. But first, I must see my flock secured. The creatures feel the shadows pressing in as keenly as I do." Her head tilted, as though following some other distant sound. "Go on ahead. I will follow in due course."

A chill prickled down my spine from her tone. It was almost as though she knew something was coming, something darker, and she meant to stand between it and the creatures under her care before turning her strength to our cause.

Shaking it off for the moment, I signaled Lance to help Gazen prepare a couple of the creatures for departure. Tala did a fresh, wide sweep of magic, plowing away a wave of ghostly soldiers to give us enough time to escape.

Catching her arm, I was still breathless. "Do you want to come to Cephiron with me?"

Even with her hair wet and flat around her face and her clothes heavy with rain, her violet eyes burned vibrant and alive with purpose. She was still achingly, impossibly beautiful.

She shook her head. "I need to go back to Ipera first. Freyjn needs to know what's going on with Brynn and the shadow warriors."

There was a twinge in my chest at the notion of splitting up, but I understood the urgency in her eyes. She needed her family to be safe, too.

I nodded. "Of course. We'll have to meet back at the boat."

"The eastern coast of Cephiro should be secure enough." Lance motioned a hand to me to get a griffin ready. "There, you will find my ships. We can rendezvous in two days."

Striding toward the first creature, Tala let Lance help her onto it. She gave him a small smile in thanks, then glanced up to meet my gaze with a solemn nod. "Two days."

With a whistle from Gazen, Tala's griffin lifted into the air.

I wanted to watch Tala until she flew out of sight, but I was busy latching supply bags onto another griffin—the one Gazen would use—before I hurried toward the creature beside Lance. "Now, let's go to Cephiron before the whole world burns down again."

"Ah," Gazen remarked wryly. "You wear your past well. The memories have made you braver—or perhaps more reckless. I'm not sure which is worse."

"Well—" I drawled with a disparaging chuckle. "You said I'm marked for death anyway, right?"

I thought she would laugh.

"Odd," she noted with a tone I couldn't read.

"What's odd?"

"What I said that time…" Gazen's weary forehead creased deeper. Her unfocused eyes seemed to turn to me. "I wasn't referring to you."

27

Fae

Tala

I was practiced enough sneaking in and out of Ipera throughout the years. I knew exactly which secret nook in the forest to stow my borrowed griffin, which isolated village paths to take to slip discreetly all the way into the infirmary.

When Freyjn's voice sailed through the room upon her entrance, I straightened up in my seat.

Freyjn's countenance carried a bit of weariness. "Come on, Renn. What's so wrong with this patient that you need my help? You know I'm not as good a healer as you anyway."

"Just come on."

His voice getting louder, Renn slipped through the examination curtain in my hidden corner to pull in a puzzled-looking Freyjn with him.

Her eyes widened when she saw me. "Tal—!"

"Shh!" I put my finger to my mouth. I darted a glance at the small gap in the curtain.

The place was quieter now. Only a handful of the injured lingered, despite the sharp tang of poultices and smoke still hanging in the air from the frantic clamor caused by the chaos at the wedding a few days ago.

But Freyjn's outburst had gone unnoticed.

Renn met my gaze, his eyebrows raised. "You good, Tala?"

I gave him a warm smile. I wasn't sure how many more favors he would let me ask of him at this point, but I was still grateful. "Thanks, Renn. You're the best."

Grinning, he gave me a wink. "It's good you know that." He gave Freyjn a nod before he stepped through the curtain again to get back to work.

Freyjn watched him leave, then turned her urgent blue eyes at me. "What is going on?"

I pursed my lips. I wasn't quite sure where to start.

Remember how we always thought Brynn might have had a different reason for hating me so much? The Fae warriors that chased me in the fourth realm weren't the ones Stellan sent. Ghost warriors attacked us in the forest. I flew in via a griffin that's waiting on the outskirts of the village. I kissed Josh—and it was *so good*.

"Um...Fae shadow warriors ambushed us at Sylvara," I began. "They wore Ipera colors. Brynn was among them. It seems the High Fae's attempts at keeping the existence of dragons a secret weren't quite as successful as we'd thought."

Freyn's forehead creased in concern. She looked me up and down. "Are you okay? What did they want?"

"They meant to kill Josh to ensure the prophecy was not fulfilled." My heart already pounding in dread at the mere memory, I dropped my gaze. "There are some Fae who have been holding a grudge against the dragons because of how their families suffered centuries ago. They believe the High Fae are in league with the enemy, against the welfare of our own people."

"That is not ideal." Freyjn's lips thinned. "I do understand their reasons, but they also need to remember it was only a small, rogue faction of dragons that had committed the atrocities. Our parents had worked together to stop them. In fact, I believe the *only* way they'd managed to stop them at all was by working together."

My chest was tight. "They don't want the dragons to come back. They'll do anything to prevent this outcome."

Sighing, she put her hand on my arm. "What's best for Arcadia isn't necessarily what everyone will think is best. The High Fae know this, too. I shall tell my father, but it may be difficult to quell a hatred that's gone on for this long."

"We need to make sure they don't hurt Josh," I said with a start, before shrinking back. "I...may have failed to tell you that, according to my findings, the prophecy requires that the 'Curse bearer' be sacrificed in order to fulfil it."

Freyjn's eyebrows rose. "Oh?"

I hissed in a deep breath in vehemence. "But I've been researching this night and day for weeks. I'm still convinced there's something I haven't uncovered yet. I'm not going to let him die. I'll read all the scrolls in Arcadia if I have to. There must be another way."

"Wow, you're really serious about this." She tilted her head at my fervor. "I know he was a huge help at my wedding ceremony, and he seems like a nice guy, but—" Pausing, her eyes narrowed at me. "I feel like I've already asked you this before—if you're in a relationship with that human, and you said no."

I looked away, a hot flush creeping up my neck. "I'm not."

"I mean, I know you have a thing for forearms, and don't get me wrong—" she added as offhandedly as anything.

Self-conscious, I closed my eyes despite the rush shooting up my spine from the mere memory of said forearms. "Oh gods, stop. I already said I wasn't in a relationship with him."

"Good."

I chewed on my bottom lip. "But what if..."

Freyjn's gaze turned searing. "What if what?" Her tone, already suspicious, shifted to authoritative as she reminded me, "The High Fae have already decided on our be-trothed—yours and mine."

I cringed. I should have known Freyjn would never con-sider disobeying the elders. This was our fate.

She took a deep breath. "Look, I'm not supposed to tell you this, but I found out that your betrothed... Well, he was chosen for you by your parents."

My jaw dropped. "What?" I had no idea. My chest tight-ened at the sudden wistful ache. Even through the centuries, and despite their passing, the mere notion that my parents had thought far enough ahead to consider my future, made them seem that much closer. Made the idea that much more precious.

"So please don't take it lightly," Freyjn went on. "I'm marrying Auric. He was chosen for me. And when the time comes, you will marry the one chosen for you."

"But you don't love Auric," I pointed out in full knowing. If she wasn't going to complain about it, I might as well. "I mean, do you even like him?"

"That's not the point, Tala. He has been chosen as my betrothed. We don't go against the elders. Our matches have been selected for the good of our people, of all the Fae. We need the strongest mage and warrior. Like it's always been."

A faint shadow crossed her eyes, but I caught it.

Freyjn's mother and father had been just such a match. And I knew even though Freyjn carried herself with composure and confidence before others, there was always that quiet fear in her—that she might never match the legacy of her mother. It was a fear that gnawed at her happiness more than she would ever admit.

My deep sigh rivaled hers. "I know you don't want to hear this, but you are not your mother. And you don't have to be exactly like her—" I peered at her face to make my point with a nod, "to be just as great."

Freyjn met my gaze, the hue of her blue eyes still tinged with darkness.

Shouts came with the doors banging open as the infirmary's hush shattered. The air filled with the metallic tang of blood.

Renn threw the curtain wide open, his usually wry face set grim. "The Fae Isles have set upon the village." Breathless, his eyes darted toward the stretchers being laid out. "Stellan's already sent troops to the outskirts to push them back. More wounded are on the way."

I sat up in alarm.

Freyjn's expression hardly flickered, but she drew herself straighter in deep thought. "The Isles have always been disadvantaged. They've never stood a chance against the mainland. This isn't strength—it's desperation." Her gaze swept over the fresh blood staining the cots, the agonized faces of those waiting for aid. "And desperation means lives lost, on both sides."

Groaning, she hung her head. "If we crush them, we only deepen the divide. If we show mercy, we risk appearing vulnerable when the land itself is faltering." Her voice nearly faltered. "I want to do what's right for all the Fae. But what is right when every path leads to more death?"

The doors slammed open again, and a commotion rippled through the infirmary as two warriors half-carried a familiar figure between them—Mead, pale and bloodied, her arm slung limply across one of their shoulders. She winced with every step, but the moment she spotted me across the room, even through the haze of pain, her lips curled into a sneer.

"Well," Mead rasped, her voice sharp despite the injury. "Look who slinks back right when the fighting's done."

I refused to rise to her baiting. She was already worse for wear—mud streaked across her face, blood soaking her sleeve. I merely gritted my teeth in frustration.

All this blood would stain the soil for nothing. Such acts of desperation would only drain the land further, pulling at what little magic remained, and shatter the fragile threads holding the realms together, leaving all of us weaker, closer to ruin.

If we couldn't even reconcile the Fae, what hope was there to restore the balance in Arcadia if the prophecy comes to pass with the arrival of the dragons, too?

As the healers eased Mead onto a cot, she caught Freyjn's attention, forcing out words between labored breaths. "Stellan... has them. The dissident leaders. They've been caught—alive." She smirked faintly, though it twisted with pain. "They're being held... for questioning."

My heart jolted. If Stellan truly had captured the Fae Isle's leaders, this could change everything. Or make it far, far worse.

Then, for some reason, a vision of Josh's wry grin popped up in my head.

Couldn't you just talk to them? Explain we're not here to fight?

Almost unaware I was repeating the words, I suggested, "Couldn't we just talk to them?"

Freyjn gawked at me. "What?" Her mouth had dropped open in full disbelief.

"Like, negotiate." I shrugged. "Not everything has to be solved with violence."

She blinked a few times. I was sure she thought she was hearing me wrong. "Are you... Are you kidding?"

"What?" I threw my hands up in ridicule. "The Fae must always be mighty. We show no weakness. We take what we want," I mocked. "Well, we've tried everything else, haven't we? Like you said, they're desperate."

Freyjn's eyes narrowed again, but she wasn't questioning me anymore.

"Plus, now knowing Brynn's people's agenda, we need to make sure their ranks don't grow in number by potentially recruiting dissidents who happen to be unhappy with the High Fae right now."

There was an odd clarity in Freyjn's expression as she considered my words. The serene look on her face seemed almost impressed. She let out a breath after a moment, clapping a hand on my back. "When the dragons come back to Arcadia, you're going to make a great leader of your people, Tala."

Grinning, I let out a chuckle. "Well, you've set an excellent example."

28

Steel

Josh

I remembered riding a griffin through a terrifying storm cloud the last time I was on Arcadia. I remembered clinging on for dear life as chaos ripped around me, around *us*. I squinted at the dipping sun of the late afternoon. At least, the weather was calm today.

Having left the rain behind, wind rushed over my face, sharp and clean, tugging at my hair. It was freeing, exhilarating—like the weight of the world couldn't quite reach me up here. Even though I was well aware I was in for another rough ride soon.

I was resolved to help Tala save the realms. With my restored memories, I was hoping too that I might find something, in all her research scrolls, a way to fulfil the prophecy without me, oh say, dying. That would obviously be a more ideal outcome.

But was I ready to give my life for her? My heart pounded in my chest at the shocking certainty of my own answer.

Abso-freaking-lutely.

Lance's deep voice behind me carried over the wind. "So, you say we've met before?"

"Oh." I blinked to amend, glancing back a bit to respond, "Well, I suppose I didn't really meet *you*. I met your descendant about several thousand years later. But you look exactly like him, talk exactly like him, and..." I paused to smirk. "I'm pretty sure I hate you just as much."

Lance understood my half-joke right away. He chuckled under his breath. "If your animosity is caused by your belief in my interest in Tala, you can set your mind at ease. Even if I did harbor romantic feelings for her..." His pause was pregnant with disappointment, but also resignation. "I've seen the way she is with you and... honestly, I don't think I can compete with that."

My jaw almost dropped. It was bewildering to hear someone like Lance—with that big sword, that blond hair, that physique, that huge kingdom—say that he couldn't compete with someone like me.

Wow...

"Um...thank you."

The land rolled out beneath us in green and gold, forest giving way to cultivated fields, then stone. Lance's kingdom appeared in the distance, perched on a rise. Banners fluttered from the ramparts, the courtyard stretching wide.

I narrowed my eyes. The courtyard often bustled with life at this time of day. However, even from up here, the unusual stillness was evident.

Lance leaned forward. He likely noticed it too.

Out of the corner of my eye, a lone figure darted across the end of the courtyard, half in shadow, and I easily recognized the outline of the armor.

It was one of the shadow warriors who had ambushed us at Gazen's.

Lance muttered a curse under his breath.

My chest already tightened in remorse. I wanted to make sure anyway. "Are they from the Fae Isles?"

"No. They are wearing Priori colors."

I cursed under my breath, too. "I thought so. They're shadow Fae warriors. They're here to kill me. And sorry to say, they're probably super eager to kill anyone who gets in their way." Groaning, I rubbed my face in frustration. "Ugh, how did they even know to look for me here?"

Lance shrugged. "Possibly because of your connection to Tala, and Tala's connection to Cephiron."

He tugged at the griffin's reins, guiding it lower, circling wide until we touched down in a shadowed copse beyond the outer wall, making sure we weren't yet detected.

He slid from the griffin's back first, his jaw set, shoulders rigid.

I followed suit, my boots hitting the wild grass.

After securing the creature, Lance motioned for me to follow him along the tree line toward a narrow service path.

From there, we crept up one of the watchtowers, and I gasped at what I glimpsed inside the castle.

Dozens of Lance's people had been corralled into a cluster. Around them, the shadow warriors stood in cold formation, spears angled, every movement disciplined and precise.

I chewed on the insides of my cheeks. This was just great. I had led the scourge to the peaceful Kingdom of Cephiron. I was fully aware that Lance wasn't even willing to sacrifice peace to help with the fighting against the Fae Isles.

I racked my brain so hard. I thought steam might come out of my ears. What could I do? What else could I possibly do?

My shoulders slumped in defeat. I let out a huge sigh. "I-I'm—*crap*—" I threw my hands up. "I have to turn myself over to them. I can't let any of your people get hurt because of this."

"Don't be stupid."

I winced at his brusque response. "What?"

His eyes narrowed on me again. His jaw clenched so tightly I thought his teeth might break. "Do you think Tala will be happy if I let anything happen to you?" His voice was barely a whisper, yet it vibrated with a looming fury.

"If I'm not giving myself up, then what are we doing?"

Lance took a deep breath, his eyebrows furrowed. "There must be a way to negotiate with them. Give them something else they want, perhaps."

I swallowed hard, the weight of remorse pressing close again. I already knew how merciless these warriors were.

And seeing them here, in Lance's home, bending his people beneath their will—it twisted something inside me.

A vision of the fire in Tala's violet eyes flashed in my mind. If she were here, I knew exactly what she would say.

"Negotiate? Tala would say that's pointless." I gritted my teeth, molten anger building inside me. "I'm sorry, Lance. I know your people value peace, but you can't let bullies push you around. These Fae are not doing this out of ignorance. They're doing this out of hate." I shook my head in resolve. "They can't be reasoned with anymore."

"I know how well you train your soldiers," I reminded him. "This is exactly the reason why you make sure to do that. Your people aren't weak. I know for a fact they kick ass better than anyone. I bet you, if you ask them, they would gladly stand up and fight to protect their homes, to protect what's important. There's a time and a place for violence. It's here and now." I peered at his face steadily. "Now, what do you say?"

Lance didn't look at me right away. His gaze was fixed on the courtyard again, his hand hovering over the hilt of his sword. His expression hardened for another moment before his response came, low but resolved. "We fight."

I blinked in surprise. I almost thought I wouldn't be able to convince him. "We fight?"

He gave me a firm nod. "We fight."

I took in a shaky, deep breath to get ready. I felt a nudge at my hand as Lance passed me his sword without even looking.

Oh boy... here goes nothing.

With a sharp cry that rang across the courtyard, Lance made a great leap and tumbled down through the narrow archways, straight into the castle.

With Lance's distraction, every head turned in surprise. I slid down toward the hostages, and with quick hands I cut their bonds. "Find cover."

The courtyard exploded in sound and fury, with castle staff scattering, ducking behind the stone pillars and side passages. Hidden doors along the walls burst open as Lance's soldiers poured out. Steel glinting, they eagerly took on the shadow warriors.

I jumped into the fight. Raising Lance's sword, my blade met the first warrior's spear, sparks bursting in the air.

Across the way, Lance had found a different sword to swing. It carved a clean arc, cutting down a warrior with practiced grace. Darting a glance at me, he barked his warning, "Left!"

I ducked, and his sword whistled above me, catching a warrior who had been ready to strike me down.

When one of the other warriors lunged for Lance's exposed side, instincts overrode my thoughts. I slammed forward, blade crossing just in time to block the thrust, shoving the warrior back.

"Nice," Lance called over the din, a wry catch in his tone. "You must have been well trained."

Breathless, I cut down another warrior, tamping down the urge to roll my eyes. "Of course, *you* would say such an arrogant thing."

Lance's answering laugh was short, fierce, and edged with humor.

Fae warriors weren't as adept with magic as Fae mages, so they were on par with Lance's human battalion. While the Fae's fighting skills were impressive, Lance's soldiers proved their mettle.

Swords clashed and sparks tore through the smoky air as I fought to keep up with their pace.

When Lance called out his next warning, "Josh, watch your left!" it was a shade too late.

A massive shadow brute slammed into my side with bone-jarring force. The impact sent me staggering as a sharp pain exploded beneath my ribs. I hit the ground on one knee, hand clamped instinctively to my side.

"I'm fine!" I yelled out before Lance could ask. The bruise already throbbed beneath my palm, hot and deep—but I forced myself upright, gritting my teeth against the pain. There was no way I was giving up. With a growl of pure determination, I charged forward once again.

Cephiron's mastery and numbers overwhelmed the shadow warriors. One by one, the enemies faltered, beaten back beneath steel and firelight.

Once the air grew clearer with the fighting receding, I planted my sword to lean against it. Panting in exhaustion, I scanned the wreckage.

All the shadow Fae warriors had been subdued and captured.

I had to give it to them though. Even with only a last few of them remaining standing, their Fae grit still prevailed. Not one of them even considered surrender.

Cringing, I clutched at my aching side.

During the battle, Lance had yelled out so many times for me to watch my weak left. My side was going to be black and blue for days. Of course, for a regular dude from Brooklyn, I was lucky that was the worst of my injuries.

As the Cephiron troops lined the shadow warriors up to lead them away, I trailed behind to make sure the tricky Fae didn't try anything.

Musty stone and hints of sewage water tickled my nose as we descended the staircase.

I cast a glance around the cold dungeons, whistling low in recognition. "Oh, yeah. This is definitely the exact same dungeon from before."

I almost couldn't believe the resonant nature of the memories that had come back to me. It had been a long, harrowing journey. At the time, I'd fought so hard to get back home. Only to find myself right back here.

Life is not a mere series of accidents...

Oh, great. Now, I was quoting Lance.

The impressive man himself, arriving behind me, slapped my back with a thump. "Thank you. For your help."

That snapped me out of my reverie, dragging my mind back to the present. "Oh. Hey. Sure."

"And for reminding me how strong my people are, that I need not fear for them, and that a good fight for a good cause is worth it."

With a self-conscious cringe, I ran my hands through my hair. "Whaaat? Is that what I did?"

Lance merely shook his head. He tilted a nod toward the shadow warriors. "We will keep them here until I can meet with the High Fae to decide their fate."

"Great. That's great." I jerked in my stance in alert. "Oh, also, dude, no offense, but these dungeons are hella easy to escape from." My eyes lit up as an idea occurred to me. "Do you have wards against Fae magic? Tala told me once in passing that wards prevent Fae from conjuring. Set them up all over the place, just in case, so they can't use their magic to escape."

Despite the odd, always amused look Lance gave me, he took on my suggestion and told his people to make sure to take care of it.

We strode back up into the castle to finally get to what we actually came here for.

A couple of Cephiron soldiers met us on the way, speaking low in Lance's ear.

His forehead creased. "Some of my men from the cursed forest have arrived. They are reporting that the ghostly army that attacked us dissipated once we had left the clearing."

I frowned. "Huh."

An uneasy stir rattled in my brain once again. Everything seemed as fragments of a much greater, hidden truth, inklings of a larger puzzle, begging to be solved.

Later.

Soon. I set my jaw in determination.

Definitely soon.

Lance gestured me toward the library wing. "Make sure to gather what you need." He headed off down a separate hallway. "I'll send my fastest riders to prepare the ship."

29

Vast

Tala

Two days passed by in a blur. Yet at the same time, it was as though they had dragged on forever.

The conflict between the mainland and the Fae Isles had reached a point of reason.

It was agreed—not with handshakes, nor with warmth, but with the slow sheathing of blades, the weary understanding that no victory could justify endless bloodshed. Both sides left the tense negotiations carrying their grudges like armor—but carrying, too, the reluctant knowledge that mutual survival lay in words, not war.

It was a precarious armistice, given the pride of the Fae.

I'd almost held back from leaving altogether. Without sufficient mediation, it was entirely plausible that such obstinate Fae tempers might easily flare up once again to reignite the discord.

Even as I'd prepared to depart, that stubborn twitch in Stellan's jaw was an obvious testament to the fact, but he maintained that I was much needed elsewhere.

It was good enough for now.

When I sprang out of the portal in a blinding rush of light, salt hit me first, sharp and raw on my nose. The fresh sea breeze whipped against my skin as I stumbled onto the wide wooden deck of the ship, berthed far across the continent from the green forests of the Fae lands.

The southern docks stretched wide before me, alive with shouts and the creak of timbers. Lance's clipper loomed above his smaller fleet like a predator among minnows. His men moved with crisp efficiency as they prepared the vessel, checking lines, hauling barrels. Soldiers in polished mail stood at the ready.

But my scanning eyes locked on the tall figure, brow furrowed in concentration, bent over a map rolled out on a weathered crate that served as a makeshift table.

The moment that green gaze lifted and found mine, I let out a breath of relief. Boots thudding, I ran across the deck.

Josh's eyes were as wide as my own. He straightened sharply, his mouth dropping open.

Nearly skidding on the deck, I stopped short of throwing my arms around him. The wind rushed past my frantic form, my hair fluttering around me in a mess.

He caught my arms and held me at a distance to look me over, his manner just as flustered. "I heard the Fae Isles attacked your village—"

At the same time, I blurted out, "I was told about the shadow warriors in Cephiron—"

We both froze for a moment, then laughed—not without an edge of breathless, desperate relief. It was almost absurd, our panic tangling together in the same heartbeat.

Josh's gorgeous smile spread slowly. Lifting his hand, he tucked a wayward strand of hair behind my ear. I thought I caught the flush in his cheeks, even as his tone lowered. "Are you okay?"

I nodded, a surge of warmth spreading through me. "Are you?"

His warm fingers trailed softly down my cheek, and I sucked in a gasp as his gaze dropped to my mouth. "I am now."

Shivers shot up my spine at the rumble in his voice. I couldn't help my eyes darting up to pin on his lips either. My heart pounded in my chest. The mere memory of our last kiss already made my toes curl. We'd only been apart for a couple of days, but it already felt too long.

I tilted my chin up in eager anticipation, eager to be in his arms, wanting him wrapped tight around me, grounding me, quieting the feverish rush of my heart.

"Oh, hey—" Lance's voice from behind us cut through the moment, sharp as a blade, his teasing tone twice as merciless. "Don't mind the rest of us doing all the work preparing for *your* mission."

Heat flaring in my cheeks, I pulled back.

Josh only flipped to his usual mischievous smirk. Dropping his arms from me, he shot Lance a suffering look. "Aw, thanks for being so motivated."

Lance strode across the deck with his usual swagger. "Map any good?"

Nodding, Josh walked around to the table again. "Yeah." He traced along the worn scroll with his finger. "The lines and ink are a bit blurred, but I think there's enough here to help guide us."

I craned my neck. "What map is it?"

"From your research at the library in Cephiron." He tapped a spot on the map. "It's faded, but I think here it says 'Nest', and from what I've read, that is what your people used to call the dragons' habitat. You even mentioned from your bedtime story that this kingdom sank in the middle of the ocean, so I got my money on that's where we're supposed to go."

Lance folded his arms. "Seems a long journey."

Josh narrowed his eyes. "You're not worried we're going to fall off the edge of the world if we keep sailing, are you?"

"What?"

Even I shot Josh a look of ridicule.

Josh blinked, then blew out a breath. "Oh, good. I was worried I was going to have to go through explaining all that again." He clicked his tongue. "This world really is slightly different from last time."

Curious, I furrowed my eyebrows. "What happened last time?"

"Last time, we were on a fisherman's beach." Josh gestured his arm behind us, where instead, jagged mountain peaks rose like watchful sentinels, lining the shore leading out to the endless ocean with waves rolling in a rhythm older than time, the horizon swallowing sky and water into one. "Then a horde of zombies attacked the boat, and you did this super awesome burst of magic that saved us."

He stopped short, darting his eyes around for a few long moments.

I met Lance's equally incredulous gaze at Josh's pause. "What are...you doing now?"

Josh pursed his lips. "Just making sure I'm not summoning them by talking about it." He glanced over the railing in suspicion at some of the deckhands supplying the ship. "I'm not, am I?"

I wrinkled my nose. If I didn't know any better, I would have been persuaded to assume that all this peril had irreparably messed with Josh's head.

Lance tamped down an eye roll. "Well, if we're done hallucinating for now, shall I get us underway?"

Josh jerked in his stance, snapping to attention. "Oh. Yeah. Great. Thanks." He glanced past my shoulder as if still on the lookout.

I tilted my head to peer at his face. "Are you still waiting for zombies?

"No." He shook his head. "Gazen's still not here. She did say she would join us later. I wasn't sure if we should wait. We might need her help, or you know, have at least someone else magical here. I'd really rather not have you always doing all the heavy lifting by yourself."

I couldn't help but break into a smile. Josh was so sweet and thoughtful.

"Also, I asked someone at Cephiron to make sure our griffin got led back to Gazen's meadow in the meantime. I hope everything went okay." He shot me a questioning look. "Hey, wait, how *did* you get here anyway? Where's your griffin?"

"Oh! I used a portal." I couldn't help the delight in my tone. "It was the strangest thing. Yesterday, when Freyjn and I were training, my magic started working properly again. No glitches. No problems. I mean, Freyjn and I were on high alert just in case, and she was there to step in, in case something happened. But it's all settled now. It's good news, right?"

Josh's forehead creased in deep thought. The wheels in his mind were spinning once again behind those green eyes.

Before I could ask, Lance's voice rang across the deck, sharp and commanding. "Raise the anchor. Set the sails—we leave with the tide." His men jumped into motion, ropes creaking and canvas snapping as the ship stirred restlessly against the waves pitching beneath the hull.

Off on the horizon, faint curtains of rain hung in distant patches, blurred gray veils that never drew closer, while the sky overhead broke in wide, pale stretches of blue—eager to carry the ship forward.

Bracing my hand on the railing, I swayed with the movement of the ship as it put out to sea. We had pushed away from the docks a few hundred feet when a piercing screech split the air, stopping half the crew mid-step.

Grinning, I cast my eyes to the sky. "Oh, finally..."

Heads tilted skyward as the creature cut across the clouds, its golden feathers blazing against the bright sky. It banked low, the downdraft rattling loose coils of rope and sending hats skittering across the deck.

Atop the beast rode Freyjn. Her cloak streamed behind her, braided dark hair whipping in the wind, her posture steady and regal as if she and the griffin were one. Her beauty was only magnified by her confident radiance. She guided the creature in a perfect arc, circling the ship once before swooping down. The landing jolted the timbers, sailors scattering with wide-eyed awe as the griffin settled with a proud cry.

Lance arched a brow. His mouth dropped open when he recognized who was dismounting from the great winged creature.

Straightening up, Freyjn gave us a warm smile.

Josh gave her a little bow. "We're honored to have you here."

Freyjn acknowledged Josh with a gracious nod.

I blinked, almost in surprise at the exchange. I kept forgetting that Freyjn was very soon to be the High Fae leader of all our people.

To me, she was my cousin who, when we were younger, roped me into keeping watch for her father while she attempted to brew elven mead in her room with nothing more than moss, cloves, and candlewax.

I swooped in to loop my arm around hers. "You're right on time—notwithstanding the grand entrance."

"I'm here to help." Freyjn inclined her head. "I understand you are planning quite a long ocean journey, and I thought you could use the favor of the wind." Without any further urging, she lifted a glowing hand, fingers splayed, and the air bent to her will—winds surging into the sails with a sudden, powerful gust that sent the ship lurching forward across the waves.

Josh's eyes lit up. "Aw, yeah! Thanks so much!"

Freyjn's laughter was light. With the breeze tugging at her hair, she already looked much more relaxed than the last few days.

Back in Ipera, Freyjn was getting overwhelmed with the negotiations with the Fae Isles, on top of the arrangements for rescheduling her wedding, and the everyday business of overseeing our people. It had been easier than I'd thought to convince her to come along, and I was glad.

Lance ordered his men to lead the griffin to a shelter at the ship's stern.

"Well, this is great." Josh went on. "You and Lance probably need to discuss what to do with those shadow Fae warriors that attacked us at Cephiron."

"Oh, I see." Freyjn turned toward Lance, her eyebrows rose in a prompt.

Lance blinked as if he was startled. "Right." He met Freyjn's gaze for a moment before looking away. "I didn't realize you were joining us." He shifted on his feet. "How was the uh...wedding?"

Freyjn's smile faded a little. "Oh, it's been postponed because of the thing that happened.

"Oh."

There was an odd tension in the air.

I could have sworn Lance's face was on the verge of flushing red.

Josh looked from Lance to Freyjn and back again. His elbow dug into my side.

Pursing my lips in fascination, I met Josh's equally astonished gaze.

Huh.

"Well—" Josh cleared his throat, bidding them with a wave. "I guess we'll leave you two crazy kids to it."

Startled at the not-veiled-at-all teasing in his tone, Freyjn's cheeks tinted pink. "What?"

Josh beckoned me over. "Hey, Tala, help me unpack the rest of the scrolls inside."

"Sure thing!" I shot Freyjn a wide-eyed, meaningful grin before hurrying away to follow Josh into the ship's main cabin.

The instant I stepped through the door, Josh caught me, pressed me back against the wall, his mouth crashing onto mine.

30

Tricky

Josh

Tala's gasp of surprise was lost beneath my mouth, the sweetness of her lips burning away everything else. We'd only been apart for a couple of days, but I couldn't help it.

God, I wanted her so much. How was I ever going to have enough of her?

She clutched at my shoulders to break off. "Whoa."

My arms fell slack to my sides in dejection. "Sorry, I shouldn't have assumed uh... I just —"

Missed you.

A bit breathless, she met my gaze. "It's not that. I..." Her fingers fidgeted with the fabric of my shirt.

Missed you too.

Pausing, her eyes darted out the window toward where Lance and Freyjn were still standing awkwardly on the deck. "It's just...we have to be careful. Freyjn's going to see."

My heart sank.

Oh, that's right.

The girl I loved was betrothed to someone else. Probably some big, strong, dreamy Fae warrior who could squash me with his pinkie.

Maybe it was even one of the reasons Freyjn had come along. Maybe she'd already noticed how crazy I was about Tala. I certainly hadn't shut up about it this whole time. Freyjn probably wanted to keep an eye on me, to make sure I stayed away from her cousin.

"No, I get it." Giving a brisk shake of my head in defeat, I walked to the table. "Um, so..." I jerked my thumb toward the couple on the deck, willing my tone to switch lighter. "Hey, who else saw that coming, huh? With Lance and your cousin."

Tala's eyes were wide again. "I know, right? Not me, for sure."

"You know, at Cephiron, Lance is always so authoritative, higher-than-thou—at least to me, anyway." I muffled my chuckle. "Now, he's kicking the floor with the toe of his boot like an awkward teenager."

Her forehead creased in thought. "They've only been friendly in the past, polite. I don't think they've spent much time together to explore anything more."

"Huh." I furrowed my eyebrows too.

I wondered if, somehow, by Lance presuming that his affections for Tala would remain unanswered, he had finally decided to open himself to feeling for others. A smirk tugged at my mouth at the amusing notion.

Perhaps Lance was right, and things do happen for a reason after all.

"Well, I think there's definitely something there." I had to add with an offhand shrug, "If you ask me, Lance is much better for her than that Auric guy."

"Freyjn cannot marry a human." Tala's response was quiet. "The Fae elders have chosen."

I dropped my gaze. We both knew we were talking about more than just Freyjn and Auric. "I really hope your Fae elders know what they're doing." Pushing papers aside to clear space for more scrolls, I cringed at the strain on my side. I was still sore from the battle the other day.

"What's wrong?"

"Oh. Nothing." I waved to dismiss it. "Still a bit battered from that thing at Cephiron."

"That *thing*?" Incredulous mocking leaked into her tone. "You mean, when you fought off dozens of highly trained shadow Fae warriors trying to kill you?" She took a step closer. "Let me see."

"I said it's nothing—"

"I said, let me see." She slipped her hands inside my jacket, pushing it off my shoulders.

"Hey—" Before I could retreat further, her hand darted out, catching the edge of my shirt. "Wait!" I stumbled back, trying to stop her, but she was already tugging it upward.

She sucked in a gasp, her gaze lowered to the horrible black and blue bruise along my ribcage. "You're hurt! Did you even see a healer?" Without prompting, she clasped her hands to summon her magic to push warmth into the bruise to attempt to reduce the swelling.

"Ahh—" Backing up some more, my leg hit the bench behind me, and losing balance, I plunked back onto it. "Whoa." I gasped when she climbed on my lap to straddle me. "What are you doing?"

"I can't see." She hooked her hands on the bottom of my shirt, and in one tug, it was up over my head and off altogether.

Heat flooded through me, my skin bared to the cool air.

With a deep frown, her fingers traced over my heated skin. "I'm not a healer, but this should help."

A shiver shot up my spine at her touch, my mouth almost dropping open. Oh, this was definitely helping. I tamped down a telltale groan. "I told you it's fine. I've survived worse."

"How can you be so careless?" Her tone was fully chastising, almost even furious.

I couldn't help an amused scoff. "Hey, I'm fine. Really." Catching her roving hand, I peered at her face. "Are you so concerned about me?"

She stopped short. The shimmering seal of the 'Curse bearer', with its dragon spiral and golden, potent fire, glowed brighter on my chest—as if it demanded attention, and it easily drew hers.

Her expression softened—clouding over, as if to realize that we'd almost lost each other again. She pursed her lips, then moved to press her other palm flat against the seal in reverence.

I almost jumped. I braced my hands on her waist to make sure she didn't fall off. There was no way she would miss how my heart hammered at her touch, raw and unrestrained, every nerve alive with the same urgency.

I drew in a shaky breath. Her body was warm everywhere we touched. That fragrant scent was playing with my senses again—jasmine, forest pine. I darted a glance left and right to make sure we were still alone before clearing my throat. "Should we be doing this?"

"No." She was still a bit breathless, but her gaze was steady when it met mine. "We shouldn't be doing this. But..." Even as she spoke, her hand slid up my arm, tracing the curve of my bicep, my collarbone. The fire in her eyes was hotter than anything I'd ever seen before. "I told you before. Fae are tricky... We do what we want."

Surely, she already knew what she did to me. I was utterly captive to her closeness. My hands dug into her waist. Was this really happening? My insides squeezed in desperate need. I wanted more. So much more.

With the prophecy that hung between us like a blade, getting even more involved was reckless enough already. Any ways out of the bleak fate of 'Curse bearer' were still eluding me. Was it a mistake to let the flame bring us this close, when the pain of parting would cut even deeper?

My soul burned with aching. "Who is your betrothed? Have I met him yet? I know it's not Lance. Was he one of those guys in your village?"

Her face somewhat draining of color, Tala bit her lip. "It's complicated."

"Why?"

Her fingers ghosting over my cheek, my jaw, her shoulders rose with a shrug. "With the High Fae, it's customary that we don't find out until quite close to the wedding ceremony. My uncle is quite strict about it—not accidentally finding out too early. I'm not exactly sure why."

I swallowed hard. "So you have no idea who it could be?"

Tala dropped her eyes for a moment, her words a mere whisper, "Freyjn said my parents chose my betrothed."

"Your parents." Puzzled, I narrowed my eyes. "But didn't they—I mean, aren't they already...?"

Tala's nod was solemn.

"Oh."

Oh.

It felt like another blow as the realization struck me—of exactly how much this meant to her. This arrangement was her legacy. It was a sacred homage to her parents. The only one she could make. And while I wholeheartedly agreed with her decision, it further solidified why she and I could never be together.

It totally sucked.

She tilted her head to one side. "In any case, I wish to honor their choice. It's the only thing I can do for them."

Crushing disappointment stung me all over.

I still couldn't quite believe the depth of it—how much I loved her. It wasn't just her beauty, though that alone could undo me with a single look. I loved her strength, the way her spirit blazed no matter how bleak the world seemed, that disarming wit, even if she tossed it like a shield to hide her own pain.

How could I not be the one for her? How could I possibly let this incredible woman go? How could I have been given this second chance only to know I was going to lose her again? How could I even let anyone else have her?

I tried to crack a pained, wry grin. "I... I don't think I'm...comfortable with the thought of someone else taking care of you."

Those violet eyes seared into me again with a new fiery resolve. "I no longer care what our destiny is. If whatever the fates have decided is out of our control, then let us just have this. This moment. Right now."

Her defiant words released a floodgate of yearning in my chest, of relief, of intense aching, and fervent anticipation. She wanted this too. I didn't need to hold back anymore. I stroked her cheek in resigned conviction. "I'll take anything you can give me."

Her attention dipped to my mouth, lingering there. She licked her lips, as if she could taste me already. Bending her head, her hands braced against my shoulders.

That voice of caution nagging at the back of my mind drowned beneath the even louder pounding of my heart.

I wanted to claim her, wanted her to claim me. There was no going back now. I was going to love her until the day I died.

If this was a mistake, it was one I'd make again and again. *Prophecies be damned.*

Her mouth inches away, those sparkling eyes fluttered closed—

The cabin door slammed open with a bang.

Tala jumped about a mile high, and the next thing I knew, I was shoved under the table. I bit my lip to stifle my groan when I hit my shin.

Several pairs of boots thudded into the room, accompanying loud voices—soldiers.

"You know the master doesn't take kindly to waiting."

"But that bird damn near bit my head clean off—"

"Just hurry on up then and shove your excuses."

My shirt hit me in the face—well, Tala tossed it in my face, under the table.

Ah, crap.

Straightening up, she leaned against the table. "Gentlemen, I trust our journey is well on the way?" Her voice was bright, maybe a little too bright, but their responses of respectful greetings didn't hint at any suspicions.

Once Lance's soldiers had gone, Tala caught my stink eye from under the table. Her serene, frozen expression collapsed to laughter, covering her mouth with her hand.

I scoffed in exasperation as I pulled my shirt back on. Even if I couldn't help my shoulders shake in mirth.

31

Forbidden

Tala

The remnants of supper lay forgotten on a tray shoved toward the edge of the table—crusts of bread, a rind of fruit, a sliver of cured fish. Their mingled scents lingered with the wax, spices, and salt.

The snug, low-ceilinged space of the cabin with its sturdy oak beams groaned softly with the ship's slow sway as the ocean breathed steady and smooth, with the dim swing of lanterns hanging from the beams, painting the room in gold and shadow.

Lance and his men shuffled in and out of the room, the rough camaraderie of seasoned soldiers lingering, subdued beneath the weight of the voyage.

Even with Freyjn's powerful wind, the wide-open ocean was proving a challenge to cross. The days blurred together, each one stitched by the same rhythm of sails snapping, ropes creaking, and the endless heave of waves against the hull.

While everyone aboard found themselves pressed into duty, I often drifted to the rail, staring out at the endless waters. The sea breeze tangled my hair, the salt spray stung my skin, but my mind remained elsewhere, caught between fear and anticipation of what lay ahead.

The crew's disquiet also mounted as the days stretched on. I almost expected it to spill into chaos, if not for Josh's quiet certainty guiding us forward.

Josh would stand at the prow at dawn, those deep green eyes fixed on horizons no one else could read. The maps helped, but it was more than that. It was as if there was a certainty in him, a gut-deep instinct, as if the ocean itself whispered its secrets to him. When others faltered, Josh simply nodded, pointed, and the crew obeyed. He knew where to go even when the sea stretched featureless in every direction.

That evening, he hunched over a spread of scrolls, elbows braced on the scarred table as the flickering light danced across ink and parchment. "This part is really cool. Supposedly, there's a precious treasure that the Dragon Heir possessed that held enormous power. Tala's mother wore it around her neck."

Beside him, Freyjn's eyes were wide, unblinking, rapt with interest.

"I wonder if what had made it into the other world as the powerful relic was a remnant of that heirloom. After three thousand years, I suppose I could understand why all the stories and legends had faded away. Nobody even remembered anything about dragons. But it was a cursed stone that held dragon magic—it seems to match. The relic must have been the last remnant of the curse beads Soleia had worn, which held the Dragon Heir's spirit."

Standing by the round window, I half-listened to Josh's excited bursts of discovery as he went through more scrolls.

"All of this started with Tala's father, Dathon, and your great-great-aunt Helene—a betrayal, a super-powerful, vengeful spell, and the spheres of protection. The magic of the land has been suffering since."

"Re-reading through the research, certain things make more sense now." His face glowed with eager anticipation. "I wonder if village boundaries can still be summoned using the spheres to protect from dangerous creatures or dark magic."

Freyjn's jaw dropped. "You've heard of them? My uncle Callan established the campaign to arm the smaller villages with protective magic. It is said that he'd started with Cephiron when it was but a small village of blacksmiths."

I hid my smile. It was for sure bewildering that Josh knew more about this land than she did, than possibly any of us did now, but it only filled me with more reassurance.

I hadn't had a moment alone with Josh since that first day. He was always in motion—consulting with Lance, discussing routes with Freyjn, fielding questions from the soldiers about his time in Arcadia.

A few times, I thought I'd had a chance—catching him by the stairs to the lower cabins, at the galley hatch during meals, or by the deck railing—only for someone else to pull him urgently away. Leaving me with fleeting glances, half-smiles, almost-moments swallowed by the endless business of the sea.

I hadn't even found out if he had discovered anything new among the scrolls that could save his life from the prophecy. I wanted to ask Josh how he'd slept, wanted to make sure he was eating, that he wasn't being too over-whelmed carrying the sole burden of our cause—my cause. This thankless cause I had forced him to take on. I wanted to make sure he knew what it meant to me, how grateful I was, and... so much more than that.

Getting up, Josh moved to fetch more scrolls across the room.

With his leather jacket off, the broad shoulders beneath the fabric of his shirt flexed under the weight of a heavy crate, the muscles in his arms tightening as he set it down. The toned lines of his biceps caught the light when he reached for another box. There was an odd stir in my stom-ach at the sight.

I already knew what it felt like to have those arms wrapped warm around me. How gentle his fingers felt cradling my face. I also knew how demanding the same fin-gers could feel wrapped tight around my hair, tugging my head back to crush his lips against mine.

I couldn't help my cheeks flame at the memory of our interrupted moment the other day. A shiver shot up my spine from the thrill of remembering Josh melting beneath my touch, the feel of his firm chest, of his heart pounding against my skin, to know that it was because of me. To know for absolute certain that he wanted me just as badly.

I still wanted to run my fingers through his hair. Was that dimple in his left cheek there before? It was taking every ounce of my self-control not to launch myself at Josh, grab his face, and kiss it.

My gaze met his almost accidentally.

One corner of his mouth quirked up in absolute knowing, as if he could read my mind, as if he knew exactly what I was thinking, knew exactly what I wanted.

His shoulder shook in mirth as he moved on.

I tried to shake it off, tried to focus on the view outside the window, even though there was nothing of note save the smudges of gray clouds against the dark skies. I frowned at the ominous shadows foreboding what lay beyond, looming over more than this quest alone.

Even if by some miracle, he survived the prophecy, Josh and I couldn't be together. Or if we did, I would have to go against my people. The notion of defying my parents stung my heart. Stellan would probably be furious. Freyjn would be disappointed. If she had to marry Auric to appease the elders, then I would have to stay away from Josh.

But weren't we already keeping secrets? The bond between Josh and me had already developed—deepened. There was no taking back what had already passed between us. Everyone in our village already thought the worst of me anyway. What difference would this one further infraction make? I'd already decided to take charge of my own fate. All we could do was make the most of our time together.

When I looked up after a moment, those green eyes were pinned on me again. So intensely, the fire seared my skin right away.

It couldn't be helped.

Dropping my gaze, I stood up to slowly make my way to the corridor.

Josh was almost a blur as he crossed the cabin. Grabbing my hand, he tugged me back behind the stairwell so we would be hidden from view by the others.

The next thing I knew, he'd pinned me up against the wall and his lips were on mine.

I barely gasped my surprise in his mouth.

His demanding kiss was all heat and urgency, stealing the air from my lungs, and every nerve in my body lit up like a struck spark, racing with a wild, dizzying current.

My eyes fluttering closed, I moaned right away.

And gods, he kissed like a man who knew exactly what I needed before I even did. I wouldn't have expected this from a weak, lightweight human like him, but Josh was *passionate, burning, insatiable—*

His kisses were almost bruising. His body was hard, un-yielding. When those long fingers dug into my hair from the nape of my neck, I couldn't help a moan. Squeezing my eyes shut, I pulled him closer. My fingertips buzzed with the need for more—more of him, more of this. Kissing him back, I crushed my lips against his, almost in desperation.

That triggered a deep groan rumbling in his throat. His tongue traced the seam of my lips, urging them to part, and when I opened for him, his entire body jerked with another groan of pleasure in his throat as he eagerly slipped his tongue inside my mouth.

Not to be outdone, I met him stroke for stroke. I clutched at his shirtfront. Every inch of my skin was burning. When Josh dragged his kisses down my throat, I moaned again. He kissed my neck, beneath my ear, the bare skin where the top of my tunic was buttoned up.

I tilted my head back to give him better access. I braced my hands on his head, digging my fingers through that soft, thick hair. His arms tightened around my body as I arched for him, against him.

"Josh..."

A whisper, a plea, a vow...

He silenced me with another kiss, fiercer than the last, and in that instant, I knew there was no going back. The world could burn outside this corridor, kingdoms could rise and fall—but right now, all that mattered was him, and the way he set me alight with nothing more than his smile, his touch.

The night shattered with the first blast of icy wind.

The ship's bell tolled out loud, and I sprang back just as the ship listed to one side, rocking in the sudden, violent waves.

One of the deckhands burst in through the cabin door, his eyes lit up in alarm. "Storm's up ahead!"

It took great effort to forcibly surface from my blissful daze.

"Hold!" Lance's commanding voice cut through the chaos as his men leapt to their posts, hauling on ropes and securing the rigging. Snow and sleet lashed the ship, the lanterns flickering wildly before two of them sputtered out altogether.

Josh steadied me against him as the deck pitched beneath us, its timbers creaking in protest as the vessel plunged into the storm. His gaze was drawn over my shoulder toward the porthole, his eyes nearly popped out of his head.

Turning, I squinted past the commotion to see.

It was still quite a distance away, but its sheer size made it appear much closer than it really was.

The horizon was split with a wall of white, a monstrous blizzard roaring across the ocean as if conjured from nothing.

Breathless, I studied the marvel in those deep green eyes as Josh stared into the swirling maelstrom of snow and wind. "Josh?"

Even as the ship lurched sideways under the weight of the storm, his certainty rang clear. "This is it."

32

Frozen

Josh

The ship moored against the island's shore, its masts swallowed by the blizzard as the vessel shuddered beneath nature's fury, sails heavy with snow and straining as though they might tear at any moment.

The gangplank groaned as it was lowered, a hollow thud echoing in the storm's muffled silence. Lance took point, leading the way off the ship with a couple of his armed men. I held my hand out to help Tala next, with Freyjn guarding the rear.

I squinted in the near white-out conditions.

This place looked different again.

The meadow stretched in all directions, rolling hills smothered in drifts that came up to the knees. No trees broke the horizon. No animal tracks marred the surface.

Only the endless sweep of pale snow and shadowed dips where the wind had carved gullies.

"So weird," I couldn't help my mumble.

"What?" Tala turned to me.

"The last time we were here, this place was a barren, centuries-abandoned field, like an ancient graveyard after some big battle."

Lance toed the tip of a flagstaff sticking out of the flurry at his feet. "Indeed." His voice rose, clear enough for all of us. "Be careful where you step. There are likely old weapons or broken splinters strewn about, buried in the snow."

Frowning, I studied the horizon where the blizzard thickened into a whirling wall of white. "According to the old records, the dragons' nest, which they called Dragoncrest, used to be a majestic floating kingdom in the sky. Apparently, it fell when the magic broke during that war. This must be all that's left."

The storm gnawed at us as we trudged forward, each gust slicing through cloaks and furs until fingers stiffened and teeth chattered. Lance's men pulled scarves over their faces, their breath pluming white as they stamped their boots in the snow up ahead.

Hissing my shiver, I looked down at my leather jacket. I was only wearing a t-shirt underneath it. Pursing my lips, I asked Tala, "Do you want my jacket?"

"Or..." Freyjn lifted her hands. A faint shimmer rippled around her, a soft glow that spread outward. The snow hissed where it touched the invisible barrier, melting before it could cling. Warmth radiated from her like a hearth.

Tala clasped her hands to copy her cousin, willing the spark to ignite, to wrap her in the same protective bubble. For a moment, violet light flickered over her skin, teasing her with promise—then sputtered, vanishing in a hiss of steam. Her eyes widened in dismay. "What? Not again." She tried once more, but the magic refused, slipping from her like water through clenched fists.

Freyjn's forehead creased. "Odd."

"It was fine yesterday!" Tala nearly screeched out in exasperation. "This is ridiculous."

The sharp edges of her frustration clawed at the back of my own mind, as if something nagging at me, a notion so close I could almost grasp it.

Narrowing my eyes, I cast a furtive glance around.

There were no ghosts this time. Every other time Tala's magic had glitched in the past, there had been those ghosts around.

I was so certain it had to be the common denominator. It was the only thing that made sense.

Unless...

"It's okay." Freyjn lifted her hand once again. With a steadying breath, the circle of her own spell widened, and warmth spread outward in a gentle wave, brushing Tala like a blanket.

Lance's forehead creased in concern. "How well do you know this place? Is there somewhere we can find shelter?"

My eyes lit up in alert. "If memory serves..." My gaze swept the snow-lashed horizon, searching for anything beyond the endless sweep of white. Then I glimpsed it—a silhouette rising above the storm, its jagged outline cutting starkly against the whirling sky. Half-buried in frost, but unmistakable.

"There." I pointed past the next ridge. "That tower—that's where we need to go."

The others turned, peering through the swirling snow until the shape became visible to them too.

Lance gestured an arm out. "After you."

Nodding, I led the way.

We pressed farther from the ship, snow underfoot crunching as the storm howled at us, and the longer we walked, the more it seemed to fold in, closing the way back.

My lips were probably blue, the snow gathering on my eyelashes. Rubbing my hands together, I glanced back to check on Tala a few times, but Freyjn's magic held steady. Tala's scrunched-up nose was more an artefact of her displeasure with the unexpected recurrence of the glitch in her own powers.

The ominous tower loomed larger with every step, its stone walls scarred by age, streaked with ice that clung like veins. At the memories of before, a sharp pang of dread rippled through me. Terror surged to the front of my mind, the agonizing pain suddenly fresh. I'd almost died then, too.

Gritting my teeth, I steeled myself. No matter what happened next, I knew I was stronger this time. I wasn't in this realm by accident, a runaway teenager trying to get home, a troubled soul only out for himself. This time, everyone's hopes were pinned on me, and I wasn't going to let them down.

Upon reaching the base of the tower, Lance halted his men. He scanned their faces, his tone brisk and commanding despite the storm. "Half of you stay here at the foot of the tower. Eyes open, weapons ready. If anything stirs in this cursed white, sound the alarm. The rest—back to the ship."

The men nodded, splitting into groups with practiced efficiency. Some trudged back toward the faint silhouette of the ship, while others formed a wary ring around the tower's foundation, spears glinting in the swirling snow.

Looking up the curved staircase along the outside of the towering structure, I made a face. It was the only way to get inside.

"What is it?" Tala came up beside me.

Lance's grip on the pommel of his sword tightened. "Are you sensing danger?"

"Nah." I wrinkled my nose. "It's just—last time, I didn't have to climb up all these steps."

The suddenly blank, slack-jawed, incredulous look on Lance's face felt like a death stare.

Freyjn's shoulders merely shook in mirth. Stepping past me, she patted my shoulder to go ahead. "I'll go first. I can clear a path if need be."

Tala's eyes sparkled with amusement.

"What?" I shrugged. "It's true."

She tugged on my jacket. "Come along, Curse bearer."

Lance probably took another moment to compose himself before following suit.

The higher up we went, the deeper into the structure we seemed to go. Soon, the thick stone walls of the tower served as enough protection against the maelstrom outside and the frigid chill.

I shook the snow out of my hair, out of my jacket.

Freyjn dropped her heat shield. Her warming magic recast itself to light the path before us, until we emerged at the very top.

A cavernous, white structure, a massive, long chamber hall, with high ceilings and arched brick windows letting the stormlight filter in, a subdued silver dulling the edges of everything it touched, despite them somehow keeping out the howling winds, the snow, and sleet.

Each column flanking the hall sculpted into beautiful, ornate fountains and waterfalls, with water that flowed from nowhere to nowhere, all washed in a pale, cloud-thick glow—dim but not dark.

It looked a bit less rundown than on my last visit.

Tala gasped, her eyes drawn to the floor.

Elaborate mosaic tiles were underfoot. The image was a bit chipped here and there, but it was very clearly of a golden serpentine creature spouting potent fire. It was exactly the symbol that was on my chest.

We were definitely in the right place, and it was still as impressive and jaw-droppingly majestic as last time.

Lance had walked ahead, but he paused in mid-stride halfway up the chambers, his gaze straying to one of the walls.

I caught his forehead crease in curiosity. My eyes lit up as I sprinted over. I knew exactly what he was looking at.

With a half-smile, I studied the first huge mural, the formidable outline of the beast, the huge golden eyes, and the glittery sweep of wings of the creature. Stepping past it, I took in the rest of the walls depicting all the other dragons taking flight in the skies above a lush land of joyous peoples, of villages, of kingdoms.

"Dragons," I murmured in awe. I caught Tala's gaze and held my hand out to beckon her over. "Look, it's your people."

Tentative but curious, Tala walked over. Her eyes widened in marvel at the majesty of the giant beasts as they seemingly owned the heavens. Her chest heaved in wonder, in rapture.

When she smiled, I couldn't help my own heart lift with hers, as though her happiness spilled into me. No matter what happened with our quest—with us—I was glad I was able to get her this far.

She was home.

"What is this?" Freyjn's voice came from the other end of the room.

Lance, Tala, and I looked over.

Freyjn was standing before a ghostly column of light.

A glowing scroll of parchment was floating delicately within a shimmery beam of gold. Every so often, a weak halo of energy pulsed in a wide, brilliant sphere around it, around us.

I squinted at it as we approached.

Tala came up beside Freyjn, her eyes glowing in the light emitted from the scroll, her whisper hollow. "It's the prophecy...but there's more here than I've found in my research."

Training her gaze on the cursive letters embossed in the mystical scroll as it sparkled and gleamed, the letters appearing on the parchment for a moment before again disappearing into the ether, Tala began to read:

> *"In realms with fading mystic might,*
> *A destined fate shall bring forth light,*
> *Where boundless power in unity reigns,*
> *A path where darkness never sustains...*
>
> *The curse bearer shall heed its call.*
> *To claim the fire, awaken the flame*
> *the dragon wakes from slumber...*
>
> *A time remade, a world made true,*
> *From fractured depths shall wholeness brew*
> *A test of the chosen to offer the cost*
> *For the world to regain the souls of the lost."*

I narrowed my eyes. "A time remade...?"

Tala turned to meet Freyjn's already stunned gaze. "Is that...?"

Freyjn blinked. "Magic beyond portal summoning...?"

"Whoa." My jaw dropped as it clicked. "It was you, Magenta. The last time I was here, it really was three thousand years from now, that's why everything is very slightly different. And when you shifted to your dragon form, you blew the fire of renewal across the Land of Arcadia. Everything had to start over. You basically... made time rewind."

Dropping my gaze, the wheels in my head spun faster. Even certain moments with her recently, I remembered time seeming to stop. It would have never occurred to me that she'd actually made time stop for real.

"You can control time—that's *super awesome!*" Sticking my two thumbs up, I broke into a wide grin. "What's that thing people say—there's no time like the present? Well, it looks like in your case, 'there's no present like time'."

"This is amazing, Tala," Freyjn breathed, her hands braced on Tala's shoulders. "This is absolutely unprecedented."

"And dangerous," Lance put in, his expression somber.

Hissing, I shot him a suffering look. "Way to see the bright side, bro."

But Tala was shaking her head. "He's not wrong. Having this sort of power is essentially tampering with the way things are, the way things are meant to be."

"Not if the way things *are* is wrong," I pointed out. "I mean, that's why Magenta—*you* had done it in the first place, the last time. To fix everything."

Freyn's lips thinned. "Not everything." She walked around in a tight circle as if to process her thoughts. "The threads of time spin from itself, each strand bound to another in secret design. Every moment is knotted to countless others. To tug at one is to summon consequences unseen, ripples that travel into shadows beyond mortal sight. Pull at too many threads, and the delicate weave may begin to loosen, the pattern unraveling until nothing of the world you know remains."

The ominous shift of her tone made my stomach sink. I supposed tampering with time itself was undoubtedly an extreme way to resolve any issue. Even if back then, it had seemed like the right thing to do.

"Everything happens for a reason," Lance supplied as if to punctuate Freyjn's point.

Freyjn nodded. "Magicks like this cannot simply stand without consequence."

Tala's eyes narrowed in deep thought before realization hit her. Scoffing, she closed her eyes for a moment. "The ghosts..."

My mouth dropped open again as everything came together. "That's why I was the only one who recognized them. The forest animals, the Guifan army—all those ghosts weren't from this world, this time. They were from the other one, the one that got rewound—" I stopped short, cringing. "Re-winded? Re-wounded?"

Lance rolled his eyes, steamrolling right over me. "Then shouldn't there be more of those ghosts showing up all across the land? If they are indeed artifacts of the other time, why have we only seen them recently, and in particularly isolated locations—?"

"Fancy meeting you folks here."

Cold dread shot through my entire body. I already recognized the malicious voice coming from behind, before we all faced the figure emerging from the shadows.

I groaned in full knowing. "Ohhh, crap."

33

Henry

Tala

A young human man with raven hair and eyes glinting like coals, dressed in royal robes, a golden crest shining on his lapel, seemingly formed from the dark, shadowy corners of a broken column. An evil smirk curved his lips as his figure visibly phased in and out of being. Dim light gleamed upon the gemstone dangling from the chain around his neck, his presence filling the ruin with a weight colder than the storm outside.

Lance instantly donned a defensive pose. "Who the hell is that?"

Josh stepped to cover me again, out of instinct. "Ahh—it's another ghost from the other time. A really nasty one. His name is Henry."

"Ah, how you've changed, my friend." Henry clicked his tongue, his sinister gaze set on us. "We used to be as brothers."

"Oh ha ha ha—shut up," Josh snapped, making a grotesque face. "Just stay away from us, Henry."

I cast my glance around the otherwise empty, but eerily elegant tower ruins. I frowned in bafflement. "Did we summon it by speaking of the ghosts?"

"No, no." Josh shook his head. "I don't think it works that way."

"Then what?" I cringed more in annoyance than in alarm.

The revelation of a new type of magic was already too unsettling as it was, the possibility that it had once been mine to wield was entirely unfathomable. Why did I have to rewind time to recreate the world before? What had I been thinking? Was it even me that actually did that? I wasn't *really* Magenta. I still couldn't grasp that I could even possess that sort of power.

Not to mention the dread gnawing on my insides at the weight of possible expectations that I might be called upon to do it again.

Remorse stung my chest. Plus, if Freyjn's analysis was correct, all the ghosts terrorizing the realms were unfortunate side effects of this rare magic. How was anyone to know that I hadn't done anything wrong with the spell last time? What if the ghostly onslaught of terror never ended? The land would be further scarred by turmoil, never to recover. And it would be all my fault.

As it was, my mind still spun with the mere discovery of this wondrous place, the mural of the dragons on the walls—my people.

Hope had started to creep back into the aching spaces in my heart where there was only desolation before. I had thought the day I found real traces of my kind would be a triumphant turning point in my mission. I was even holding on to the tiniest wish that it might mean my search was finally over.

Alas, perhaps my penance had only just begun.

Freyjn shifted her stance in front of Josh to block both of us. "Stay back, you two."

Lance moved to stand beside Freyjn. He glanced over his shoulder at Josh, his steely blue eyes urgent, alert. "How do we get rid of this ghost? Are there more coming? What could possibly be summoning them in these very specific times and places?"

My heart pounded in my chest. Almost unaware I was doing it, I took Josh's arm, my nerves easing instantly. It always happened with him. I always felt safe.

Josh's eyes lit up. "Lance, your men reported that the ghost army in the forest disappeared as soon as we'd split up and left the forest?"

"Yes, and?" Lance snapped.

Josh let out a slow breath, glancing down where I was gripping him like a vise. When he lifted his eyes, those deep, green depths seared into me. There was a new light in them.

An epiphany.

As if I'd read his mind, I blinked. "Oh."

"Oh? Oh, what?" Freyjn prompted, stepping back a touch as Henry's ominous steps continued to wear slowly across the marble floor toward us, his dark eyes pinned on us as he approached.

Foreboding dread surged through me, my skin running cold. I swallowed hard. "The ghosts only turn up...when we're together." I took a deep breath, my heart sinking to my stomach. My insides felt as though I'd been tossed in a bottle and shaken vigorously.

I wanted to scream. It was as though Josh and I needed even more reasons to be apart.

Except, of course, for, out of all the equally valid reasons thus far, this one was absolutely indisputable.

"You mean...?" Lance's forehead creased.

"This ghost, Henry," Josh said, "is part of all the things from the last version of this world. They're all colliding with this one. They're going to keep causing all kinds of chaos. And it's not going to stop unless..."

I met Josh's solemn gaze again, my heart right about breaking. "Unless we part ways..."

Henry's loud cackle echoed from halfway across the chambers. "Who wants to die today?" His shadowy figure lifted into the air.

My grip on Josh's arm tightened with alarm. "What's going on now?"

Josh groaned again. "Ah, hell. He's transforming into a dragon."

Henry's form began to ripple, bones stretching, flesh tearing away into shadow. The smirk twisted into something monstrous as his body expanded, limbs snapping into talons, wings unfurling with a thunderclap of blackened air.

I winced at the cracking of bones as Henry's shadowy form developed a long scaly tail. His face morphed into the hideous skull of a huge, glossy black dragon, scaled in midnight armor, eyes burning red, a specter of malice given form. When he flared his wings out, the light glanced off the multiple spikes protruding from their edges.

"He's a dragon?" Freyjn gasped, unable to hide her horror.

"Not a real *real* one," Josh explained flatly. "He did this last time, too."

Henry's dragon puffed smoke out of his nostrils as though in a chuckle, smooth, venomous. He glared at us through the slits of his eyes, still a hint of mischief in them.

The beast's roar nearly shook the tower to its foundations. The murals shivering under its fury, ancient paint crumbling as the air filled with the stench of sulfur and ash. Then, without warning, the huge dragon whooshed straight at us, its razor-sharp wings scraping at the marble floor.

"Whoa—!"

"Look out!"

Henry lunged, massive jaws snapping shut where moments ago we had stood.

I dove aside, snow spraying across the marble as the dragon's teeth shattered a pillar into dust.

Josh skidded to a stop beside me. He caught my arm. "Are you okay?"

"I...I think so."

He peered at my face, an almost imploring prompt in his eyes. "Maggie, last time, you shifted into a dragon and kicked Henry's ass."

Something twisted in my chest. I wrung my hands out. "B-but I'm-I'm not a dragon! I can't shift. I don't know how. I've never done it before. I don't even know if I can. I'm only half-dragon. I might not even be the same person you met last time. I—"

Muted sounds of yelling floated from below the tower.

"What fresh madness is going on down there?" Freyjn was braced against the arched windows, peering out.

Josh peered over the edge to squint. "It looks like..." He cursed under his breath. "It looks like Henry's zombie army is finally making its appearance. They've engaged Lance's soldiers below the tower, and probably the ship too."

Straightening up across the way, Lance gripped his sword tight. His gaze was pinned on the monstrous creature, terrifying wings spread, veering around for another go. "My men are capable. We need to deal with this monster first."

Freyjn signaled a nod. "Agreed."

Lance's steel flashed in the dim light as he lunged at the dragon's legs.

Freyjn raised her hands, conjuring a bright flare of power and hurling it at Henry's wing. For a moment, it staggered the beast—but then the magic fizzled, guttering out like a candle in a gale.

Henry's jaws snapped down, and Lance barely rolled aside, the teeth slamming into the ground where he had stood. Shards of stone flew outward, grazing his cheek.

Freyjn cried out, "Lance!" She thrust her palms forward to summon a plume of fire—but the blaze of magic splintered off the creature as though it had merely been swallowed by the specter itself.

Josh's eyes popped wide. "Whoa." So far, he had been oddly calm, almost bored by the ghost. This time, a hint of fear leaked into the surprise in his tone. "He wasn't fireproof last time."

Lance groaned, his attempts to push up off the floor seeming weak.

Freyjn scrambled back up, shooting me a wide-eyed look. "How exactly are we supposed to fight a Deathbringer?"

Her question stabbed at my heart.

No...

My chin quivered in apprehension.

Maybe Brynn had been right. Maybe bringing back the dragons would only cause chaos, unrest, and deaths in Arcadia. Maybe *everyone* was right. Maybe it wasn't worth attempting to restore my father's legacy. Maybe I really was nothing but a threat to all the realms.

The monstrous dragon reared back, wings beating like thunder, ready to strike again—then suddenly, a piercing shriek split the air.

From the broken ceiling above, several griffins burst through in a spray of ice and stone, feathers gleaming gold against the storm.

Upon the back of the magnificent beast leading the charge sat Gazen, her short hair wild in the wind, her eyes blazing with battle-fire. She dove low, her griffin's talons raking across the dragon's muzzle, forcing Henry to recoil with a furious bellow, while the other griffins flew around, distracting his maneuvers.

"Gazen!" Josh cried out his relief.

Gazen's griffin hovered beside us, stirring the air, whipping at our clothes, at my hair.

I beamed at her. "Thank the gods, you're here to help."

Steadying her mount, Gazen pursed her lips. "I am afraid I also come with unpleasant news."

Josh rubbed his face with his hand. "Oh, jeez, what the hell else is going on now?"

Gazen's lips pursed tight. "Darkness spreads on the mainland," she stated. "Both the Fae and the human kingdoms are up to their necks fighting ghostly armies, similar to the ones we'd encountered in the forest. And as soon as one battalion is quelled, more pop up in its place."

Josh hissed another curse.

Henry's dragon roared as he fought off Gazen's griffins. He spread his wings, pumping to flap straight at us again.

"Take cover!" Lance yelled out as we all scattered.

Josh bolted to duck behind a column. I dove to plaster myself right beside him.

"Shoot," he muttered. "It's no good. If we can't stop him, Henry and his minions are going to destroy this world."

I clutched at my chest. "As long as we're together, the darkness spreads."

Unless...

The prophecy.

A test of the chosen to offer the cost...

I already knew the cost.

The Curse bearer needed to be sacrificed.

No.

No.

I gave a brisk shake of my head, my heart pounding in my chest in a frenzy. "Let me try. I'll do as you said I did before. I'm sure if I focus hard enough, I can conjure the renewal fire and turn everything back once again. Perhaps this time, I can rewind time all the way back to Helene and my father, so that none of *any* of this ever even happens."

Josh shook his head. "We can't. We can't keep turning back time."

"Why?"

"All this is already happening *because* of the renewal fire. Freyjn already said it. We can't remake an entire world over and over and turn back time without consequences. At some point, we have to deal with what's here now. At some point, we have to move forward."

His resolution was almost punctuated by a crack of thunder. The storm outside had not relented, the windows dripping with pale gray light.

Josh staggered, one hand flying to his chest. His voice broke, strangled with surprise. "Tala—"

My breath caught.

The mark on his chest, usually not even a faint shimmer, blazed like a star beneath his tunic. Light pulsed through the fabric, radiant and insistent, spilling golden-white beams that painted the walls. It was not merely glowing—it was calling.

He clenched his jaw, shoulders tense under the weight of revelation. "The prophecy. We must go and fulfil the prophecy." His hand pressed against the glowing mark, though the light only flared brighter, spilling between his fingers. The air around him vibrated, the light thrumming in rhythm to his heartbeat.

"Curse bearer," I whispered, unable to help the lump in my throat. I could feel the pull of the mark too now, as though the light itself reached through my chest, urging us on. "Is it trying to lead us somewhere?"

The glow on Josh's chest grew blinding, a steady beacon piercing through the madness. I realized with chilling certainty, the prophecy had not just awaited us. It had carried us, wave by wave, step by step, to this very place.

"It's probably what brought us here to begin with, what helped me navigate the ocean." Josh's eyes shone with determination. "Everything is connected. All this is part of the same problem, and there's only one solution. We have to fulfil the prophecy."

Offer the cost...

My chest stung with fresh anxiety.

There had to be another way.

I clenched my jaw tight. "No."

His matter-of-fact gaze met mine. "Tala, we have no choice."

Taking a deep breath, Josh's gaze shifted to Lance, Gazen, and Freyjn, who were preoccupied getting ready to engage further assaults by the ghost dragon.

The set of his jaw was steady, a quiet pride in his eyes, gratitude for friends who had fought by his side, while a faint sorrowful shadow softened the lines of his face—an unspoken farewell.

Henry's dragon roared again, the storm screaming through the tower ruins.

Seeming not wanting to distract the others with good-byes, Josh seized my hand. His voice was fierce, urgent. "We have to hurry."

Slipping past the fallen columns, Josh's other hand pressed to his chest as he followed the Curse bearer mark's calling—his calling.

To his fate.

To his doom.

And all I could do was grip his hand tighter.

34

Succession

Josh

Tala's hand in mine, we plunged deeper into the stone structure, the scrape of claws, steel, and shouts echoing as the battle with Henry's dragon continued behind us.

My heart pounded beneath the glowing Curse bearer mark on my chest, even as it led us through a narrow passage behind the dais.

Below the elegant waterfall chambers revealed a labyrinth of passageways, grand staircases, large rooms, and compartments. A few paths were blocked by crumbled debris, but we followed an unfailing path into the depths of what appeared to be the ruins of a once-majestic palace.

As the stairway spiraled down, the air grew thick, heavy with dust, mildew, and centuries of neglect. Every footstep stirred hollow, swallowed and distorted by the stone walls until it seemed the crypt itself was breathing back.

The fighting all but muted from down here, the groan of shifting stone and a low hum of air moving through cracks sighed as though from long-buried throats.

"What place is this?" Tala's voice resonated beside me.

"Honestly, I'm not sure. I never made it this far last time." I tamped down my nervous jitters at the unexpected turn of events. Up until this point, I'd been relieved and comforted by the notion that I should already know what to expect. There was certainly none of this before. "Last time, you and Henry had a dragon showdown upstairs, and you kicked his ass—" I gave her a wink, then shrugged. "Then you summoned a portal to send me home. By 'you', I mean, when you were Magenta."

Tala winced.

Stopping, I blinked at the hint of displeasure on her face. "What is it?"

"Um... I just thought maybe... can you not call me Magenta anymore?"

"Oh."

That was the last thing I was expecting her to say.

My eyebrows furrowed in curiosity. "Why?"

"Well, first of all, according to you, Lance gave me that name. And second of all..." She propped her hands on her hips, her face crumpling up, but she didn't continue.

"Second of all, what?" Her grimace hinted at something very distinct. My jaw dropped in disbelief. "Wait, are you jealous? How can you be jealous of Magenta? She's you."

She shot me a suffering look. "Oh, what, like you're not jealous of Lance? Or Dantilian, or whoever that man was from before?"

Despite my good sense, the mention of Dantilian struck a nerve. I cracked my neck, attempting to shake it off. Surely, I didn't care anymore if she was head over heels for some other guy from a different time? Right...?

Sighing, Tala turned away. "Maybe it doesn't make sense, but this Maggie... Magenta—she has a hold on your heart, it's obvious. She and you share so much history that I'll never know anything about."

I let out a half-scoff, half-chuckle. I caught her shoulders to peer at her face. "Look, it's your name. Just tell me. I'll call you whatever you want."

The pout on those luscious lips was the cutest thing. Despite all the world probably ending around us, it took everything I had not to take her face in my hands to kiss her senseless right then.

"Just... just call me Tala," she said, almost diffidently. "I was named for my mother, Soleia. Sol. The sun. 'Tala' in the old Fae language means 'star.'"

I couldn't help a smile. "That's beautiful." I cradled her face in one hand, my smirk slightly mischievous. "How about... Tallie?"

Her cheeks flushed in pleasure.

Self-conscious, I ran my fingers through my hair. "I know...we haven't had a chance to talk about that—kiss." My pulse raced in anticipation at the mere recollection.

She cracked a wry smirk herself. "Which one?"

"The ones you didn't regret."

Her violet eyes shone. "So...all of them?"

My chest felt like it was about to burst, but I dropped my rueful gaze. "Given we're about to sacrifice me right now, I know we already knew it was a bad idea for us to—to *you know*, and given everything else, all the other reasons..." I trailed off with another shrug, almost at a loss.

"What, you mean like how I'm already betrothed to someone else—someone who was approved by my venerable deceased parents, and that every time we're together, violent, horrific ghosts from a different time turn up to terrorize all the realms? Those reasons?"

Sticking my hands in my pockets, I cringed. "Well, yeah."

Tala grasped my cheek in her hand, a resolute set in her chin. "I am not some fragile thing to be shielded from scandal. All those reasons mean nothing against the truth in my heart. If it's power they fear, then let them tremble. I'll wield mine to protect you for as long as I can."

A sudden gust swept through the shadowy crypt—as if responding to her vow.

The clammy air chilled my skin. I squinted to see in the dim light where the disturbed dust seemingly unveiled a darkened tunnel up ahead, and at its far end loomed a massive stone door, its surface smooth, pristine, despite its age. The door stood sealed, immovable, as though it had not been touched for centuries.

The air rippled, and suddenly a male figure glimmered into being before us—misty, half-formed, his face blurred as if seen through water.

"Whoa." I jumped, already moving to a defensive pose just in case.

"*There is only one... The same one the Dragon Heir himself withstood for five nights to gain his position,*" he said, voice thin and muted, like wind through a cavern.

Before I could blink again, the apparition dissolved, vanishing into wisps of smoke that curled away into the crypt's stale air.

I gawked at Tala. "What the crap was that?"

Tala's eyes were as wide as mine. She'd taken her stance in front of me, her hands clasped together in alert to call on her magic.

Two more phantoms reappeared, women this time, their forms trembling like candlelight. One voice was harsh, one soft: "*You don't know anything. Emberheart Fire is a very potent form of dragon fire.*" "*...sacrificed himself in the Fire, not only to establish a ruling power but also to abolish this tradition.*" Their words lingered, chilling and sharp, before their forms unraveled into mist once more.

I stood frozen, trying to make sense of it. My skin crawled with the weight of something I didn't understand.

Tala drew a sharp breath, her gaze fixed on the place they had been. "They're echoes—people who lived here before. People of Dragoncrest—my people." Her certainty pressed against the pit of my stomach, heavy as the crypt stone around us.

As though obeying a rite, the massive stone doors before us began to groan open on their own, their grinding creak followed by a sharp draft escaping like secrets too long entombed.

"Whoa." I craned my neck to peer warily past the entryway before glancing back at Tala.

A shade of curiosity in her violet eyes, she gave me a nod in response. We slipped through the gap in the door.

Inside, the air shimmered with age. A pedestal of blackened stone stood at the center, upon it a shallow bowl where a tiny flame flickered, sporadic, delicate fingers of searing heat seemingly reaching out as it sputtered and swayed—so faint it could have been mistaken for a candle. Yet its glow was unnatural, ancient, pulsing with power.

"Wicked fire."

Tala surveyed the dimly lit crypt of wall-to-wall forbidding stone. "Emberheart Fire..." she recited from the ghostly apparitions. "I remember stories... my father was said to have survived five days of agonizing torture in a chamber of fire. He was weakened immensely, near death at the close. But unlike those that came before him, he'd withstood the full trials of the flame. He was thereby awarded the throne, proclaimed as the true king of the dragons."

"Wait a minute." I snapped my fingers a few times. "I think I also read a notice about someone else having survived something called the Emberheart Fire trials centuries later. I think it might have been your uncle's brother?"

"Uncle Callan? Yes." Tala's eyes narrowed. "Since he was Fae, he was given only three days, though I believe he nearly died as well. Only dragons can survive the Emberheart Fire."

Even as she spoke, the air stirred again, colder than before, and the ghosts blipped back into sight. Their faces were sharper now, figures glowing faintly, their words falling in a single, united voice: "*This tribulation was meant as a test of succession due to the past chaos in the Houses. Whatever the results of the test, it will be as the gods have willed it.*"

The declaration shuddered through me, deeper than sound, before the figures unraveled once more, vanishing into silence and shadow. But the word 'test' pricked my ears up. "Oh, this is it. This is the test. This is the solution to everything."

A faint shadow crossed Tala's face. "The test of the 'Curse bearer'..."

"This is my destiny, my sacrifice." I took a step closer toward the pedestal.

"Wait." Tala caught my arm. "This—there has to be another way."

"Tala, we've been researching this for weeks. There is no other way. We have to fulfil the prophecy." I clenched my teeth in resolve, refusing to give room to doubt or hesitation. "I need to be sacrificed. All this ends if we are no longer together. Henry, the ghosts, all of it. All the realms will be fine as long as you don't see me anymore, as long as I'm gone."

Tala's eyebrows furrowed in irate disbelief. "And your solution to us having to split up is to sacrifice your life to some dangerous fire trial?"

"Isn't that what the 'Curse bearer' is meant to do?" I threw my hands up. "Lance, Freyjn, and Gazen, they're desperately fighting Henry upstairs right now. All the other Fae and the rest of your world, they're going against an endless horde of ghost armies—who won't stop coming unless..." I sighed, my entire body heavy as lead. "You know, as long as we're together, it's not going to stop. The darkness will keep spreading."

Seeming to absorb my words, Tala chewed on her bottom lip for a few moments. But then her eyes lit up. "Well, wait. Then doesn't that mean the sacrifice can be either of us?"

I blinked, completely off-balance by the notion. "What?"

"All this ends if we are no longer together. Doesn't that mean I can be the one who's sacrificed? Doesn't that fulfil the conditions of us splitting up too?"

My eyes widened in aghast, in stunned indignation, my chest tightening so hard I could barely breathe.

Oh no, this must have been what Gazen was talking about before when she'd foreseen that I wasn't the one marked for death.

Tala was going to sacrifice herself in my place.

Those violet eyes burned with grim resolve. "It *doesn't* have to be you. This whole time, I thought it had to be you, but the prophecy never said that. The two of us are causing all this chaos, but only one of us needs to be sacrificed." Her voice rose as if prompting the crypt for a response. "Right? I'm right, aren't I?"

"*A test of the chosen to offer the cost...*"

"Jeez!" I jumped at the eerie voice coming from everywhere and nowhere all at once. I darted my own gaze up and around us in the near darkness. "Okay, this whole thing just escalated from mere straight-up creepy to downright terrifying. Are those ghosts actually watching us right now?"

Tala ignored my outburst. She turned to me almost eagerly. "I'm right."

"Wait, what?" I protested, rubbing my face with my hand. "Tala, no!"

"But this is the test. A test of sacrifice." Tala squared her shoulders, stepping forward. "And I can sacrifice my life instead for you. In fact, if you really think about it, this is all actually *my* fault to begin with. I'll do it."

"No! That's crazy." I snapped, grabbing her wrist and tugging her back. "I'm the one who doesn't belong in this world. You have family, friends. I've already prepared myself for this."

"No!" She spun on me, eyes blazing hotter than the flame. "I won't let you—"

"Hey, I said I wanted to save your world. I'm prepared to die. You need to be prepared to live." I tried to edge past her, but Tala's hand shot out, shoving square against my chest.

"But I'm more likely to survive it!"

"You—" Catching her by the shoulders, I walked her toward the door again. "Need to restore your father's legacy, your kingdom, find your people. Your whole life, you've been searching for where you belonged."

"No. No!" Shaking her head, she blocked the doorway with both arms, face set in mock fury. "If the price of finding who I am is your life, then I don't need it. I already know where I belong. I belong with you. You need to be in my life. It just doesn't work without you."

I lunged for the gap, and she darted sideways, hip-checking me back like we were children fighting over the last dumpling. "I want to do this. I don't have any magic or kingdoms or castles. This is the only thing I can do for you. I told you I'll do everything to help you save your world. I've already made my peace with it. If I have to sacrifice my life, so be it." I caught her shoulders, gently but firmly, and pushed her back toward the arch.

She dug her heels in, gripping my shirt, dragging me with her. "And I won't watch you die again." She tried to push me toward the door, but I caught her wrists, holding her fast despite her struggle.

"But I'm supposed to die," I pointed out with a groan as we pressed against each other, both trying to force the other away. "That's like the job description of the chosen one. You have to be the hero who survives this."

"No!" Tala's shoulders shook. "When you almost died from that memory restoring potion, I..." Her fingers still clutched at me. "I-I can't sacrifice you to the prophecy. I just can't."

I loosened my grip but didn't let her go, my chest already aching at the memory. "Well, I already lost you once before. Hell if I'm going to lose you again."

The Emberheart Fire burned low and blue from its vessel a few steps away. The flame pulsed, as if listening, the air tightening around us with unseen power. In mere moments, it would likely envelope the entire room with its terrifying, lethal blaze.

"Oh, dammit." Tala's eyes blazed with unshed tears.

"A-Are you crying?" My mouth dropped open. "What's all this all of a sudden? Didn't you say the only reason I was even here was to fulfil this prophecy? You were always so determined to complete your mission when all this started. What's changed?"

"Nothing's changed." She shot me a furious look, her tone cutting sharply despite her words. "I'm in love with you, you idiot!"

It seemed even good news struck me like a blow to the face. "You... you what?" Okay, maybe *that* was the last thing I was expecting her to say.

I love you.

I heard the words again in my mind, her voice soft and distinct, wrapping through me like a whisper meant only for my soul. My heart surged, my breath caught, and every part of me ached with fierce wonder.

I love you.

I'd surely hoped for this. Except, I'd always thought it was too far to reach. I knew she'd felt a certain way about me, she definitely liked me—she'd said as much, and the attraction was undoubtedly there. But I had never let myself believe her feelings for me could ever possibly run this deep.

My mind spun. I staggered back, my knees almost shaky with disbelief. I almost couldn't speak. "You said you love me. I don't believe this..."

Giving me a wry glare, my beautiful fuchsia fairy lifted one nonchalant hand, her fiery, long hair floating about her as if it had a life of its own, her violet eyes glimmering in the dim light. "Hi, I'm Tala. I'm in love with you." Her eyes narrowed stubbornly. "And I'd rather die fighting you over this than let you go without me."

My breath caught in my throat at her words, at her fierce resolve.

All my control shattering, I surged toward her, seizing her face in my hands and crushing my mouth to hers, desperate and unrestrained.

Tala's hands gripped my face, trembling, intense, as though she could anchor me against the inevitable. She pressed harder, gasping against my lips, and I kissed her back with everything I had left. Desperation, love, terror, hope—pouring into that single, burning moment.

"Your offering is acceptable."

That ominous voice filled the chamber once again, ethereal, vast, resonant with power—as though it came from the flame itself—and the heavy stone doors groaned shut once again, sealing us in.

I froze, meeting Tala's equally stunned gaze.

The tiny flame on the pedestal shivered once, then burst outward in a blinding surge of light, a flicker developing into a firestorm, a cleansing blaze that leapt from wall to wall, swallowing the chamber whole.

Heat slammed into me like a hammer, searing my skin before I could even cry out. My breath turned to ash in my lungs. The stench of burning stone, of flesh, of smoke thick and acrid filled my nose. My ears rang with the roar of it—like a thousand furnaces opening at once, deafening, endless.

"Ahh..." I grunted, trying to numb myself even as my every nerve screamed in agony. My skin blistered, my muscles clenched, my body begged me to flinch away. But I didn't. I couldn't. Because Tala was in my arms.

Through the fire's blaze, through the torrent of pain, I fixed my eyes on hers. Even as tears streamed down her cheeks, even as the light reflected in her pupils like molten gold, she held my gaze steady. Her hands clutched mine, her grip fierce despite the agony that wracked us both.

I pulled her close, the heat scalding even where our bodies touched, and yet it felt right. If this was the cost, if this was the prophecy, then I would pay it. We would pay it.

The fire roared higher, charring the air itself, the world dissolving into searing white. Still, I held her tighter.

"I love you, Tallie."

"I love you, Josh."

Panting, I tamped down another groan from the crackling pain seeping through my skin, spreading to my insides. I cracked a casual grin. "What if everything still gets worse from here?"

Tala's lips curved into a trembling smile. "Then we'll be together anyway."

I almost laughed. In that moment, nothing else mattered—the agony, the fear, the ruin of the world around us. As the fire closed over us completely, I welcomed it.

I'm staying right here, with you, if this is the end...

And in each other's arms, the Emberheart Fire claimed us.

35

Hold

The tower's upper chamber shook as Henry's dragon ghost's massive tail whipped across the floor, scattering shattered stone and nearly sweeping Lance off his feet. He staggered but raised his sword, his face grim.

Freyjn scrambled to her feet after diving clear of another tail strike. She flung her hands outward, forcing every scrap of magic she had into a blazing orb. For a heartbeat, it flared, bright as a star—then guttered out against Henry's black scales as though the dragon had swallowed the light itself.

Gazen wheeled her griffin in tight arcs around the dragon's head. "I got him!" Her blade flashing, she slashed at one burning eye.

Henry reared back with a bellow that rattled the very pillars, his jaws snapping dangerously close.

The griffin screeched, feathers bristling, its talons raking at the dragon's face only to strike through smoke and shadow where flesh should have been.

Cursing out loud, she met Freyjn's fierce gaze, then Lance's bloodied one. "Its form won't remain intact!"

Henry's enormous head swung toward Gazen's griffin, jaws opening wide, the heat of his breath searing the air.

Lance charged forward, slamming his sword at the dragon's neck in a desperate strike. The steel bit deep enough to spark against shadow, but Henry's laughter rolled like thunder as the wound closed instantly. With a violent twist, the dragon's claws came down.

"No!" Freyjn hurled herself forward, shoving Lance back as the dragon's maw snapped down where he had stood—so close she felt the air tear as it scraped the stone beside them.

Gazen swooped low again, her griffin's wings buffeting the dragon's snout. She struck at the beast's face again and again. Sparks flew as steel met scale, but every blow glanced off, leaving only shallow streaks of light.

The dragon's roar rumbled like laughter, cruel and un-yielding.

Freyjn stumbled back, panting, anxiety and fury mingling in her wide eyes. "We need to hold the beast for as long as we can." She summoned her last reserves even as exhaustion sapped her magic. It crackled weakly in her palms. "I am certain Tala will find a way."

Lance wiped the blood from his cheek, steadying his sword again despite the tremor in his arm. He stood shoulder to shoulder with her, battered but unbroken. Above them, Gazen and her griffin circled for a dive, her face set with grim defiance.

Henry's massive wings beat the air, sending shards of stone raining from the crumbling ceiling. The ruined tower groaned with every deafening clash—dragon roars, griffin cries, steel ringing futilely against black scales.

Gazen drove her griffin into another dive, blade raised high. The creature's golden talons slashed across Henry's muzzle, but the dragon only snapped back with jaws wide enough to swallow them whole. She leaned low against her mount, the breath of the beast scorching past her as they pulled away just in time.

"I can't find a weakness in the beast." Gazen circled higher. Her eyes blazed as she wheeled around.

On the ground, Lance braced himself, his sword arm shaking from fatigue. Each swing of his blade felt heavier, a fresh storm pressing down on him. Henry's tail swept across the chamber again, striking him square in the chest and hurling him across the marble floor. He slammed into a pillar, the air punched from his lungs.

"Lance!" Freyjn rushed to his side.

Shuddering against the floor, Lance coughed. "Where the hell are they?"

Freyjn caught his shoulders to keep him steady. She pressed her palms against his chest, forcing warmth into his battered ribs. The glow flickered, sputtering. Despite the remorse in her grimace, she willed the magic with stubborn determination. "I'm not as good a healer as my mother. I'm so sorry."

With a growl, Henry's dragon lowered his head toward them, teeth glinting, breath steaming with death.

Gazen and her griffin dove again, striking the dragon's flank, her blade sinking deep into the shadowy form. For one terrible heartbeat, Henry faltered—then his massive body rippled, the wound closing as though it had never been. His tail lashed upward, catching the griffin mid-flight.

The griffin shrieked as it was slammed against the wall, and Gazen was nearly thrown from the saddle. She clung with desperate strength, her sword slipping from her hand to clang uselessly against the stone floor below. The griffin flapped wildly, feathers scattering, blood staining its golden wing.

"No, no, no—Gazen!" Freyjn shook her head in alarm. "We can't keep going like this!" She staggered back, frustration stinging her eyes.

Lance forced himself upright. His voice was hoarse but fierce. "We have to. No matter what it takes."

The dragon's eyes glowed hotter, burning pits of crimson locked on the three who dared defy him.

The storm outside howled louder, the tower structure trembling as though it too bowed before the ghost of time.

A different piercing roar split the storm.

It wasn't Henry.

The walls trembled as a second bellow followed, this one deeper—so deep it almost shook the very stones of the pillars loose.

Lance whipped his head up in time to see new shadows sweep across the ceiling.

From the storm outside, two colossal forms burst through the gaping cracks in the ruined ceiling. One shimmered with all the colors of the rainbow, its scales gleaming with silver light, wings unfurling like a banner of purity. The other carried a darker gleam, gold tinged with streaks of black, as though fire and shadow had been forged into its hide.

"Tala's done it..." Lance breathed, stunned. "The dragons have returned."

Both beasts' eyes burned with fury. Their roars thundered straight at Henry, and the nightmare dragon's massive head snapped upward, his red eyes flaring.

With an ear-splitting shriek, the silver dragon dove first, colliding with Henry in a whirlwind of wings and claws. Scales ripped, teeth snapped, and the chamber filled with the deafening sound of titans locked in battle. The golden-black dragon circled from the other side, its wings slicing through the storm, and it dove low, slamming into Henry's flank with bone-shaking force.

The three dragons tumbled into the air, swooping and slashing with razor-edged wings. Henry lashed out with jaws wide enough to crush stone, snapping at the silver dragon's neck, but it twisted away, raking bloody gouges across its muzzle. The golden-black dragon came from below, clamping its jaws into Henry's leg and wrenching it savagely.

Stone crumbled from the ceiling as their battle shook the ruins. Gazen's griffin screamed, banking hard to keep from being swept into the storm of wings and talons. Freyjn pulled Lance back against a column, shielding him from the hail of debris as scales and blood rained down.

The dragons whirled, massive bodies blurring with impossible speed, their wings slicing the air with whipcrack sounds. They tumbled, snapping and clawing, biting with brutal fury. For a moment, it seemed the two might overwhelm Henry, their combined strength forcing him back.

Henry's tail whipped around, slamming into the golden-black dragon and sending it sprawling against the far wall with a thunderous crash. The silver dragon lunged for Henry's throat, teeth sinking deep. But Henry twisted, his own jaws clamping down on its wing. The silver dragon shrieked, the sound tearing the air like lightning splitting the sky.

Then Henry reared, his chest swelling, his throat glowing with a terrifying light.

"No..." Freyjn's eyes widened in dread.

The monstrous dragon's maw opened wide, and with a deafening roar, a torrent of fire spewed forth. Not ordinary flame but black and red, a storm of fire that lit the chamber like a forge from the underworld.

The two other dragons reeled back, wings buffeting frantically to escape. Lance, Freyjn, and Gazen could only stare, stunned, the searing heat washing over them in waves.

Henry's growl of triumphant laughter rolled above the roar of fire.

"I thought Josh said Henry wasn't a real dragon," Freyjn murmured in bewilderment.

"Things aren't exactly the same as Josh experienced before," Lance recalled.

The ruin blazed with the impossible sight of a monstrous dragon belching fire. The crumbling tower became an inferno.

Henry's black-red fire poured like molten death, searing across the chamber, licking over stone columns, painted dragon murals blistering in the heat.

The silver dragon rallied with a piercing cry, chest glowing as it unleashed a stream of silver-white flame that clashed against Henry's. The golden-black dragon followed, exhaling a torrent of molten gold fire laced with streaks of shadow. Their flames hammered into Henry's own, the collision exploding in the center of the chamber, waves of scorching heat radiating outward.

Her reflexes quick, Gazen yanked her griffin low, pressing her body against its neck as fire rained around them. Shielding her face from a rain of falling embers, Freyjn bent over Lance's figure to cover him from the heat so intense it stole the breath from her lungs.

The clash raged above, torrents of flame twisting together, sparks showering like stars ripped from the heavens. The chamber filled with smoke so thick it choked the air, shadows of wings flashing through the haze, the roar of dragons drowning every other sound.

Without warning, Henry lunged, his jaws clamping down on the silver dragon's neck. With a savage twist, he wrenched it to the ground. The silver beast shrieked, body crashing through shattered marble, wings flailing as Henry drove it down mercilessly. With one last, agonized cry, the silver dragon stilled, its glow flickering out.

The golden-black dragon roared with a bloodcurdling fury that shook the ruins and the very storm outside. Rearing back, its eyes blazed with wrath. Its chest glowed molten, brighter and brighter, as though it gathered the sun itself within.

Across from it, Henry crouched low, wings spread wide, his throat burning with hellfire once more. Both dragons poised—then unleashed.

The very air split as torrents of fire from both beasts collided mid-air, gold-and-black flame crashing against red-and-shadow. The explosion of heat was apocalyptic. Flames seared outward in surging waves, marble tiles cracking beneath the strain, the ceiling shedding chunks of burning stone.

The firestorm's roar was deafening. The chamber was choked in acrid smoke, thick and suffocating. Sight was smothered, the world reduced to hacking coughs and the sting of burning eyes. Nothing but a roiling shroud of gray, curling through the broken arches.

Freyjn conjured a faint magical bubble to surround the shelter of their crumbling column, while Gazen's griffin fought against the backdraft, its wings straining.

For a long, tenuous heartbeat, there was only that—smoke, heat, and blindness. Seconds grew into eternity, the tension excruciating. It was impossible to tell the outcome of the devastating firefight.

Then, through the thinning haze, restless currents carried the veil aside inch by inch, and shapes emerged through the pall.

Framed in drifting tendrils of smoke, the golden-black dragon stood. Its wings stretched wide, the ember-light of its scales still glowing, smoke rising from its jaws in curling wisps. Beneath its talons lay the husk of the black dragon, charred and broken, its vast body reduced to little more than a scorched crust.

The golden-black dragon lifted its head and loosed a thunderous roar of triumph rolling through the chamber—so formidable, so majestic, even the tempest outside faltered in awe of its power.

36

Here Be Dragons

Josh

I stumbled forward on human legs that suddenly felt too fragile, too thin, as though they might buckle under me. My muscles ached, every joint screaming from exertion. My skin prickled, somehow stretching too tight over bones that had been vast only moments before.

Squinting through an indeterminate mist covering my form, I flexed my fingers, so much smaller compared to the talons I was pretty sure I'd had before. I winced at the soreness threading through them. My body felt both mine and not mine, as though I'd been too big for too long and was crammed back into a shell that barely fit.

Whoa. I couldn't imagine ever getting used to this.

Though the memory of fire still clung to my lungs. The beat of colossal wings, the taste of smoke, the power that had surged through my veins. The pure thrill of triumph in battle.

Realization dawning over me at exactly what had just happened, my heart pounded in my chest. I whirled around in a panic. "Tala!"

That same mystical white fog was dissipating over her slumped body across the marble floor, a few feet away.

Tala, no...

I sprinted over, dropping to my knees by her side.

Her eyes were closed, her face pale, her pink hair splayed like a crown around her face.

My pulse hammered so hard it drowned out every other sound.

Her skin was clammy, there was a gash along her neck, blood matted her hair, and bruises down her arms and legs. I was sure I had the same bruises, something warm trickled down my temple. I clasped her hand in mine—mostly in fear, but also in reverence.

Tala's dragon had fought alongside mine with effortless grace and tenacity. I was sure I would never stop being in awe of how magnificent she was—in any form. She and I had fought the monstrous dragon—together. And we had won.

But had I still lost her? Was this the cost we inevitably needed to pay?

I squeezed her hand, clenching my fists. Remembering how to breathe felt futile while the woman I loved slipped out of my grasp.

When her chest rose—faint, shallow—relief hit me so hard, my vision blurred.

"Oh, thank freaking god."

The pounding of boots thudded behind me. Lance skidded to a halt on my left, eyes wide. "Is Tala okay?"

Freyjn dropped to her knees opposite me, already clasping her hands together to summon her magic. "She's still bleeding—move your hand." She held hers hovering over Tala's form, a warm yellow glow of magic spreading across them both.

Gazen's shadow fell over us, walking over. Her statement was directed at me. "You're also bleeding."

My eyes intently on Freyjn's healing magic over Tala, I waved my hand to dismiss her concerns. "It's nothing."

But the dry catch in Lance's tone made me look up. "So..."

"So?" I echoed blankly.

Exasperated, Lance rolled his eyes. "What the hell—both of you are dragons?"

"Oh." I scratched my head before shrugging. "What can I say? We both survived the Emberheart Fire trial. Legend has it, only dragons can survive it. Hurt like the devil though."

Regular, weak human boy...

My eyes lit up at the soft teasing voice in my head—unmistakably Tala's. When I glanced down, those sparkling violet eyes were finally open. It looked like she was going to smile, but winced instead.

"Ahh—" Tala lurched forward in her slump.

Freyjn was already cringing. "Your injuries are quite severe."

"We should take her back to the ship." Lance's words rang with authority. "She needs blankets, water, and fresh air so Freyjn can do her work."

I nodded right away, bending down to scoop Tala in my arms. I chewed on the insides of my cheek, already concerned about the strain the long trek back across the meadows to the ship might have on her. "Can you hold on until we get there?"

But as I shifted her in my arms, Tala's eyes narrowed at my shirt again. The Curse bearer mark on my chest was glowing golden beneath my shirt once more.

Reaching up, she pressed her hand against it—seemingly out of curiosity.

The air split without warning, the bluish-white watery sphere of a portal flaring wide. It burst into existence so suddenly, I sputtered out, "Whoa—!"

Freyjn yelped in surprise.

Lance nearly stumbled back.

Through the haze of magic, the wooden deck of Lance's clipper appeared, with a handful of soldiers looking on in bewilderment from the other side.

My jaw dropped. "Oh, awesome!" Without any hesitation whatsoever, I crossed the threshold, quickly finding myself, as expected, on the deck of the boat near halfway across the island.

The rest of the group emerged out of the portal behind us, right before it crackled closed.

Lance eyed where the swirling whorl had been in suspicion for a second, but he quickly recovered. "Call back the rest of the troops," he said to the nearest soldier.

I set Tala down on the cot that another soldier brought over. Tucking her fuchsia hair back behind her ear, I couldn't help but beam. "Your portal magic is back."

Tala's beautiful face smiling up at me right that moment was the most right I had ever felt in my entire life.

The prophecy has been fulfilled.

"Huh." Freyjn's gaze was cast across the landscape.

The howling blizzard that earlier seemed like it was going to swallow us all had died altogether. Snowflakes drifted lazily in the sudden stillness, catching the first shafts of sunlight breaking through the storm as the sky split wide with blue.

"Huh." Gazen's eyes were unfocused as she let out her huff.

"What is it?" Lance peered at her.

Gazen was seeing across the land with the help of her griffins. "All the armies of ghosts have dissipated as well, vanishing as though they had never been. Fae and human soldiers are left standing in their wake, staggered, stunned, weapons slack in their hands." She broke a faint smile, murmuring, "It's over."

Freyjn moved back to Tala's side so she could continue with her healing magic. She clasped Tala's hand for a moment, remorse already curling her lips. "I'm so sorry. I'm really not the best healer."

Tala gave her a nod. "I trust you."

Lance's strong hand found Freyjn's shoulder. "I know you can do it."

Freyjn's posture straightened at Lance's reassurance, his solemn encouragement. Her eyebrows furrowing in concentration, she clasped her hands together and cast her magic.

These two...

I blinked, my gaze veering back to meet Tala's. *Was that...?*

Even as Freyjn was doing her magic, Tala's lips were quirked up.

I really wish the elders would reconsider.

My mouth almost dropping open, I let out a scoff in marvel. "Oh my god, I just heard that. I-I can hear you in my head."

Tala's face fell in surprise. "What?" *"That's impossible."*

"I heard that too," I chuckled, averting my gaze for a moment. "This is amazing."

Lance looked from Tala and me and back again. "What are you two on about?"

I met Tala's eyes, tilting my head in amusement. *"You know, I'd always thought it was weird how I sort of felt like I could read your mind before. I thought I was just really intuitive."*

Her violet eyes widened in pleasure. She'd definitely heard me, too. *"Legends do say the dragons could read each other's minds."*

"Do you know what's going on here?" Lance asked Gazen.

Gazen merely shrugged, a mysterious smile lacing her features.

I couldn't help my grin. All the little pieces of the mysterious puzzle I'd been trying to solve my entire life were coming together.

Shouting and clattering of boots up gangplanks stole Lance's attention. He straightened up. "We'd better get started on our journey back. We have a long ocean to cross once again." Calling out instructions to his men, the crew hurried to ready the vessel—rigging checked, sails unfurled, anchors weighed, every rope and spar set in place for the voyage ahead.

There was a momentary weight in my chest as the ship pushed off the mooring. I glanced back across the endless meadows, where the thick blanket of snow was already melting upon the green, green grass, toward the white tower standing tall, faint through the mystical haze.

There was still so much to discover, so much to know. I was sure this would not be the last time I would be on this shore.

Tala's hand grasped mine.

I looked down to see her smiling again, her contentment easily funneling into me.

Yes, we would return.

Together.

Freyjn stepped back, the yellow glow fading from her hands. Her shoulders were heaving slightly from the strain. "This is the best I can do for now." Rueful, she shook her head. "We should get her back to the Fae lands as soon as possible."

Lance's forehead creased. He likely knew, as well as pretty much everyone else, that it would be a near-impossible task. It took us days to get here, even with Freyjn's wind magic pushing the ship. A shadow of agony crossed Lance's features for a moment, the consequences of any such delay plainly wearing on his mind.

Josh.

"Yep." My gaze snapped instantly to Tala's.

Tala raised her arms in my direction. She wanted me to help her up off the cot. Obliging, I carefully braced my arms around her back, taking her weight as we both straightened.

With a small frown of concern, I assessed her up and down. "Are you feeling much better? Did you want to go somewhere?"

Freyjn's sharp blue eyes were on us. I thought she was going to disapprove of how closely I was holding her cousin. I almost jerked my arm away.

Except, Tala easily met her gaze with a pointed nod. "Yes, we are in a relationship."

Freyjn's jaw dropped.

I bit my lip at the wide-eyed shock on Freyjn's face, even as a sudden warmth surged through my chest. It sounded like the tail end of a different conversation altogether. My eyebrows shot up my forehead. I gave Tala an expectant look. *"What was that all about?"*

Tala's smirk was mysterious. *"I'll tell you later."* "But first—" Closing her eyes, she pressed one hand against my chest once again.

This time, a powerful force shunted clear through my body, a searing energy so intense I almost couldn't breathe. My heart hammered in my chest, my ears popped. "Aahh—" I gasped, trying to blink through the sting.

The wide ocean before us heaved as the air split open with a thunderous crack, light flaring brighter than lightning across the horizon, and a bluish-white sphere of searing energy clawed its way into existence, towering as tall as the ship itself, its edges rippling like molten glass.

The brilliant, not-quite-liquid silvery sphere crackled and roared, a grinding howl that rolled over the waves, shaking the masts and rattling the rigging. Mist boiled up around it, hissing where raw power met the water, until the vast circle loomed like a storm-born gate, alive with fire and thunder.

"Holy crap!" I cried out.

Lance's eyes were wider than ever.

Freyjn's jaw was nearly on the floor.

Gazen, to her credit, merely looked mildly amused.

The incredible portal split the horizon in two, one half surging with rolling waves, the other stretching out into a cracked, drought-stricken plain. The ocean spilled eagerly through the rift, frothing water rushing across dry earth in a torrent that sent dust flying and people scrambling. On the other side, men and women on the field stopped in their tracks, staring up in awe, mouths agape at the impossible sight of a ship's prow jutting through the sky itself.

With a groan of timber and a snap of rigging, the vessel lurched forward, sails billowing as the wind caught them even in this strange passage. The crew shouted, rigging taut, as the entire ship hurled itself through the glowing breach.

With a thunderous crash, the ship landed on the plain. Wood shuddered, anchors rattled, and the masts swayed under the impact, a hollow thud echoing across the flat land. Dust and sea spray mingled in the air, the ship standing impossibly solid on sun-cracked earth where no tide had ever reached.

* * *

"You are a crazy person." Renn fussed over Tala in the infirmary at Ipera. Shaking his head, he bustled about the room, casting healing magic, grinding herbs for a replenishing potion, forcing water at his patients to keep hydrated.

I folded my arms across my chest as I sat on the cot across from hers. I still had some internal injuries that stung when I coughed, but for the most part, my injuries were healed.

Except I also had to wait for some of that replenishing potion. My entire body felt drained of energy—from helping summon that ginormous portal. "What did you call it again?" I peered around Renn to catch Tala's eyes.

"A magic amplifier," Tala replied, an adorable quirk to her grin. "It seems the Curse bearer has an innate ability to make my portal magic stronger. I couldn't have done it otherwise."

Renn stopped to shake his head at her yet again, his forehead creased in disapproval. "You. Are. A. Crazy Person. What were you even thinking, conjuring a behemoth-sized portal in the middle of the ocean whilst being so badly injured like this? And what do you think the settlement of Willowfen is going to do with a clipper ship on their corn field?"

Tala's laughter was airy. "I'll help them portal it away, of course. Later. Once you've made me all better." She flashed him a cheeky grin. "You're the best, Renn."

Renn's shoulders shook in mirth. He tossed a warm cloth at her before turning to leave. "You two stay put. I need more herbs for this potion."

I caught Tala's gaze and we both laughed.

Pausing for a moment, she wrinkled her nose. "Sorry about that, by the way. I should have given you a heads-up before using your powers."

I flashed a suggestive grin. "I'll tell you this, babe—feel free to use me however, whenever."

Her cheeks flushed a soft rose, the color creeping up to her ears as she tried to look anywhere but at me. Damn, she was beautiful like that—so unguarded, so real—it was all I could do not to close the distance right then and kiss her until that blush deepened.

Almost impatient, I checked the doorway. Aside from Tala and me, as it happened, the infirmary was empty—easier to keep the cots clear when people weren't at war—so it was easy to see who was coming and going. And I was eagerly expecting a certain someone to be coming.

"Do you think Freyjn told your uncle about us?" I was nervous about it, sure, but mostly, I was antsy. I was determined to conquer that one last barrier standing between me and all my hopes and dreams.

"Probably." She studied my expression, a mischievous catch in her tone as she looked around. "Do you want to run away? We could run away together."

Despite how awfully tempting the notion was of riding off into the sunset with the most beautiful woman across all the realms, I squared my shoulders, clenching my jaw in resolve. "No. I'm done being the nice guy. I want to fight for you. Tell me what I need to do."

Her eyebrow rose. "What if you have to duel my betrothed? He's probably going to be a monster Fae warrior like Auric."

I shrugged, all casual. "Whatever. Maybe I'll just shift into a dragon and eat him."

Tala burst out laughing.

I stifled my own chuckle, my chest right about to burst with happiness already just being able to laugh with her.

The two of us were still getting used to the knowledge that such majestic beasts were sleeping within ourselves. Though I was eagerly looking forward to training how to use our shifter forms, flying across the realms together, owning the skies with Tala.

Only if her uncle didn't zap me out of existence beforehand.

I caught sight of Stellan's forbidding form entering the infirmary. I straightened up in my seat as he approached, trying to muster up as much respect and courage as I could.

Freyjn was right in his wake. Serene and refreshed, if still looking a bit worse for wear from our quest.

I didn't know how she had left things between her and Lance. All I could do was hope for the best for her, for them. I did know that Freyjn's wedding to Auric was still on hold. Nobody was rushing to get onto it. Perhaps that was encouragement enough for me.

"Thank you, sir, for your urgent attention and hospitality." I gave a slight bow. I still wasn't entirely sure how things were done in the Fae lands.

Stellan inclined his head as the slightest acknowledgment. "Freyjn has reported some quite incredible things to me."

Wary, I bit my lip. *Uh-oh?*

"I understand you endured the Emberheart Fire trials with Tala, protected her against a monstrous dragon specter, and fulfilled your duties as the Curse bearer. We owe you our deepest gratitude."

My eyes widened in surprise. "Oh." Shrugging, I ran my fingers through my hair. "Um, you're welcome…?"

Freyjn hid the chuckle she couldn't help behind her hand.

Behind me, Tala scoffed in mocking. I almost felt her eyes roll even without looking.

Steeling myself, I took a deep breath before I psyched myself out altogether. *Here goes nothing.* I stood up, cleared my throat. "Sir, respectfully, I would like to be considered as Tala's betrothed."

I wasn't sure what to do with the silence that followed my request. I shifted on my feet. Freyjn's gaze darted from person to person, breath held—she was curious what would happen too. I assumed I'd see the magic blitzing me out of existence before it actually happened. I resisted the urge to cringe in dread while waiting.

Stellan's eyes narrowed. "I am not certain if you have been told, but for the High Fae, we often wait to reveal a betrothal until a few weeks prior to the wedding ceremony itself. We believe it's better not to know too early. And I know this from experience." He also took a deep breath before going on, "But I believe in this case, we will allow an exception."

I nodded, taking a curious mental note to ask Tala later what exactly had happened with Stellan and his mate for his staunchly firm conviction in this matter. But I really shouldn't have been musing about that at all because I almost missed what Stellan said next.

"Tala's hand has been promised to the young man who survives the Emberheart Fire trial."

WHAT?

Tala screamed in my head.

"Ow!" I winced, rubbing my ears, even though obviously I didn't technically *hear* that.

"What?" Freyjn's eyes bulged in disbelief. "Then..." She looked from me to Tala and back again.

When I turned to Tala, her eyes were shining with tears—of elated relief.

My heart pounded in my chest. I was literally too overjoyed, I could barely speak. Wide-eyed, I looked up at Stellan again to make sure I hadn't simply hallucinated the last ten seconds.

"Strange." Stellan shook his head. "My first thought upon meeting you was that you do somewhat resemble my brother, Callan. I didn't mention it since it was highly unlikely. Now, I know it is no coincidence. He had gone to the fourth realm too, willingly exiled himself to be with the love of his life—Mina, a dragon Princess from Dragoncrest. You must be a distant descendant of their line."

I almost choked. "I'm also half-Fae?"

Tala's voice shook with delight. "Something else your father forgot to tell you." Pushing up off her cot, she walked over to me, hands already reaching for my face. "It's you, Josh." Those sparkling violet eyes gazing up at me as though I put the stars in the sky, Tala said the words I never in my wildest dreams thought I would ever hear. "I am betrothed to you."

My face felt hot. I still couldn't quite believe it. I dropped my gaze, biting my lip. *Shoot. I better not cry in front of my future in-laws.* "Are you sure? I mean, I want..." I cracked my neck, hesitating. "I want you to choose me because you want me. Not because your parents chose me."

Tala tilted my face up so I would meet her earnest gaze. "My parents loved me. They chose you because *I* chose you. Because I love you."

I couldn't help my smile widen.

The girl I loved was mine.

***

Epilogue

A few days later

Josh

"You did well in there." Tala tilted her head toward me with a smile.

I glanced back at the large assembly rooms. Fully recovered from our ordeals, Tala and I had attended our first diplomatic meeting as official ambassadors of Dragoncrest. I had to admit—surprisingly, that it wasn't as boring, or as bad, as I'd thought.

The meeting had let out mid-morning. Sweet scents of the forest swirled all around the village of Ipera, the sun, bright but gentle, spilling gold over the half-bustling path as Tala and I walked side by side down the main road.

"You certainly have a way with people," she went on. "And you really *are* knowledgeable and good at so many things—various occupations, reading maps, fighting battles, even talking policy. You're going to make a great leader."

My cheeks warmed self-consciously. Her words lingered in me, stronger than any applause from the High Fae council. But I flashed an airy grin. "Yes, yes, flatter me more."

Tala gave me a playful shove. "You're such an idiot."

We reached the corner where the path broadened, leading down toward the cluster of homes.

A Fae couple swept past us, the man's silver-blond hair braided back tight above a green coat edged in silver thread, the woman's obsidian-dark hair spilling over a pale blue gown that shimmered unnaturally.

But all the while, their judgmental glares never left us.

Tala's face fell, her aura dimming as it often did whenever the Fae badgered her.

My eyebrows furrowing in annoyance, I whipped around to yell, "That's right, people. We saved your world." I snapped my arms out wide, fingers spread. My hands cut the space between us like blades—like a dare, a mic drop, a swaggering gotcha. "You're welcome."

Tala shook her head in hilarity. Her violet eyes bright once more, she didn't seem embarrassed at all, even though the Fae couple continued to glare at us over their shoulders.

Perhaps it was better for them to think we were crazy than to think we were threats?

Admittedly, it was a slow start. Making the people of Ipera trust that dragons didn't inherently mean others any harm was an uphill battle.

But I was fine with taking it slow.

I knew I still had a lot to learn about how everything worked here in my new home, in this new-to-me world. I needed to get to know my own people—tricky business that it was, since I was half-Fae and half-dragon but raised among humans in the fourth realm.

I supposed I was a little bit of everything. Both Tala and I. I dared to believe that perhaps we were even exactly what the Land of Arcadia needed.

I didn't even mind that Stellan had insisted on an extended betrothal period for us. No doubt he wanted to thoroughly vet me first, get to know me a lot better, before letting me officially join their illustrious family.

Even Freyjn's wedding to Auric had been suspended for a spell—watch this space.

As far as I was concerned, everything was on the up and up.

Casting her eyes around, Tala let out a soft hum of contentment.

The forest village thrummed with new life, its cottages draped in fresh blossoms and its trees heavy with green, as though shaking off years of shadow. Magic shimmered in the air like dawn mist, a bright reminder that the strife across the land had ceased and the land was healing in abundance.

"Everything is so much more beautiful since the prophecy was fulfilled." Her hand brushed mine as we passed the fountain in the square.

I nodded. "I heard the drought in Willowfen has broken. Dried-up springs started flowing again, farming fields gone from cracked dirt to green shoots in a matter of weeks."

"And orchards are bearing fruit early, even in the Fae Isles. The river fish have returned, in numbers no one remembers seeing before. Magic flourishes everywhere."

Seeing her joyful smile lit something in me. I was lighter than air. Nothing in all the realms could touch me. I gazed down at her face. "Is it everything you were hoping for?"

Her sparkling eyes were full of wonder. "Oh, I don't think I dared hope for anything close to as wonderful as how everything turned out." She took my hand in hers. "Though we still have so much to figure out, so much to discover. We need to go back to Dragoncrest, of course. Then we must find all the exiled dragons in the fourth realm and bring them home, too."

"Ooh..." My eyes widened. It struck me that this meant I would actually be able to return home after all, if only for short stretches at a time. My mother would probably insist on meeting my supposed fiancée. Of course, my sister would be so thrilled.

Tala tilted her head in suspicion. "What are you thinking about?"

I stifled my chuckle.

We were both also still getting used to our new way of communicating—quickly discovering that it wasn't necessarily a good thing that dragons could very easily read each other's thoughts.

"Nothing." With a mysterious smirk, I slid my arm around her shoulders. "A new mission sounds like fun. You bring the portals. I'll bring the fish crackers."

Her curiously narrowed eyes told me she was going to nag me about that dodged question later.

Tala's forehead creased with her musing first. "Hmm... do you ever wonder about why or how the timelines diverged last time? I mean, presumably, my parents left me in Stellan's care exactly the same way, but in your version of things, three thousand years from now, everything had changed so much, the Fae were wicked, dragons had been forgotten, and I was..."

"A sassy, lonely fairy guarding a lake?" I quipped.

"Was that what I was?" she scoffed a chuckle.

I almost ached at the mere recollection of how dreary her life had turned out—would have turned out? I was determined to make sure, this time around, that Tala's life would be marked by lots of fun, happy memories with me.

I pressed a kiss to her temple. "Well, who knows how time works?" I shot her a curious look. "*Have* you been experimenting with your time messer-upper powers?"

Tala shook her head. "I think your guess might have been right. I can only use it in my dragon form, and let's say *that* still also needs a lot of work." She wrinkled her nose. "In any case, it's a bit disconcerting that even *I* forgot the time I myself had recreated. You seem to be the only one immune to my powers."

"Well, we don't know that for sure." I pursed my lips. "It's just I'm the only one who remembers what happened during my time here before."

"Will you tell me all about it?" Her eyes were wide with eager interest.

Smiling warmly, I nodded. "Of course." I gave her shoulders a light squeeze. "You know, I almost stayed here that last time, then I would have forgotten everything, too. I insisted that I wanted to be destroyed with the world, just so I wouldn't have to leave you."

Turning to bury my nose in her fragrant hair, I murmured low, "I'm so glad you talked some sense into me and sent me home instead. So we could find each other again. Even if it took a few more years, I wouldn't have had it any other way."

Her scoff was haughty, even as her lips quirked in pleasure. "Good. Then I'm happy you listened to me."

"Well—" I gave her my most disarming, most charming grin. "I'm yours, so I have to listen to you."

My eyes widened again when Tala lunged at me.

The next thing I knew, her mouth was on mine, her arms around my neck, her fuchsia hair wild all over the place.

A bright light flashed in my periphery, as though she'd portaled us out of the brisk, outdoors air, and we were suddenly inside a bedroom—woven rug on the tatami floor, a low side table beside a mattress, a small bookshelf against one wall of a cottage, the curtains letting in streaks of light—

Hell if I cared where we were.

I let my eyes shut, in complete surrender, willing all my senses to be overwhelmed by her.

So sweet. She tasted so sweet, like tea, and peaches, and heaven.

Groaning in my throat, I wrapped my arms around her. I wanted to feel every inch of her against me. My one hand found the nape of her neck, my fingers tangling in that silky hair. I tilted my head to kiss her back deeper.

Closer. I want to be closer.

Somehow, my back found the wall. She'd pushed me against it. When I slid my hands low to clasp her hips, she moaned in my mouth.

I wanted to drown in her, in her scent, in the feel of her. I dragged kisses down the side of her neck, indulging in that fragrant, soft skin.

Gasping, she tilted her head back, as if to give me better access. Her fingers slipped beneath my shirt, grazing against my burning skin.

My control broke in an instant. Growling, I spun us around, catching the bottom of her thighs to lift her up, straddling across my hips. I pinned her to the wall, my lips crushing hers, my hard body pressed against every soft curve of hers.

A strangled moan tried to escape her mouth, but I muffled it with mine.

Her fingers dug into my hair, and my mind clouded with pure desire.

She broke off kissing for a moment. Catching her breath, her eyes closed as she leaned her forehead against mine. "Josh." She laced her arms around my neck.

I met those sparkling violet eyes when she opened them again. I pressed another kiss to her forehead. "Yes?"

Her throat bobbed as she swallowed hard. "Put me down."

I almost winced like someone had thrown a bucket of cold water over me. "Oh." I quickly set her down and stepped away from her warmth. Crap. I'd gone too far. I knew it. So much for taking things slow.

Tala stepped around me, careful, deliberate.

Chest heavy, still heaving with desperate want, I dropped my gaze to the floor. We probably were moving way too fast. What was I even thinking? Either way, I was going to respect her decision.

I turned quickly, ready to apologize, only to see Tala perch herself on the bed. My heart thundered in my chest once again as she scooted backward a little to make some space.

A shy smile lacing those red lips, her violet eyes dancing, Tala held her hand out to me. "Do you want to—?"

My mouth was back on hers before she even got the rest of the words out.

* * *

The End?

Don't miss an epic ending!

S. R. BREAKER is a USA Today Bestselling Author of non-stop action adventure, offbeat YA/NA fantasy romance books. She lives in New Zealand with her husband and two kids.

Suburban mum by day and author by night, she loves to live vicariously through her characters. They don't have to vacuum all day long and are almost always guaranteed to survive any fantastical or thrilling incidents, no matter how treacherous she writes them.

She likes binge-watching TV shows and reading books that take her to far enough unknown worlds—but then still have enough time to wash the dishes after.

Subscribe to her mailing list now for bookish news and get a FREE e-book!

https://subscribe.breakerworlds.com/fantasy

Sneak Peek: Trapped by Clocks and Hearts

He stole her heart for the Queen
But now he wants it for himself
Will he sacrifice everything
To unlock the magic of her heart?

Tulgey Woods was a deceptive place. From a distance, it appeared to be a serene and peaceful forest, filled with charming little animals, and trees and flowers that were wont to chat you up if you dallied for too long.

But it was actually the home of a monstrous creature.

With eyes of flame, jaws that bite, and claws that catch, it would arrive like a dark shadow to engulf the entire forest if it sensed even a smidge of mystical power on its grounds.

Not exactly an ideal place to go gallivanting.

Spotting the girl emerge from the darkness of the forest, my breathing eased a little. She probably almost got suffocated by the trees and flowers in the thick woods, but had fortunately made it out before any of the more carnivorous plants caught her scent.

Folding my arms across my chest, I hovered atop a Tum-tum tree a few yards away.

Walking up toward a giant mushroom in a clearing, the girl tucked back her long, unruly brown hair blowing in the slight breeze, her long, white lab coat fluttering behind her like a cape.

The mystical fungus a shade too tall for her to prop her elbows on, the girl leaned the tiptoes of her loafers to regard an inordinately large caterpillar that was perched upon it with a narrow-eyed look. "Hello?"

Not startled at all at the sight of her, the languid blue creature, three feet tall with a slimy, semi-transparent body, puffed smoke out from his gaudy hookah. "Who are *you*?"

The girl's nose wrinkled in deep thought. "You know...I actually really *literally* don't know."

The pipe of the hookah poised near its mouth, the Caterpillar shot her a look of ridicule. "What do you mean by that? Explain yourself!"

She chewed on her inner cheek, her tone matter-of-fact. "Oh, I don't really understand it all myself so I'm afraid I can't tell you who I really am. See?"

The Caterpillar folded its arms across its chest. "I don't see."

"It's just...I can't seem to remember things."

"Can't remember *what* things?" the Caterpillar prompted.

Her forehead creased in contemplation. "Well, I heard I was found in an icy cave in the frozen wastes, left for dead. One of your world's wizard guys rescued me. But when I woke up, I didn't remember anything. Who I was." She twirled a lock of hair around her index finger. "How I got here. Where I'm from."

Wizard? My eyebrows snapped together in distaste at the term.

She wasn't even telling it right—since I absolutely *did not* rescue her.

I wasn't supposed to be at the frozen wasteland that day. I was in the middle of an assignment from the queen.

But when I reconned inside that small, nearly hidden cave, I'd found her.

Alone. Frozen. Nearly dead.

After a quick assessment determined that the girl was still alive, naturally, my first instinct had been to harvest her heart.

It should have been simple.

I would have left her body, delivered her heart to the Queen of Hearts, and gone back to my clock tower to enjoy my life of solitude until I was called to duty once again.

End of story.

It wasn't.

For the last couple of weeks, the strange girl had spent delirious days in bed, indisposed, recovering from frostbite and near death. Installed in the little storage studio beneath my loft, I had successfully hidden her presence from the queen's envoys and the rest of the world—for now.

Since she'd thawed, I hadn't spoken more than five words to her. Of course, there was no accounting for her guile. For starters, I couldn't fathom how she'd escaped my tower to get all the way to this forest. She must have recovered faster than she was letting on. She *must* have been sneaking around and eavesdropping the other day when that cat had dropped by again to snoop around and prattle my ear off about things.

A nerve ticked in my cheek in my annoyance. *I swear to god—*

I was going to gut that cat the next time I saw it.

After I gutted *her.*

"Who are you?" the Caterpillar snapped again.

The girl winced at the creature's brusque response but she probably figured she might as well respond. "I guess you can call me Allie," she declared, looking a bit miffed. "Honestly, it's been quite a rough few weeks. I mean, if you forgot who you were, and found yourself in a strange place, you could probably really use something to relax too, couldn't you?"

"Not a bit."

Allie's forehead creased. "Why am I even having this discussion with a talking caterpillar?" Shaking her head, she blinked a few times before turning away.

"Come back!" the Caterpillar called out. "I've something important to say!"

She glanced over her shoulder. "What is it?"

"You'll get used to it in no time," the Caterpillar stated, put the hookah back into its mouth, and began smoking again.

She blinked, looking around at a loss. "What, you mean being here?"

The Caterpillar took the hookah out of its mouth once more and yawned. Then it began to slither slowly down off the mushroom, crawling away on the grass, merely remarking as it went, "One side will bring you up, and the other side will bring you down."

Her lips pursed. "The sides of *what?*"

"Of the mushroom," the Caterpillar finished before it disappeared into the woods.

Just then, a low rumbling from across the valley caught my attention. Glancing up, I clenched my jaw.

Here it comes.

The shadow.

A large flock of birds squawked and flapped upward from a clump of trees on the horizon, a flurry in their efforts to escape the eclipse that blotted out the light like a tidal wave of darkness visibly coming closer and closer to the clearing where the giant mushroom stood.

Letting out a haggard sigh, I rode the air to coast swiftly down, scooping the girl up in my arms before she even noticed I had arrived.

"Whoa—" She grabbed my neck to secure herself against me before she looked up to meet my gaze. "It's you!"

I was sure she could read the disapproval in my eyes, the wind whipping past us as I flew us away from the forest.

But her cheeks were pink, her smile wide with pleasure.

It was odd. In our previous very brief encounters while she recovered from her state, she had never once expressed pleasure at the sight of me.

The last time I'd had to physically come downstairs to deliver her food rations, the expression in her eyes was most definitely not delight. Apprehension, yes, but not delight.

Definitely not pleasure.

This situation did not warrant the pleasure in her eyes.

Then it hit me.

That damn caterpillar.

"What did you just eat?" I asked in suspicion.

Her pupils clearly dilated, she laughed merrily. "Oh, don't be such a downer."

I shook my head again. "Don't you know what magic mushrooms do?"

"It didn't look poisonous. It didn't say poison on it." Her face fixed into mock sobriety. "Besides, you know what they say. If at first, you don't succeed, try two more times so that your failure is statistically significant."

I scoffed in ridicule. "You are so high right now."

She smacked her lips out loud. "It tasted like waffles. Did you know everything here tastes like waffles to me? Besides, the caterpillar made it sound so fascinating. I was just curious."

"You are much too curious for your own good," I mumbled.

"I'm a scientist." She threw up one hand as if to gesture the obvious.

I narrowed my eyes at her. "How is it that you remember you are a scientist when you don't remember anything else about yourself?" Even with my arms hooked under her back and legs, I motioned air quotes with my fingers. "*Allie.*"

Laughing again, she pinched my cheek. "Are you always this surly?"

Flinching in horrified protest, I recoiled away. "Stop that!"

My god, she was so annoying.

I was severely tempted to shove her away and toss her against the rocky mountain peaks beneath us to her certain death.

If only her entire existence wasn't potentially the answer to my biggest problem.

* * *

Enjoyed the preview?

Read **Trapped by Clocks and Hearts** by **S. L. Breaker** now!